Karen Hayes is the autho
novels and a volume of
Mornings. Her most recent novels, *Still Life on
Sand, Cloud Music* and *A Patch of Green
Water*, are also published by Black Swan. She
lives in Devon with her husband and children.

PRAISE FOR KAREN HAYES

A PATCH OF GREEN WATER

'A powerful story about love and the illusions people
weave about it . . . With a fast-moving plot and deftly-
sketched supporting cast carrying their own emotional
baggage, Hayes keeps her readers involved to the last
page' *Home & Country*

'This dreamlike love story will linger in your mind for
ages after reading it' *Prima*

CLOUD MUSIC

'A dreamy story of musicians, families and the effects
places have on dreams' *Prima*

'Magic, music and sorcery come together in this
passionate romance . . . A tale of unrequited love, longing
and triumph over despair, *Cloud Music* can't fail to cast its
spell on you' *The Sunday Post Magazine*

'Enchanting' *Candis*

STILL LIFE ON SAND

'A beautiful, perceptive story' *Women's Realm*

'Written with zest and shrewdness' *Helen Dunmore*

'What Karen Hayes does, with disarming skill, is to
describe the hopes, fears, jealousies, dreams, pride and
illusions that rumble beneath her characters' inner lives'
Tim Pears

Also by Karen Hayes

STILL LIFE ON SAND
CLOUD MUSIC
A PATCH OF GREEN WATER

and published by Black Swan

BRIDGE OF SHADOWS

Karen Hayes

BLACK SWAN

BRIDGE OF SHADOWS
A BLACK SWAN BOOK : 0 552 99779 X

First publication in Great Britain

PRINTING HISTORY
Black Swan edition published 1999

1 3 5 7 9 10 8 6 4 2

Set in 11/12pt Melior by
County Typesetters, Margate, Kent

Black Swan Books are published by Transworld Publishers Ltd,
61–63 Uxbridge Road, London W5 5SA,
in Australia by Transworld Publishers,
c/o Random House Australia Pty Ltd,
20 Alfred Street, Milsons Point, NSW 2061,
in New Zealand by Transworld Publishers,
c/o Random House New Zealand,
18 Poland Road, Glenfield, Auckland
and in South Africa by Transworld Publishers,
c/o Random House (Pty) Ltd,
Endulini, 5a Jubilee Road, Parktown 2193.

Reproduced, printed and bound in Great Britain by
Cox & Wyman Ltd, Reading, Berks.

For Adrian

ACKNOWLEDGEMENTS

I would like to warmly thank Rossella Bongi for her invaluable help in so many ways, from Italian lessons to introductions to her native Florence and her welcoming family there. A big thank you, also, to Alberto Bongi, who kindly let me share his home to live and work in while I wrote this book.

And to all my other Italian friends, both new and old, my grateful thanks.

1

Della sees Stefano for the first time at the Villa Tiglio, playing tennis on the grass court behind the house. Two separate sensations, which from now on will always be linked with this first sighting, assail her senses: the scent of the lime trees now in flower, and the sharp, stunned sound of the ball hitting the ground hard as Stefano serves an ace.

'Well done,' says Hunter, Stefano's opponent. He doesn't sound as if he means it.

Neither of them have seen Della. She's half hidden behind the trunk of a lime tree. If they did see her they wouldn't care; they are too intent on their match.

Stefano serves again, and this time Hunter effortlessly returns the ball. Della's attention is not on the rally but on Stefano, who is not at all as she'd imagined. He is both lighter and more powerful, yet more graceful and vibrant than his photographs suggest. Even as she thinks this, he wins another point with a smash into the far corner. Hunter, foolishly trying to reach what is an impossibly far and fast ball, only succeeds in making himself look ungainly and cross.

Della inhales the scent of lime-blossom perfume, which hovers over the garden like a swarm of sweet-smelling insects. She watches Stefano move, stretch, run and sees how his body inhabits its space like a relaxed hand inside a soft, worn glove. Turning to Hunter, she notes how the older man is not on such friendly terms with his body, his space; it's as if he's been ill measured for both.

Stefano holds his serve easily. This is when Della

should make herself known and be introduced, finally, to Stefano, but she holds her place behind the lime tree. The garden is hot, too hot for this time of year. It's too early; it is still spring, with the rich scents clogging the air to prove it. Beyond the garden the hills around Florence look musky under a heated blue sky. Della thinks she can smell the faint oriental scent of the cedar trees beyond the garden and the clean woodsy smell of the cyprus even further on.

And mingled with this she is sure she can inhale Stefano, who is much nearer to her than Hunter. Mixed with the sweetness of the lime blossom and the other intoxications of the garden she is sure she can smell the clean, young sweat of Stefano.

Della closes her eyes for a moment, just a moment. When she opens them she sees Stefano break Hunter's serve with a graceful lob over the far side of the net, where Hunter hasn't a chance of returning it. Stefano grins, not maliciously but happily, like a child, wanting to be praised for doing something well. Hunter doesn't praise but frowns, turns his back on Stefano and pretends to retie his shoelace.

Stefano's smile, tossed so confidently into the air, wavers as it isn't caught and falls crashing to the ground. For a moment he looks sad, so sad that Della takes a step forward to reach him. But Hunter is serving again and the game continues.

Della, still hidden, cannot take her eyes off Stefano. He looks solely Italian, though, of course, he is half English and has just come from London. But his skin is that of his mother's, the colour of old gold, rich and sultry, and his hair too is not Hunter's, who was all sandy beige before he imperceptibly turned pale grey. Stefano's hair is black and curly, almost to his shoulders. Hunter too wears his hair long, but it's straight, fine, thinning and dying. Stefano's hair is like a growing animal, thick and frisky, alive.

Della has seen photographs of Hunter's son, a skinny, lanky boy with large bewildered eyes, too much hair and teeth. This was the image she had of Stefano, and this is why she cannot move from behind the lime tree. She had expected a child. Even knowing that he was – how old? Twenty-five, twenty-six? – Della had been seduced by the old photos, expecting to see the same gangling adolescent, expecting to be coerced into the unknown and unwanted territory of surrogate motherhood.

But it's the man, not the child, who is taking her into uncharted waters, causing her to remain immobile, breathless in the hot, perfumed air of the Villa Tiglio. He is, simply, beautiful. She wants to stand and look at him, just as some days she stands and looks at certain paintings, like the one by Pontormo in the church just down from the Ponte Vecchio. Just as there is something deeply sensual in the painting, something that compels her to return again and again to stare at it, so there is that same intensity in Stefano. There is also the same quality of light and colour. Like the painting, Stefano seems to be lit from within rather than taking his light and colour from the world outside himself. Even the deep green of the headband round his forehead seems luminous.

'Christ. Della. What are you doing lurking there? No wonder I'm off my game, with you spying on us in the shadows.'

Hunter, who has just lost another game, leaves the court and goes to Della. He is distracted and irritable. He doesn't often lose at tennis, and never to his son. Through his anger runs the smooth silver thread of relief, that the game will now be interrupted because of Della's arrival.

Stefano has followed Hunter, though seemingly reluctantly. Whether it's because he wanted to continue the game, or because he doesn't want to meet Della, is not quite clear.

Della, usually so strong and confident and able, finds herself leaning against the rough trunk of the lime tree like some kind of shadow, overcome by the presence of

Stefano. It's as if a powerful painting has come to life, the main figures in it suddenly breathing, moving, holding out a hand to her as Stefano is doing now while Hunter says, 'Della, this is my son, Stefano. Stef, this is Della. My, uh, my partner.'

The words are superfluous. Stefano knows who Della is and Della knows who Stefano is. She takes his hand and says, with the banality born of confusion, 'I've heard a lot about you.' His hand feels warm, damp with sweat, but the grip is strong. Its wetness is erotic.

Stefano nods. He doesn't add that he has heard about her. But his hand holds on to hers for longer than is necessary; he is looking at her longer than is necessary. A spark of excitement – crazy, irrational – pulses through Della.

Stefano says, 'The tennis court hasn't changed much since my last visit. Dad is still on form.' He hasn't let go of her hand. He needs the contact, to get a grip on exactly what it was that changed his past so dramatically.

'That must have been about three years ago,' Hunter says.

'Yes. When *Mamma* was still here.'

Stefano says the word the Italian way, though the rest of his speech sounds thoroughly English. Hunter looks down on the ground, as if his son has committed a great social blunder. Stefano, noticing, goes on defiantly, '*Mamma* loved it here. She used to say that the Villa Tiglio was always home to her, even before you moved here permanently.' He drops Della's hand.

Della watches, fascinated, as Stefano fills the space around him. He seems to overlap, taking up much more room than he should. He is taller than Hunter, who's an inch or two under six feet, but it's not that. It's as if his spirit, his personality, cannot be contained by his body and so must inhabit a wider area around it.

Hunter says stiffly, 'How is Chiara? I suppose she's happy to be back in Italy.' He doesn't want to talk about his ex-wife, but since Stefano brought her up, he will meet the challenge.

'Italy is her home,' Stefano says. 'She hasn't been happy in London.' He looks accusingly at Hunter, who refuses to drop his eyes and acknowledge any guilt.

Della says, 'And you are going to live with her in Siena?'

'I did ask you to stay here, Stef,' Hunter says petulantly. 'The villa is your home, after all.'

Stefano looks at him as if he's on another planet. The comment is far too ludicrous to be answered. Della says, in the sudden silence, 'Shall we have a drink on the terrace, and celebrate Stefano's arrival?' She smiles at him, and is rewarded by a brief smile in return. His smile is like the olive trees, old and wise, yet silvery and light. She would like to wrap it in grapevines and store it under her pillow. She knows she should run like hell, thinking these whimsical thoughts, but her feet remain solidly planted in the fine green grass under the lime trees.

Hunter says, 'We'll have a drink shortly. Stef and I haven't finished our match yet. It's the last set, nearly over. Stay and watch, and then we'll celebrate Stef being in Italy and my win at the same time.' He smiles at Della, suddenly happy, suddenly sure that he has gained back his concentration, his equilibrium, his prowess on the tennis court. He is still king, after all, for hasn't he got everything now? The one thing missing had been his son, and now Stefano is here, is *his*, is not only back in Italy for good, but will be working for Hunter at the Villa Tiglio.

Stefano picks up his racquet and looks coolly at Hunter. Hunter turns to Della, kisses her hard on the mouth with open lips. 'For luck,' he says to Della as he draws away, glancing slyly at Stefano as he does so.

Stefano thinks, What a fucker you are.

He knows that he will lose this last set and so the whole match, for his father is on a high and there will be no stopping him now. But Stefano doesn't really care. He knows there is more to life than tennis.

He also knows that Della cannot keep her eyes off him, even as he succumbs to Hunter's skilful serves and rallies, even as Hunter wins and kisses her again, victoriously. Even then he feels Della's eyes unable to unglue themselves from him.

'Well, you've got to hand it to your old dad, I haven't lost it,' Hunter gloats. He says the *old* mockingly, as if he could never be old, and indeed, he knows he cannot. He is fit and strong and forever youthful; doesn't he have Della at his side to prove it?

Stefano says nothing. His face is inscrutable, but his thoughts are troubled. His father's like an old rooster, crowing with pride, strutting through the henyard as if he's conquered the world, rather than winning an unimportant tennis match. So everything, and yet nothing, has changed. Stefano remembers other, earlier games during summers at the villa, and not only tennis. One year, when Stefano was eight or nine, Hunter became fanatical about croquet, and had a croquet lawn set up in the gardens. Stefano remembers crying bitterly in the shade of the lime trees when he lost humiliatingly, time after time, and in front of guests, too, to his father. He remembers Hunter finding him and scolding him for being a poor loser.

He shakes these thoughts from his head and turns to see Della staring at him oddly. What does she want to see, for God's sake? What has Hunter told her about him to make her gape that way?

Stefano decides he doesn't really give a damn. He's young; life passes over him like clear water over smooth pebbles. Della – and, yes, his father, too – are as unimportant to his life as the tennis match he has just lost.

Or so he tells himself.

2

The back terrace of the Villa Tiglio overlooks vineyards and olive groves and wild meadows covered in red poppies. The hills of Tuscany ripple like purple-blue waves behind the fields and poplars, but no-one is admiring them now, though Stefano, preoccupied, is staring out into the distance. He doesn't really see what he is looking at; he is still too preoccupied, thinking about his father. Though he knows he must stop diving into the past if he is to live comfortably in the present, memories keep floating, like weeds, to the surface of his thoughts.

One memory is intruding now, as his eyes take in the lime trees beyond the garden, the trees for which the villa is named. In front of them is the low brick wall that surrounds the tennis court, and Stefano sees himself as an adolescent, bringing back a girl, his first girlfriend, sitting with her against the wall and kissing, touching, hesitantly and tremulously. Oh, the sweetness of it, the mind-blowing bliss! And then Hunter, looking for them, asking them if they wanted coffee. *Coffee*, for God's sake! And when they said no, Hunter sitting there on the damp grass with them, trying to act like a mate instead of a father, talking to the girl in his halting, stilted Italian. Flirting with her, Stefano realized, but not until much later, not until it happened again and again. Every girl he brought home, those summers in Florence, was monopolized by Hunter, mocking, prancing, showing off his croquet or basketball or tennis. Insisting the girls have a go, and if, politely, they said they would, it was always Hunter

15

that took the ball or racquet from Stefano, saying, 'No, no, that's not the way to do it, Stef. Here, let me show the young lady the right way.'

Della has brought a bottle of chilled prosecco outside. It stands sweating on the white garden table, which is shaded, like the entire terrace, by the leaves and branches of a couple of ancient olive trees. The terracotta paving is framed by huge pots of the same clay, filled with plants: hibiscus and gardenia. The white flowers of the gardenia penetrate the air with their heavy scent, as does the jasmine blossom growing over the brick wall between the garden and tennis court. Della feels she cannot breathe, that she is caught in the middle of this battle of scents.

Hunter pours the cold wine into long-stemmed glasses. Stefano turns his face away from the hills, watches the bubbles fizzing gently in the pale-gold liquid and wonders if he was right to have come back. It was his mother, Chiara, who had urged him to take this job with Hunter. She didn't want him to hate his father, she had told him. What had happened between herself and Hunter should not affect the father-and-son relationship.

What had happened was that Hunter had left Chiara for Della a year and a half ago. Stefano had been in London at the time, at loose ends after university, using his degree in French and Italian to haphazardly teach private students at his own convenience, having decided that he wasn't yet ready for a serious career commitment. Chiara had arrived unannounced and distraught, nearly mad with grief and shock.

Later, she'd apologized to Stefano, said that she bitterly regretted dumping all her pain and distress on him, but at the time she had not been capable of rational thought. Whatever she thinks of Hunter now, of what he did, she doesn't want Stefano to hate him. She thinks this chance for Stefano to work with his father will give them time to become reconciled.

Hunter lifts his glass. 'Cheers,' he says. 'Here's to you, Stef. Welcome home.'

Della raises her glass. 'Good health. And yes, Stefano, welcome home.'

Stefano doesn't drink. He says, seemingly casually, 'Shouldn't we say *salute*? After all, we're in Italy.'

Hunter recognizes the challenge. 'But we are English.'

'I'm not.'

There's a pause. Hunter says reasonably, 'You were born in England. You grew up there.'

'But my mother is Italian.'

Only Della seems to recognize the absurdity of this conversation, but she says nothing and lets it meander on, which is unlike her. Della, with her fine English accent, which the students admire hugely, would normally interrupt assertively, tell an anecdote, steer the conversation to a different shore. But she remains quiet.

Hunter says, 'Well then, *salute*. But I have to warn you, Stefano, that here at the Villa Tiglio we speak only English. It's a rule of the school.'

Still Stefano hasn't touched his drink. 'But there are no students here on Sunday.'

'No, but I'm advising you for tomorrow. Our students are here to learn English and, even on our breaks, both they and all staff members must speak English. But I'm sure you remember, from your last visit home.'

Stefano says sharply, 'Not home. Florence was never my home. You and *Mamma* moved here permanently when Granddad died. I was in college, remember? I stayed in London.'

Hunter is losing patience. Della can see his face tighten in that way it does when he's becoming angry but doesn't want to appear bad-tempered. He says, with exaggerated patience, 'Ah, Stefano, not only do I remember, but I remember a great deal more than you do, obviously. Surely you haven't forgotten that every summer, every single summer of your childhood, you came with us to Villa Tiglio when my parents owned it. It was our second home, even though we lived in England. Surely you have some leftover fondness for it even now, even if you do feel you've outgrown us here.'

Della wonders why she hasn't noticed before how pompous Hunter sounds when he is being sarcastic. This first meeting is difficult for him of course, but doesn't he recognize how much harder it is for Stefano? It's time she stepped in, before Hunter totally blows it.

She says to Stefano, 'It must have been wonderful, coming here from London every year. Like a different world.' She smiles at him sympathetically, encouragingly.

Stefano's face softens, becomes open, vulnerable. 'It *was* a different world. We all changed, every summer, the minute we got here. Or rather *Mamma* and I did. We became wholly Italian, do you remember?' He looks appealingly at Hunter. 'You used to tease us about it. When the summer was over and we went back to London, *Mamma* had practically forgotten all her English, said she had to learn all over again. And I had to change from being an Italian kid into an English one.'

There is a moment of awkward silence. Hunter, instead of using this moment to save something which is nearly lost between him and Stefano, refuses to be pulled into a past he has chosen to distance himself from. He says, 'Yes, well, no point in looking back, is there. Let's drink to the future, shall we? It's much more promising.' He finishes off his glass of prosecco and pours himself another.

Stefano looks startled, then bewildered, then angry. Della watches his expressive face change from a stunned defencelessness to a hardened determination. He looks suddenly much older. 'The past *exists*,' he says, putting down his glass and standing up. 'You can't rewrite it, much as you would like to.'

18

'Where are you going?' Hunter says, alarmed. 'You haven't touched your drink. You're staying for dinner, aren't you?' He is almost, but not quite, pleading, but it's far too late.

'I'm going *home*,' Stefano says, and then repeats it in Italian, *'Vado a casa.* To Siena.' He nods a goodbye to Della. Looking at Hunter he says scornfully, 'Oh, don't worry, I'll be back tomorrow morning bright and early, ready to take on my class. I won't let the school down by mixing my professional life with squalid family stuff.'

The relief in Hunter's face is obvious to both Della and Stefano. 'Good, good,' he cries. 'I cannot tell you how pleased I am to have you on the team.' He tries to clasp Stefano on the shoulder, but the younger man steps aside slightly, just enough to cause Hunter's arm to float aimlessly, like a leaf in autumn, through the scented spring air.

Stefano says softly, 'Everything always comes out right for you, doesn't it. You have me here at your language school, working under you; you have the Villa Tiglio. You're lord of it all, aren't you.'

Hunter starts to speak, but Della interrupts him quickly. Standing up from the table where she had been watchfully sipping her wine, she says, 'Stefano, we both think it's marvellous that you've joined us, and I hope you will thoroughly enjoy working here.' She puts her hand lightly on his arm. 'And it was jolly nice of you to come by today to see us before you start on Monday. Classes begin at nine, but if you can get here an hour early, Hunter or I, or one of the other teachers, will show you the work books we're using and brief you on your students.' She drops her hand from his shoulder and holds it out for him to take as she adds, 'I'm so pleased that I've finally met you.'

Stefano understands that she's dismissing him formally to prevent him from walking out in anger, so that she can save Hunter's pride; so that the two of them can pretend the meeting went well, that there is no rift between father and son. For a moment he struggles against his instinct to ignore her outstretched hand and walk away from them both, but then he remembers he came here by his own choice. Though his mother had wanted this, it was Stefano himself who had determined he would be civilized about his father and his new woman.

And so he takes Della's hand, and once again startles her by holding it for longer than is necessary. The fact that Stefano doesn't let go electrifies her; he too must feel the same current that she does.

But what Della doesn't know is that this is the way Stefano learns about people. He makes his judgements through his senses rather than through rational thought processes. He is trying to get a handle on Della, see what she is like, understand why his father left his mother for her.

At last he lets go of Della's hand. 'See you Monday!' she cries, and her voice is as eager, as hopeful as a child.

Hunter says, far too heartily, 'Yes, Monday. Tomorrow. First day of a new term, a busy day for all of us. Please be on time, Stef. There's so much we have to sort out before we actually begin teaching.'

Stefano thanks his father for the wine he didn't drink, and then for the tennis match he didn't win. Hunter isn't sure whether his son is calling a truce or mocking him, but Stefano's face, usually so expressive, gives nothing away.

When he is gone Della drops her smile and says to Hunter, 'Well, that was a fucking balls-up, wasn't it.'

Hunter, who ordinarily loves the way Della never loses the purity of her accent – so necessary for a teacher of the English language – during her frequent lapses into the blustery vernacular of the streetwise, is annoyed. 'I thought it went well, all things considered,' he says. He has decided that Stefano's parting politeness was an apology for the childish, churlish manner in which he'd behaved.

20

Della considers contradicting him, but decides otherwise. There are other ways of handling Hunter, just as there were, in the past, other ways of handling parents, friends, lovers. It had taken Della a long time to learn this. The youngest in a family of three brothers, she had grown up pert and spoiled, her bossiness interpreted by her doting parents as jaunty self-awareness. Her brothers, though not so doting, contributed to her feisty confidence by teaching her rugby, swearing and the unsubtle art of self-defence on the plush back lawn of their fine Tudor house in Buckinghamshire. But as the children grew up, and their parents grew old, Della began to realize her cockiness and contrariness were wearing thin with all of them. She quickly learned that she could get through the opposition far better with clever manoeuvring, rather than blundering straight on down the middle. She had her rugby-playing brothers to thank for that.

And so she decides not to plunge into Hunter's psyche, making him look at the situation honestly and admitting that his first meeting with Stefano after all this time was not exactly happy families. If Hunter needs to maintain the illusion that one tennis match and a bottle of prosecco in the garden is all the bonding that is needed to bring Stefano around, let him enjoy it while he can.

Hunter is brooding now, forced by Della's remark to go over the scene with Stefano in his head, replaying every word. Della sees his tight mouth, his slight frown, and shakes her head to rid herself of the irritation she feels with him. She reminds herself that this is Hunter, her partner, her lover. The man who stayed when all the others left. She remembers how grateful she was to Hunter when she'd realized that this one was not going to leave her. There had been too many who had, over the years. Married ones, who went back to their wives, or the single fickle ones who had stayed for a time until someone else came along. Then there were the ones that couldn't commit, and the others that wanted so much commitment she felt as if she were being swallowed whole. God, she was lucky to be out of all that!

Della goes to Hunter, perches on his knee and peers into his face. She makes herself forget about Stefano, forget about the sharp shock waves, like little jolts of electricity, that went through her when she first saw him. 'Don't brood about it, darling. You know Stefano better than I do, and if you feel our first meeting went well, I'm sure you're absolutely right.'

Hunter is mollified. He hasn't yet learned that, though Della may placate him at times, it doesn't mean she agrees with him.

Stefano walks quickly out of the staunch iron gates of the villa and down the narrow stone street of the Via San Leonardo towards the centre of Florence. Behind the high stone walls on either side of the street, olive trees droop their silvery branches against a scorched sky. It is late afternoon, almost evening, and still hot. The road curves and winds, followed by a trail of lime-flower scent. It drifts over the tall walls from the trees surrounding the houses and villas behind.

Stefano thinks of his father and the Villa Tiglio. He had been more moved than he'd let on when he'd first walked in to see Hunter standing outside the front door under the rounded archways. The house looked much the same, the walls painted a deep mustard colour, the wooden shutters dark green, the burnt amber tiled roof.

Hunter had not looked the same. Stefano had been shocked at how much older his father had become, belying the letters he had written, describing his new-found youth and fitness since being with Della. Stefano had been prepared for the greyness of his hair – Hunter's light-beige colour had begun to bleach out years ago – but not for his face, which looks parched, fallen in on itself. It's now framed by much longer hair than Stefano can remember on his father; so long, in fact, that Hunter had tied it back in a short ponytail for the tennis. Stefano had noticed that, by some twisted coincidence, the band around Hunter's ponytail was exactly the same shade of green as *his* headband, the one he'd put on for the match.

When Stefano had arrived at the villa, Hunter had immediately challenged him to a tennis match, as if nothing had happened, as if Chiara were still inside the house, cooking her special risotto for them both. Hunter was in high spirits, joking that since he'd taught his son the game in the first place, he was anxious to prove he could still win, was still the champion. But behind the teasing, Stefano knew that Hunter was deeply serious. With sad resignation he had realized that some things are for ever doomed to remain the same.

Yet everything *has* changed. Stefano thinks of his mother now, sitting in her sister's comfortable but not overlarge apartment in Siena. Chiara has been to hell and back, he thinks bitterly, while Hunter reaps the rewards of the language school they both set up six years ago at Villa Tiglio, when his own father died and left the property to Hunter.

Stefano is hardly aware now of the balmy evening approaching, of the way the sky is mellowing and the air is softening after the harsh heat of the day. He is too lost in remembering. All those hard, bleak years in England when his parents struggled to make a living, particularly those last years in London, when Hunter was an underpaid teacher and Chiara struggled with her freelance work as a wood-restorer. They got by, but London was expensive and inhospitable to the only marginally successful. Both Chiara and Hunter longed for Italy: Chiara because it was home, and Hunter because he was ambitious and knew he would never get ahead in England.

How happy they were, Stefano remembers, when they made the move permanently to Villa Tiglio. Especially Chiara, who had sacrificed her own work for that crucial first year to help Hunter with the administration, the publicity and organization of his school. The waste, the sadness of it all, Stefano thinks; and then all his thoughts are scattered as he is nearly run over by a scooter racing in the wrong direction along the one-way Via San Leonardo. The rider is female, young, with long hair blowing out behind her, like a dark, triumphant flag. She smiles at him both apologetically and appreciatively as she flies by, but she doesn't slow down.

Suddenly Stefano is fed up with thinking about his father, his mother, Della and Villa Tiglio. He is newly returned to Italy after nearly three years; he has a job with good money and few hours; he is free, young and ready for anything.

Jauntily, he begins to walk faster, past the massive fortified walls of Forte Belvedere on his left, with its grassy verges filled with poppies, red like bloodstains against the stone structure. He walks through the old gate of the city and down the tiny steep Costa San Giorgio, past Galileo's house on the left with its frescoes and portrait of the astronomer, and, further on, past the church of Santa Felicita as he turns left in front of it down the Via Guicciardini.

His steps lighten and quicken. He wants to get to the Piazza Santo Spirito, go to a bar he knows there and look up the friends he drank, picked up girls and played football with during the long summers he used to spend in Florence.

He has not yet let himself think about Della. Instinctively he knows that this, when it comes, will be a minefield.

3

Stefano walks into his mother's apartment, or rather the one belonging to her married sister, who has moved permanently to California but wants to maintain her little piece of Italy. It's eleven o'clock, but Chiara has not been worried. Stefano, a good Italian son, phoned her from Florence to say he would be late. His voice sounded excited, happy even. Chiara had felt desolate, thinking these emotions came from his meeting with Della, his reunion with his father. Later, desolation was replaced by guilt, for wasn't this what she had wanted? A son needed his father, even though his father was a *porco*.

'*Allora, hai fame?*' Chiara asks as Stefano sprawls at the kitchen table, opens a can of beer he has bought and offers her one. She refuses and asks again, 'Are you hungry?'

He assures her that he's not, only thirsty. Chiara persists, as mothers do, and asks, 'So, you have eaten then? At the villa?'

'*Non ho mangiato alla Villa Tiglio, Mamma,*' Stefano says impatiently. Though his mother speaks very good English, having lived most of her married life in England, they always speak in Italian.

Chiara says, 'So where did you eat, if you didn't eat with your father?'

'In the city, in Oltrarno,' he says, naming his favourite area in Florence, the part around the Piazza Santo Spirito on the other side of the river Arno. 'The Sabatino place, don't you remember? The trattoria on the Borgo San Frediano.'

'Is that still there, then?'

'*Mamma*, it's been there forty years, in the same family.'

Chiara smiles. 'So it has. It's good to know that some things never change, eh?'

Stefano is relieved at this lightness of tone. He had half feared a heavy scene after his first visit to the Villa Tiglio, though he knew his mother would try to keep her own emotions under control because of him. 'Sabatino's will never change, *Mamma*. The tables and chairs must be the same ones they had when they first started, and so is the decor.'

'That was always part of its charm.'

'Is it? I think it's the food. And the fact that it's cheap.'

They are talking easily. But Chiara is fidgety and gets up, gets a bottle of mineral water from the fridge and pours some in a glass. Neither want to talk of Hunter, but Chiara knows they must. 'So did your father take you to Sabatino's?'

'No, no, I met Marco.'

'Sadie's son? How is he?'

'Great. I went with him for a meal. He's got an apartment on the Piazza Santo Spirito.'

'Does Sadie still teach at the school?' Chiara feels suddenly sad that she has to ask. Once she and Sadie were friends, but when she left Florence, close friends from the Villa Tiglio felt like rampant vines threatening to strangle her with memories. Cutting them away had been the only way she knew to ensure her survival.

'Yes, Sadie's still there,' Stefano says.

Chiara steels herself. 'And Hunter? You did see him, didn't you?'

'Yes, of course I saw my father. That's why I went, you know that. I wanted to get all this family stuff out of the way before starting work tomorrow.'

'So? He is well?'

'He beat me at tennis, so he must be all right.'

Chiara laughs, but it's forced. Still, she's trying, Stefano thinks. A rush of love sweeps through him for

26

his feisty mother, dumped but not defeated.

His mother certainly doesn't look like a discarded old wife. She looks younger than Hunter, though they are more or less the same age; somewhere in their middle fifties, Stefano seems to remember. True, her hair would be grey like Hunter's if she didn't dye it its original dark brown, but it's still thick and curly like his own. Like Hunter, she has remained slim, but where he has become all bones and veins and sinew, she is gently rounded. And where Hunter's face has caved in on itself like a pie crust which has risen and then fallen, Chiara's face has grown plumper with age, which suits her. It is only the deep black smudges under her eyes, which appeared a year and a half ago and have never gone, that mar her face, but they are enough. They are only the visible scars, Stefano thinks. The others are worse.

Chiara knows that if she doesn't say it, Stefano won't either. She refuses to have the spectre of Della hovering around her new home here in Siena, her new life, Stefano's new life. Determined to bring the ghost out into the open, she asks, 'And Della? Did you meet her?'

Stefano gets up, takes another beer from the fridge, offers Chiara one again, which this time she accepts. His mother hardly ever drinks beer, he remembers. The kitchen is cool after the heat of the day; a breeze moves the white curtains with the red poppies on the open kitchen window. Basil and sage plants thrive on the window sill and fresh lilies stand on the wooden table. Chiara, with her weakness for plants and flowers, has already made the unused apartment seem as though it's been lived in for years, though she has been here only a couple of months.

'Yes, I met Della. She interrupted our tennis. I think Dad was pleased because he was losing.' He grins mischievously and raises his glass to her. Chiara is breathless with love for this son of hers who is trying to make this easy for her.

And so she is able to ask, as lightly as Stefano,

'And is she what you expected?'

Stefano is perplexed by this question. He hadn't expected anything, to be honest, for he had been so busy being angry at Hunter that he had no room to think of the woman who had caused all this. He wonders now why he does not, and never did, blame Della. Perhaps he knows intuitively that his father is weak, that if Della hadn't come along it would have been someone else.

'She's ordinary enough,' he says now. He grins again. 'She's not a patch on you.'

This time Chiara laughs out loud. 'She's younger than me. Lots. She can't be forty yet. And she's quite attractive.' She is forcing herself to be fair.

Stefano forces himself to be truthful. 'She *is* good-looking, I suppose, but in a very ordinary way. *Mi capisci?* She's not, like, wow!' He emphasizes this with a very Italian macho gesture, which makes Chiara laugh again. Encouraged, he goes on. 'Maybe Dad needed someone, I don't know – someone less vivacious as he grew older. Maybe he thought you'd be too much for him.'

'*Madonna,* Stefano, the things you say.' Chiara shakes her head, but he knows she's pleased; pleased and grateful. 'And was Della happy to have met you at last?' she goes on.

'*Penso di sì.*' Stefano shrugs and nods, but now his voice is doubtful, no longer relaxed and easy. Chiara notes this and wonders if the woman was rude to him, unwelcoming.

She is about to ask when Stefano leaps up from the table and says, 'Never mind them. Come see what I've been doing all evening, after leaving the villa.' He is bouyant and excited again, as he was on the telephone. He pulls Chiara to her feet and pushes her towards the front door of the apartment just off the kitchen. 'Come on, it's outside.'

'What is?'

'Come see.'

They tumble out of the green painted door and down the two steps into the steep tarmacked road. The apartment is right in the heart of Siena, only a short walk from the Campo, the massive, splendid medieval piazza where the ancient horse race, the Palio, takes place every year.

'So what am I supposed to be looking at?' Chiara wants to know. The street is deserted, but from the Piazza of San Francisco near by there's the sound of laughter: university students returning home after a night out in one of the local bars.

'This,' Stefano says, hoisting his leg over the seat of a small, slightly battered, but still sturdy Vespa. 'I bought it from Marco tonight. He's just got himself a newer model.'

'But . . . you drove that thing home, tonight? I thought you came in by bus.'

Stefano grins and shrugs. Chiara thinks how at home he looks, perched on the scooter. Like all the other young Italians sitting on their *motorini* or scooters or mopeds, in groups or in pairs, ready to talk for hours, just as their parents talk in cafés, their grandparents on benches in sunny piazzas.

'I needed wheels, *Mamma*, and soon. I hate being tied to bus schedules.'

'Maybe you should take up your father's offer and live at the Villa Tiglio. There is plenty of room as you know. It would be more convenient for work.'

'It does seem stupid to commute all that way every day when I could live in Florence,' Stefano says, and Chiara feels her heart muscle ripple, as if preparing to ward off a blow.

'Well do then.' She makes herself smile at him encouragingly.

'You don't mind?' he says, and his voice is lilting with relief.

How quickly they – Hunter and Della – have captured him, she thinks bitterly. But she says, dissembling, 'Of course not.'

29

He gets off the scooter and hugs her impetuously. 'I'll tell Marco tomorrow. It's a great place, right on the Piazza Santo Spirito. I can get to the Villa Tiglio in a few minutes on the Vespa. Marco has two big bedrooms looking right over the piazza. He's been trying to find a flatmate for ages.'

'Marco? But . . . I thought we were talking about . . . about your father's house, about the villa.'

Stefano's face darkens. '*Mamma*, I would never stay there. Never. *Ma va.*' How could you even think that?'

Relief radiates Chiara's face, lighting it from within, just as the moon lights it from without. It is half full tonight, covered by a fine white mist. 'I'm so pleased that you'll be in Florence. It would have been too much of a worry you making that long journey twice a day and on a Vespa too. As long as you come see me sometimes,' she burbles happily. Then, teasing, 'You *will* come see me, now and again? You won't forget your poor old *mamma* on her own in Siena?' In the gauzy starlit night she looks about thirty, he thinks, and hopeful. He wishes for it to last, wishes that finally she is over the worst of Hunter's betrayal.

'You know I will,' he laughs. 'If you stop trying to get round me with that poor and old crap. Anyway, I hope you're going to come see me too, in Florence. I'll buy you a meal at Sabatino's.'

He watches her face as she hesitates. She has been in Italy for two months and has not once contacted any of her old friends in Florence, though she has been in touch with childhood friends here in Siena, where she grew up. It's as if she has cut the twenty-eight years of her marriage out of her life, out of her past. Even in London, which was Chiara's home for so long, she didn't see any of the friends she shared, as a couple, with Hunter. Instead, she sought out old colleagues from her days as a picture restorer, men and women who knew her through her work, not through her marriage.

Stefano says, 'You have to go back, you know. You're

too addicted to Florence to abandon it completely. I can't believe you never intend to see your beloved Fra Angelicos again.'

He knows he has her. One of his earliest memories is standing with her in the quiet starkness of the old monks' cells in the Convent of San Marco gazing up at her favourite frescoes. Before he could read or write she had taken him to see these and other favourites, which she revisited each summer when they returned to the city. The treasures of Florence are part of her life, of her soul, of her work too. She has lived without them for nearly two years already; he cannot believe she will live without them for ever.

A *motorino* passes them noisily on the street and breaks the mood, preventing Chiara from answering. 'Let's go in,' she says. 'It's getting cooler. Tomorrow it will not be so hot, *grazie a Dio*.'

As they say goodnight and go upstairs to their separate bedrooms, Chiara lets herself think for a moment about Della. She wonders how she reacted to Stefano, this grown son of the man she lives with. Stefano had, of course, been in London when Della was hired to teach at the school, and by the time he was due to visit his parents in Florence, Chiara had fled to London and Della was ensconced in her place.

There are still particles of emotions on the floor of Chiara's heart when she thinks of Della, not so many as before but still there, like thin shards of broken crystals. Pain, grief, jealousy, anger – she thought she had picked them all out, bit by bit, over the past long months, but now she sees she has missed a few. Once again, she struggles with bitterness; it's not an emotion she knew before Hunter left her, nor is it one she wants to remain in her heart. It's the irony, she thinks as she runs a bath, putting in lavender foam oil and swishing her hand around in the hot water to create even more bubbles. All those years with Hunter in England, soothing his simmering rage and frustration as his teaching career didn't prosper as spectacularly as he believed it should. And she longing to return to Italy but keeping her own dissatisfaction to herself.

And then, finally, relaxing, thinking the difficult times were over with the language school on its feet, Hunter crowing with delight and satisfaction, and herself settling once again into her beloved Firenze. How complacent she had been, how happy, how smug in her belief that the rough years were over.

She steps into the bath and vigorously begins soaping herself, too tense now to relax in the steamy foam. She knows it's being back in Italy that is stirring these sharp molecules of dusty emotion back into her consciousness. It will settle, she tells herself. Everything does, finally. But she's not convinced.

Stefano, undressing for bed and lying naked on top of the light summer duvet which is still too hot for this strange spring night, thinks about Della too, wondering what indeed she did make of him, her lover's son, on this their first meeting. He lets the thought take hold, invade him. He is, after all this time of avoiding the fact of her existence, focused on Della.

He wonders, idly, if his father will be pleased that his son has begun to acknowledge, at last, the new woman in his life. Then Stefano hardens his heart and decides he doesn't really care what his father thinks.

4

Della wakes early on Monday morning, but Hunter is earlier. It's well before six o'clock and he is already putting on shorts, a T-shirt and a light sweatshirt. 'Up you get,' he says buoyantly to Della. 'It's a perfect morning for a run.'

Though they run three or four mornings a week together, Della would prefer today to have the time to shower slowly, dress carefully and get her head together before facing the new input of students who will be arriving at nine. Or, if she were honest, before facing Stefano, who will be here at eight.

Reluctantly, she makes herself join Hunter for their usual run. Pulling on her own shorts and top quickly, she goes downstairs to meet him in the small courtyard at the front of the villa.

The early morning is pleasantly cool, the sky stained with crimson streaks, as if the poppies in the fields below have bled into it. Della and Hunter walk briskly down the gravel path to the iron gate in the high stone walls which lead from the Villa Tiglio to the Via San Leonardo. Lime trees line the path and drive as they do behind the house near the tennis court, and already their scent sprinkles the morning air like dew. Della thinks of Stefano.

Before they head out through the gates and into the street they do a few standing trots and stretches to warm their limbs and ease them into their run. Then they go down the hill on the narrow stone-paved road towards the centre of Florence, the same way Stefano had walked the day before.

Luckily there is little traffic down the winding road

at this time of the morning, for the footpaths on either side under the stone walls are so narrow that they're nearly impossible to walk on, let alone run. Della waits for her mind to empty, as it does when she runs, but the welcome euphoria eludes her today. There are too many heady sensations bombarding her mind and emotions: the stark white lilies in the little church of San Leonardo on the right, the perfume of jasmine flowers toppling over the wall further on, on the left, the clear notes of a blackbird as they go through the archway of the old gate into the city. Intermingled with all this Della remembers the clean, hot young scent of Stefano, vying with the lime blossom.

The Ponte Vecchio is blessedly empty as they run across it over the river Arno, the jewellery shops shuttered and locked, the bronze bust of Benvenuto Cellini free of tourists clamouring for photographs. The series of bridges beyond the Ponte Vecchio cross the red-tinged river like elongated shadows stretching from shore to shore, the sky above them still flushed with early morning. Turning right, Hunter and Della head past the vast gallery of the Uffizi on their left and then run down the Lungarno, the road alongside the river.

Hunter, spry and athletic, runs slightly ahead of Della today. He is feeling exhilarated, powerful, at his peak. He has managed to obliterate from his mind the unpleasant things about his reunion with Stefano yesterday and recalls only the highlights: his win at tennis, Stef's polite acquiescence as he was saying goodbye, and, perhaps most importantly, the way Stefano looked at Della, held her hand for those extra few seconds when she reached it out for him to shake.

Hunter noticed these things, for Hunter notices most things. Unfortunately, he often interprets them in quite the wrong way, but he doesn't know this.

And so Hunter is feeling smug today. He is sure that Stefano is totally bowled over, mesmerized by Della. *That* will show him, Hunter thinks gleefully as he runs alongside the sludgy water of the Arno, now turning

34

into a yellowy brown as the sun rises higher. That will show Stefano that his father is still a force to be reckoned with.

Hunter likes this. When Stefano grew up, far too quickly for his father's liking, and far too tall, too handsome, too Italian, Hunter had felt it an affront somehow to his own shorter, slighter frame; his own Englishness; his own pleasing boyish looks, which Stefano's sudden, striking maturity seemed to make insignificant. Being the father to this strange progeny was off-putting. Hunter, now in his prime, with lovely youthful Della at his side, feels more at ease being a mate to his son, and so, yesterday, he jumped at the way Stefano watched Della, as if he could eat her there and then. Hunter almost nudged him, almost said something laddish, like, She's a bit of all right, eh, boy? He didn't, of course, for he is far too cultured to be quite so boorish; there is a time and a place for everything. But the more he thinks of that meeting between the three of them, the more satisfied he feels.

Hunter puts on a bit of speed, leaving Della even further behind. He is grinning slightly as he runs, remembering the look of almost astonishment – certainly perplexity – on Stefano's face as he'd stared at Della. Hunter could feel himself gaining stature in his son's eyes with that look; and so it should be. Stefano has not been at all supportive of Hunter's union with Della; perhaps now he will be a bit more understanding and sympathetic to his father, instead of standing by his mother in that typical Italian manner.

Turning right at the next bridge, Della and Hunter cross over the Ponte alle Grazie. The sky has changed colour again; now it is stained with a haze of white, as if a milk jug has been tipped over it. They leave the river and zigzag up and down some back roads until they come to the long road leading steeply uphill, the Via di Belvedere. This is usually a killer, but Hunter feels so full of zest that he holds his pace while Della lags a short way behind. He almost said to her last night, after he had successfully made love to her for an hour and twenty minutes – he likes to time his lovemaking – that it wasn't a bad thing for one's son to be a bit jealous of his father. But Della had been in a funny mood. Though she had said and done all the right things during their lovemaking, he had a nagging feeling that she wasn't all there. Perhaps she wasn't well; certainly she'd tried to get him to finish quicker than usual, but he wasn't having any of that.

Or perhaps, he thinks now as he flies like a god towards Olympus up the steep hill of the Belvedere, leading up to the fort on the top, she was simply overwhelmed by meeting Stefano. It can't have been easy, confronting the fact that she had a grown-up stepson. Well, not exactly a stepson, for she and Hunter weren't exactly married, but they were living together, as an established couple. Perhaps it had made Della feel she was getting old, this sudden would-be stepson in his mid-twenties appearing before her.

Della, several yards behind Hunter, doesn't feel in the least bit old. The immense fortified wall of the city towers on her right, and at its feet, on the grassy verges, poppies splatter like drops of blood. Like Hunter, she finds she is running easily up the steep, winding road. The only reason she has lagged behind is that she wants to be alone, with her thoughts scattered haphazardly, like the poppies, in her head.

For they are growing wildly, these conflicting emotions, a jumble of weeds and blossoms in the compost of her mind. First there is a peculiar feeling of happiness, odd because it seems to have no roots in anything other than the sheer delight of meeting Stefano. Growing with that is a kind of black hopelessness, because she hasn't forgotten that Stefano is Hunter's son. Yet clinging to all this is another, greener vine, choking everything else: the knowledge that she, unlike Hunter, is still young. Not as young as Stefano, perhaps, but she is closer to his generation than to Hunter's.

She wonders, as she runs, if Stefano finds her at-tractive. He must do — the way he held her hand yesterday, the way he looked at her. She liked that; she likes men to stare at her in the street, likes to know she is still noticed by them. The Italians are es-pecially good at making a woman feel admired. Far from annoying her, like they do some women, these men make her feel whole and complete, when they boldly stare and murmur '*bella*' as she walks by. They remind her sometimes of her brothers' friends, after they outgrew their rugby-tumbling days, hanging around the spacious house, with clandestine joints and cold cans of exotic lagers, eyeing her sixteen-year-old body with blatant appreciation and hot, bold lust. They'd spoiled her too, these spoiled young men, with their flattery and leers, their suggestive eyes, their open propositions when her brothers were out of earshot. It made her feel powerful, as she'd felt when she was a child, when she was still young enough and new enough in the family to be a novelty; the only girl in a riot of boys.

And so Della likes living in Italy, where she is indeed still a novelty — despite the influx of English — with her pale colouring, her well-bred voice, her cool yet assertive manner. She enjoys the attention of the Italian men, likes knowing that if she walks out of the house with a short, well-cut skirt, or her snug white jeans, her pale golden hair high, high on her head in a sophisticated twist, she will be noticed. Even now, running with Hunter, she is not unaware of the long lascivious stares from the men in cars, who drive past, admiring her well-exercised thighs and the flash of firm buttock under her shorts.

But now they are at the fort, the sky above its tower-ing stone no longer skimmed milk, settled at last into the day's enamel blue. From the fort Hunter and Della turn on to the Via San Leonardo as the road levels out towards the Villa Tiglio. Hunter is running on the spot, waiting for her. His long hair, hanging loose below his ears, is wet with sweat and plastered to his head, making his bones more emphatic. As he turns to her with a smile she sees for a moment not his face, but a skull, his skeletal self.

'You're not doing too badly,' he says condescendingly. 'I thought you were a bit slow on the hill.'

'I'm fine,' she snaps, not even stopping but running past him towards the house and towards Stefano.

The first person Stefano sees when he arrives for work at eight o'clock is the young woman who nearly ran him down on her scooter the day before. This time she almost ploughs into the back of his bike as he slows down at the gates of the Villa Tiglio.

After five minutes or so of flirtatious apologies, they discover that they're both going into the same place. '*Allora, devi essere uno studente,*' she says.

He explains that no, he is not one of the language students, but the new teacher at the school. She frowns, disbelievingly, and says, still in Italian, 'But that's not possible. You're Italian. Hunter never hires Italian teachers, only native English speakers.'

'I am,' Stefano says, reverting to English for the first time. 'I was actually born in London.'

A torrent of Italian hails on him. 'Ah, I understand. You're Stefano, Hunter's son. You're taking the place of that teacher who quit unexpectedly. And you're Chiara's son, but you've been working in London as an Italian teacher. But now you've come back to Italy for good, and so has your mother. You're sharing her sister's house in Siena, right?' She leans back triumphantly on the saddle of her scooter, pleased with her knowledge.

They are both still sitting on their bikes, blocking the entrance to the villa, but luckily it's early, not quite eight o'clock. Stefano asks drily, 'My father has been talking a lot about me?'

'Not Hunter, but Sadie, one of our other teachers. You remember her, don't you? She told me you were coming to work for us. She is so pleased that Chiara has come back to Italy.'

'Yes, I know Sadie, she was here when my father and mother were still together.'

'That was such a sad thing. We all liked Chiara. I hope she's coping now. Is she all right? We were all disgusted with your father for leaving her for Della.'

Stefano is momentarily disconcerted by her frankness. He has forgotten how upfront the Italians are. He has also forgotten how gorgeous they are too; the young woman in front of him is a stunner. She has long, rumpled deep-red-brown hair which tumbles halfway down her back – hair that he would love to spend hours untangling; startling ocean-green eyes; and plump lips, which she seems to have outlined in a dark-purple pencil and coloured in with the pale shades of a heather plant. 'Do you like it?' she asks ingenuously, as he stares at her mouth. 'It takes me hours to get the exact colour.'

He grins. 'It's weird, but yes, I suppose I do.' He doesn't say that he'd prefer to see her lips naked, say in bed, for a start. Instead, he asks, 'If you know my mother, you must have started as a student here ages ago.'

She is indignant. 'Student? Mother of God, not a student, thanks to every saint in heaven. I work here, of course. I'm your father's secretary.'

They are interrupted by the friendly honk of a small Fiat now trying to get into the drive. An ample woman, with large green-framed sunglasses and dyed orange hair which frizzes in all directions from her head, leans out the window and shouts, '*Ciao*, Bettina, I see you've got Stefano panting at your feet already. Wait until I tell my son. Stefano, great to see you. Marco said he'd run into you. And I'd recognize his old scooter anyway. How's your mum?'

By this time they have, between them, totally blocked the Via San Leonardo. Several cars behind Sadie, who is the woman in the Fiat, are honking noisily. Eventually they all get inside the villa with their various vehicles, park them and walk together through the front courtyard and under the arches into the house.

The language school occupies the entire first floor of the villa, with the other storeys remaining as living quarters for Hunter and Della. A wide corridor tiled with pale grey and pink marble leads to the main office, which is through an open archway. Here Hunter, as owner and director of the school, reigns, with an alcove for Bettina, his secretary and reception-ist, at the side.

It is the first day of a four-week session – always a slightly frenetic day for the school. The students are mostly Italian, but not all are from Florence; many come from quite a long way and have to be found accommodation. They are of all ages.

Stefano, Bettina and Sadie are still chatting as they approach the office, where Hunter is sitting at his king-size desk, looking through some papers. He looks up and frowns. 'No Italian, please. You know the rules. This is a school of English, so we speak English here at all times.'

Sadie says reasonably, 'But there are no students here yet, Hunter. We have so much to talk about, see-ing Stefano, and you know Bettina isn't comfortable in English.' Sadie herself, married since she was nineteen to an Italian, feels perfectly at home in either language.

'I quite understand,' Hunter says, 'but really, Bettina, you have been with us for well over two years now. Surely you *should* be comfortable with English, work-ing in an English school. Perhaps if you made some effort you would be.'

Bettina snaps. In rapid Italian she gives Hunter an earful, as Stefano puts it later to Chiara. She tells him she is not a teacher, thank the blessed Madonna and the Holy Spirit, and so she has no need for English, for that is the last country in the world she would visit, if all the people there are as fussy and rigid as Hunter.

And besides, she adds as Hunter tries to interrupt, since the students at the school are Italian anyway, and many of them are beginners in English, it's a shame only she, and Sadie of course, speak decent Italian to help them with their problems.

The telephone rings and Bettina is forced to break off her tirade to answer it. Hunter, not at home with the Italian language, despite his many years in the country, has by now switched off from Bettina's prattle, as he always does. Turning instead to his son, he says, 'Stef, glad to see you're nice and early. Ready for work then?' He puts his hand in a comradely gesture on Stefano's shoulder.

Bettina, her hand muffling the telephone, interrupts them with some questions for Hunter, so Stefano is left alone as Sadie has gone off somewhere. He wanders down the corridor and into the first room he comes to, an airy, spacious room with double windows, looking out over the lime trees. The room is furnished with tables and chairs and a large writing board at the front, with a wide oak desk at its side.

Della is at this desk, looking through a workbook. She doesn't see Stefano at first and he has a moment to study her. Yesterday, when he thought about her, trying to figure out what there was about her that had made Hunter choose to leave Chiara, he had realized that he didn't remember what she looked like. All he remembered was a vague impression, as he had said to Chiara last night, of a rather ordinary woman; attractive perhaps, but not in an extraordinary way.

Now that he studies her objectively, he sees that she has pale-brown hair, with so many yellow streaks it seems blond. Her hair hangs loose today, not quite reaching her shoulders, and is brushed away from her brow, which is clean-cut, unlined. Her face is oval, the features regular. He can see that the word attractive could be applied to her, though he himself does not find her so. There is a slight hardness to her face, a toughness of expression which to him is unappealing.

41

He cannot quite grasp what it is that has so besotted his father.

Della looks up from her paperwork to see Stefano once again staring at her. She smiles at him with a slight, almost coy, turning of her head, which he finds irritating. Nonetheless, trying to be grown-up and civilized about all this, Stefano smiles back. Having given up the perplexing problem of what his father sees in Della, his mind turns to what she sees in Hunter.

What Della sees in Hunter is something that would be too complex for her to explain to anyone, let alone Stefano. On the surface it seemed simple enough: new teacher at the language school falls in love with the boss, boss falls in love with her, ditches wife, and new teacher and boss live happily ever after. But the reasons why Della fell in love with Hunter were far more complex. Bluntly, he had saved her pride and her self-respect after a humiliating affair in Rome, where she had lived and worked for nearly seven years. She had thought she was settled permanently in Rome, after years of building her career as a teacher of English as a foreign language in various grim Eastern European countries. She hadn't much liked the travelling, but she was determined to succeed. She knew it was the only way to the top, these tough jobs teaching English in office blocks that looked more like army bunkers, in vast industrial units, where she taught Polish, Russian and Slovakian middle managers the business English necessary to communicate with similar businesses in Spain or Portugal. It was the universal language now, and Della's hard work was finally rewarded when she landed a top job at one of the best language schools in Rome. Thinking she was settled for good, she had rented a tiny but exquisite apartment off the Campo de' Fiori in the heart of the old city, believing that now her professional life was sorted, her emotional life would be too.

But her affair with a married politician, who lived in a separate house from his actress wife, was the last in a trilogy of ruinous Roman affairs, and Della, as she had done once or twice before in her life, simply turned her back and ran. She quit her job, moved to Florence and was promptly snapped up by Hunter, who, unlike the Roman politician, charmed her, wooed her, fussed over her and, most importantly, left his wife for her, instead of just making promises.

Della desperately tries to think of Hunter as his son sits himself in front of her, in such close proximity that she can smell the faint scent of soap – something green, olive-like, earthy. She remembers how Hunter was at the beginning: so kind, so eager to let her confide in him, so helpful and loving. And later, so grateful to her for revitalizing his life, extricating him from a marriage that had grown stale years earlier. After the disaster in Rome, after the years of failed relationships, Hunter appeared like a god in a golden chariot; a miracle if there ever was one.

Yet perhaps, Della thinks now as she meets Stefano's eyes, which are looking intently at her, perhaps gods are not to be trusted. Perhaps they are, in the end, merely illusions: what we want to see when we reach for the heavens.

The silence is lengthening between then as they look warily at each other. Della refuses to speak first. The stubbornness that so infuriated her brothers nonetheless very often worked, as it does now. Stefano is the one who breaks the silence. 'I give up,' he says, shaking his head in perplexity. He notices that her eyes are of a deep, almost navy-blue colour.

'Give up what?' Her smile wavers slightly. His proximity is powerful, startling. She feels as if she has lost control somewhere. He is just as she remembers, only more so. The light, airy room seems cramped and suffocating with Stefano in it, as if he is using up far more than his fair share of light and air.

'Give up what?' she says again, raising her eyebrows at him, looking at him sideways from under brown eyelashes. He realizes she is flirting with him, and is embarrassed for her. He doesn't understand that this is what she does, what she has always done, since her childhood, to try to gain authority over men whom she is afraid may dominate her.

'I've given up wondering why my father did it. Left my mother for you, I mean.'

She feels as if he has slapped her. 'That's not very complimentary. In fact, that sounds to me like an insult,' she says, her face stony.

Stefano is genuinely surprised. 'Is it? I'm sorry, I didn't mean it like that. The thing is, they were together for so long. There wasn't any warning, no previous separations, nothing like that. They were . . . they were, I don't know, a couple. A family. I can't get my head round it, you know? Like, why break up something that, you know, was older than *me* even.'

'Just because they were together a long time doesn't mean that it was a good thing,' Della says. She feels very much on the defensive, not a position she is often in.

Stefano sighs and looks away from her out of the window. He cannot explain that if his parents' marriage was not as he had thought it all those years of growing up, if the past he remembered was a lie, then how much else in life was a delusion?

Almost as if he is talking to himself, he says, 'I also can't get around the feeling that my father is a shit. I'm sorry, I know you love him. Well, I assume you do. If you don't, then what you did was inexcusable: letting him dump my mother for you.' He turns to look at her again. 'You *do* love him, don't you?' His voice is not accusatory, only curious.

Della hesitates. Twenty-four hours ago she would have said unhesitatingly, Yes, of course I love Hunter. But something strange is happening to her. She feels that she has never felt for Hunter what she is beginning to feel for this man sitting opposite her. She has never wanted to reach out and touch Hunter's face the way she wants to put her fingers on Stefano's lips, the curve of his cheeks; the way she wants to know what the texture of his hair feels like in the palm of her hand. She has never wanted Hunter the way she wants – suddenly, blindingly, without warning – Hunter's son.

Stefano is waiting for an answer. Della would like to say truthfully, No, perhaps I do not love Hunter. Perhaps I have yet to learn what love is.

But as Stefano has just said, if this were true, it would be inexcusable what she did: let Hunter break up his marriage, his family.

She knows she should just say, Yes, I love Hunter. After all, what business is it of Stefano's who Della loves and who she doesn't love?

But she cannot say this either. Not because she cannot lie – Della, like most people, is not averse to the occasional untruth – but because she wants Stefano.

'You do love him, don't you?' Stefano's voice is not unkind, but gently persistent. What had been uttered almost casually, almost rhetorically, suddenly seems significant. He has noted her hesitation, her discomfort.

Della begins to speak, but closes her mouth again before anything can come out. She looks at him in such confusion, all games and coyness forgotten, that Stefano, for the first time, warms to her.

Then she puts her head in her hands and covers her face.

'*Gesù, Madonna*,' Stefano says softly. 'So that's how it is. What a fucking mess.'

Della lifts her head, not sure what it is she will say to him. But it is too late: he is standing up, walking out of the room, no longer looking at her.

It is just as well, she thinks. She knows she would have betrayed herself to Stefano had he stayed another moment.

5

Hunter waylays Stefano in the corridor, just after his encounter with Della. 'Ah, there you are,' Hunter cries. 'Come with me to the office and I'll show you the books we use.'

Stefano follows his father. Bettina, in her alcove off the main office, looks up and grins at Stefano, then goes back to her computer.

'Here is the main workbook.' Hunter hands Stefano a fat, loosely bound sheaf of papers. 'I compiled it myself, actually. I've made a list for you of the exact number of pages you are to cover each day with the beginner's class.'

'Give or take a page or two, I hope,' Stefano says lightly, leafing through the workbook.

'No, I didn't say that. You are to follow, exactly, the lesson plan I've written for you.'

'Well, right, fine. I intend to follow your lesson plans – you know the business – but, like, in a classroom situation, it pays not to be too rigid, right? So if we fall behind a page or two one day, it's no big deal. We make it up by doing more the next day, or the next week.'

Bettina, in her alcove, has stopped typing. The silence in the office is broken by the noise of the first batch of students arriving, but this is still in the distance as they hang around the door, mingling quietly. Hunter says, 'Stef, let's get this clear. You may be my son, but here, during working hours, I'm not your father, I'm your boss.'

'Dad, what is this all about? I know that. What's the problem?'

'Just because you have a degree, just because you've done some piecemeal teaching, doesn't mean you know more about the education business than me.'

'Christ. Dad—'

'Let me finish, Stef.' Bettina, openly staring now, shakes her head, straining to understand the English. Hunter goes on, 'I've been doing this a long time. It might seem simple to you, this language teaching, but it's an extremely precise skill, an art even. Don't think that you're going to catch me up that easily. You've got a long, long way to go, if you think that.'

Before Stefano, who is too bemused to answer, can speak, Hunter is distracted by the incoming students and goes off to greet them.

Stefano looks at Bettina. 'Does he lecture all his teachers like that?' he asks her in Italian.

Bettina shrugs. 'Just ignore him. I do.'

Then suddenly the hallway seems filled with students. There is a babble of Italian, mixed with halting English from those who are now into their second or third session. Sadie appears with Hunter and Della, and the students are given written and oral tests and sorted out into classes: beginners, intermediate, higher intermediate, advanced.

Bettina is inundated with questions and comments about the rooms or apartments she has found for those coming from outside the city; her desk is constantly surrounded by bemused students. She doesn't even try to speak English, even to the advanced students, despite Hunter's admonition earlier. Stefano notices this with some amusement. He also notices her long brown legs in a black mini-skirt and the red T-shirt made of some shiny clingy material.

Stefano is given a beginner's class in the same room where he left Della earlier with her head in her hands. He has seen her since then, but only at a distance, as she handed out test papers, told new students where to go and answered questions. She looks both formidable and competent in a long rust-coloured skirt, with a

47

dazzling white sleeveless shirt tucked into it, emphasizing a small waist. She wears no jewellery, only a watch, and since her meeting with Stefano she has obviously put on fresh make-up and combed her hair. It is now swept to one side, pulled into place with a small comb. It nestles neatly onto the collar of her shirt, the blond streaks in the pale brown smooth and stark. She looks cool and businesslike, a different person from the first coy and flirtatious, then distraught woman he'd spoken to this morning.

Stefano finds himself watching her as their paths cross on and off through the morning. Not as he sometimes watches Bettina, with healthy appreciation tinged with not a little lust, but suspiciously, as he would watch a feral animal. There is something about her that makes him uneasy.

After the first two hours there's a twenty-minute break. Stefano leaves the classroom to find Sadie walking past with a tray of coffee. 'Come into the front courtyard; that's where the staff usually have their break. We let the students roam around the back terrace and garden; there are more of them than there are of us. They can use the communal kitchen downstairs to make themselves coffee, if they want, or there's a machine, but we make ours in the main office.'

Hunter and Della are already sitting on the garden chairs in the courtyard beyond the archways. Here, as on the back terrace, there are terracotta pots filled with plants, the red hibiscus flowers shining like beacons, the white gardenias fragrant with scent. Two large cedar trees stand on either side of the path, leading to the stone wall and the gate to the street, and the lime trees beyond them are pulsing out their morning perfume. A blackbird is singing loudly. Stefano sees a pale-orange lizard scuttle under one of the terracotta pots.

Sadie's hair is the same colour as the lizard, frizzed up high from her forehead as if in permanent fright, and she's still wearing her huge green-framed sunglasses. She bustles past them, her plumpish body in a yellow flowing garment and orange sandals, wriggling gracefully between the chairs. Putting a tray on the table, she cries, 'Here, coffee everyone. Bettina kindly made it for us, but she says, after today, we do our own.'

'Doesn't Bettina get a break?' Stefano asks.

'She can take one any time she likes,' Hunter says with a slight frown. 'She's not tied to classroom hours like we are; she has much more free time.'

Stefano says mildly, 'I haven't seen her stop working since she got here. She seems to do everything, and all at once.'

Hunter's frown deepens. 'Not exactly everything. In fact, I would say she has the easiest job here.'

Stefano takes a coffee from the tray and adds sugar. 'D'you think so? I'd rather have my job any day. Standing up in front of a dozen students seems a whole lot cushier than listening to fifty or sixty of them complaining about a dozen different things.'

Sadie sees Hunter's face get that pinched, tense look which means he's getting annoyed and trying not to show it. She says quickly, 'Coffee, Hunter? Della, this one is yours, slightly weaker. Bettina remembered to add hot water.'

Hunter is not to be distracted. 'I can see you have a great deal to learn about teaching,' he says to Stefano.

'Oh, probably,' Stefano agrees.

'I hope, Stef, that you're willing to be taught, now that you're older. You used to be a bit of a know-it-all, if I remember.' His voice is determinedly pleasant, his face fixed in a stiff smile.

Sadie looks pleadingly at Della, who can usually be relied upon to barge in and change the flow of conversations that don't appeal to her. But Della is strangely quiet, watching both Hunter and Stefano with an expression that Sadie can't quite put her finger on.

Stefano has stopped drinking coffee to look at Hunter. Putting his cup down carefully he says, 'Is that what you remember, Dad? Funny, but I remember other things. Would you like to hear what they are, since we're talking about the past?'

He looks at his father defiantly. Hunter, after a pause, backs down. 'There's hardly time, break is nearly over.' He picks up his coffee and drinks it quickly.

Della and Sadie both smile at Stefano. Their unspoken support diffuses the moment, but makes Hunter cross. He is the boss here; he is the one that they should be supporting.

Stefano, knowing exactly what his father is thinking, is suddenly determined to get through this first day at work without a scene with his father to spoil it. He says impulsively, 'Dad, by the time classes finish today I'll be fed up with being inside. Fancy a tennis match later this afternoon?'

Hunter beams and his face loosens, the skin becoming slack with relief. He had felt at a disadvantage for a moment, something that seldom happened, and in front of Sadie and Della too. He must be careful; he must not let Stefano get to him so. After all, he loves the boy, and he has him here now, at the Villa Tiglio, where he has wanted him ever since Chiara left and tried to turn Stefano against him.

He cries heartily, 'Won't give up, eh, Stef? Still determined to beat me? Fine, fine, let's give it a go. You're a glutton for punishment, though, after your thrashing yesterday.' He winks broadly at Della, who looks away.

Sadie, watching, says to Della, 'You're quiet today. What's up?'

'Nothing. Why, should there be?'

Sadie looks at her keenly. 'You usually have more to say than any of us. Something wrong? Are you ill?'

Hunter turns to Della. 'You *are* unusually preoccupied, darling. Sure you're not ill?' His face takes on an exaggerated look of love and concern, which Stefano finds offensive. He decides that it's because Hunter is so *aware* of the way he is looking at Della. It's as if he has been practising how a man newly in love should look.

50

Della doesn't even answer. By now all three are staring at her, Stefano included. Even he knows she is acting strangely. From what little he has heard from his mother, and from Hunter's letters, he knows that she's a tough, independent woman, one who knows her own mind and doesn't suffer fools gladly.

Yet this is not the Della Stefano has met here. This Della is erratic and uncertain, flirts boldly with him one minute, yet stands meekly in the shadows of the lime trees the next, hiding, instead of striding boldly out to meet her new – what? Stepson?

This Della lets him take the initiative, letting her hand rest in his, standing acquiescently while he scrutinizes her with curious eyes. Puts her head in her hands when he tries to confront her about his father as he tries to sort out in his head why his father did this monstrous thing to his mother.

They are all looking at Della now, but she no longer sees anyone but Stefano. He is wearing black chinos, a deep-red shirt, with long sleeves rolled up to his elbows. His hair curls and lifts at the collar of his shirt as his head turns to look at her. He is sitting on the chair next to her; she can sense again the clean showered smell of him mingled with lime and gardenia.

Hunter says again, 'Are you feeling all right, Della?' but she's saved from having to speak by Bettina, who comes bounding into the courtyard, all legs and hair and chatter, complaining about one of the students who is already moaning about his landlady. When she stops for breath Sadie says, 'Why look, Bettina, you and Stefano are dressed alike, black bottoms and red tops. A perfect match.'

Everyone looks at the two. For a moment Hunter is disconcerted, overwhelmed by their beauty, their youth, the golden colour of their skin and the dark richness of their hair. Then Bettina laughs and moves closer to Stefano, scrutinizing him and then herself. 'So we are. The perfect colour co-ordinated couple. Better not tell Marco.'

She laughs again, then looks at the others. '*Madonna benedetta!* What a lazy bunch you teachers are! All the students back in their classrooms and you lot sitting without a care in the world. Not like me, putting up with a thousand questions, a hundred problems. And who gets paid the most, eh?'

Hunter frowns but rushes back inside the villa, indicating that the others should come too. They follow more languidly, Della lingering until last, walking back into the house behind Stefano. But at the doorway, instead of walking straight on to his classroom, he turns suddenly so that she cannot help but walk right into him.

'Oh, sorry,' he says, instinctively reaching out to hold on to her arm to steady her.

'It's OK.'

He doesn't let go of her arm. He doesn't see that the pressure, far from steadying her, is making her more agitated.

'Look,' he says softly, 'I'm sorry about the remark I made this morning. About my father. And about prying like that. Whatever I feel about my father doesn't involve you; it's all between me and him.'

'I'm not sure I agree. I can understand that it's natural for you to feel resentment towards me too.'

'I don't think I do. I think it's just him. That's what I have to sort out – on my own.'

He looks into her face as if, belying his words, he's trying to find answers there. He is standing close, very close to her. Della is tall and, though he is much taller, the angle they are standing at makes her face not much farther below his. She can feel the softness of his breath and catch the aroma of the coffee he has just drunk.

She nods, unable to say more. He turns and is gone. Della leans against the open doorway for a few moments, until she can find the will to go into her own classroom.

6

Hunter wins the second tennis match easily. He is spurred on by Della, who this time doesn't hide behind the lime trees, but sits on a garden chair on the sidelines, watching them. Hunter is slightly surprised that she isn't louder in her approval of him; she usually shouts things like, 'Bloody good shot, Hunter,' or, 'Oh, well done, darling,' after a good rally, but today, though watchful and attentive, she is silent. He decides that she is being tactful around Stefano, and discreet. After all, the boy is virtually her family too, now. Hunter feels a flush of love for her, for this; for he knows that Della is not naturally tactful, nor discreet. She likes to shock, surprise. She maintains that life is too dull without a bit of drama. Hunter sometimes thinks that her childhood and young adulthood, when still at home in England, must have been exhausting. All that vying for attention in that energetic, mostly male family. But he approves of the way it has made her single-minded, determined. It matches his own determination and ambition. It thrills him when he thinks of the two of them together, a team, both working for the good of the Villa Tiglio School of English. It was one of the things that had initially attracted him: her passion and enthusiasm for her work, for the school, for *his* school. She had praised it highly, and Hunter too for the way he ran it. Coming from a woman who had worked for seven years in the most prestigious institute of English in Rome, this was high praise indeed, and Hunter had immediately loved her for it.

Now Della is watching the game quietly, her face

devoid of any expression. Despite himself, Hunter feels disconcerted, and finds himself looking over at her when he plays a particularly exquisite shot. But her face is still, impassive.

Hunter wins the match easily. But now he's becoming seriously annoyed, not only because Della's congratulations are so off-hand, but also because it seems Stefano doesn't really care, despite suggesting the game in the first place, whether he wins or loses. Hunter likes his opponents to care. It makes beating them so much more satisfying.

Stefano doesn't care about this game not only because tennis is quite unimportant to him, but also because the afternoon, this first day at the Villa Tiglio, has changed his mood again, made him mellow, relaxed. He enjoyed the classroom teaching, much more than he thought he would, and felt that zing at the end of the day brought on by mutual respect and admiration between himself and his new students.

This has dissipated his anger and frustration with Hunter, exacerbated this morning by his father's constant need to treat him as a child, and a recalcitrant one at that. Since his return, Stefano's feelings for his father seem to vacillate between a tolerant, almost affectionate amusement and a deeply rooted hatred.

This afternoon, or early evening, a kind of easy nostalgia has infiltrated Stefano's emotions. Spending the whole day here at the Villa Tiglio has transported him to his childhood, to those long summer visits with his grandparents, Hunter's parents, the original owners of the villa – members of that group of earlier English expatriots who had discovered the joys of living in Italy and had bought the place on a whim for a song.

As the day progressed Stefano began to drift away from the present into nostalgia. He remembers both his father and his grandfather teaching him to play tennis on the newly installed grass court at the villa; Hunter trying to teach Chiara, and how she dissolved in giggles when she lost, teasing Hunter into almost believing it really didn't matter that much: winning or losing.

Stefano remembers other things too, on and off during the day: Chiara's ageing parents, visiting from their cramped little house in Siena, sitting on the terrace and nodding off in deckchairs. How they spoiled Stefano, their only grandson: Chiara's mother bringing over her special pasta sauces, still warm from her own cooker at home, and Chiara's father slipping him a thousand-lire note when he thought no-one was looking.

Being back here at the Villa Tiglio, Stefano remembers those summers, realizing, now that they are gone, how special they were and how fortunate he had been to grow up with such magical Italian holidays. All that sun and space; the open, exuberant affection of his grandparents making up for the rest of the year back in England, when his father drove him either to tears or rage. He wants those memories to remain clear, not watered down and dissolved by this thing that has happened to his parents.

Later, when Chiara and Hunter moved permanently to Florence and Stefano stayed behind to go to college, the summers changed, of course. One by one his grandparents grew older and died. Suddenly Chiara and Hunter were the older generation, busy setting up the language school, struggling to maintain the villa as a place of business, no longer their carefree holiday home.

For Stefano, no longer a child, the summers changed too; they became sultry with sex, with the teasing laughter of girls on scooters – girls like Bettina – with going to clubs down on the Piazza Santo Spirito, thrumming with rock music. Summers were hanging out till all hours of the night in clubs and discos, or in the piazzas, with Sadie's son, Marco, who was Stefano's age and as eager to have it all as Stefano. Then it was going back to London and college in late September, golden skin tanned deeper from the Italian sun, and either his own heart, or some girl's heart, broken with the end of summer, only to be mended by the start of autumn, when old ties back in England, unknotted by absence, tightened again, and Italy receded into dreams and memory.

Stefano's tennis game this early evening with Hunter is haunted by a dozen other games, games of the past both on and off the courts, and so Hunter has easily won in three straight sets. Stefano finds that he's glad Hunter has beaten him. It proves that he's not quite grown up yet, and during this day of nostalgia, the years of childhood and those of that heady post-adolescent stage seem cosy, safe. Stefano has a sudden longing to remain there just a little longer.

'Well played!' Hunter cries as the match ends. He is always magnanimous in victory.

Della claps politely. Hunter once again thinks crossly that she could be a bit more enthusiastic, but reminds himself that she must be restraining herself in front of Stefano. But Stefano is a grown man; he doesn't need to be tiptoed around like a petulant child. He decides he will tell Della this later. She's certainly been acting strangely since Stefano arrived. Trying to be tactful is one thing, but to mollycoddle him is another.

Hunter, victorious, leans over Della to kiss her full on the mouth, and is irritated further as she turns her head slightly so the kiss lands awkwardly. Yes, he'll definitely talk to her later. She looks distracted, as if she's not quite there.

Hunter is soothed somewhat in the next twenty minutes or so as Della brings out fresh orange juice mixed with sparkling mineral water. Ice cubes tinkle in the crystal jug and Hunter feels his well-being return as the cold, refreshing drink goes smoothly down his throat. He feels more kindly towards Della, realizing again how difficult this must be for her, this sudden appearance of a grown man to whom she is, after all, a surrogate mother.

Looking gratefully at her, conveying with his eyes the tenderness he is now feeling towards her, Hunter puts his hand on her bare thigh, which is exposed by the slits in her long cotton skirt. They are all sitting down on the terrace chairs, relaxed in this extraordinarily warm spring evening. Hunter's hand, seemingly absent-mindedly, begins to knead the flesh of Della's thigh.

Stefano stands up. 'Well, thanks for the game. I'll be off now.'

Della looks startled. 'I thought you'd stay for dinner. Please, won't you stay? I'm making a risotto. Hunter says it's your favourite. He also says I make the best mushroom risotto he's ever eaten.'

The fragile tissue of the day's nostalgia rips as Stefano comes back to reality. In his head he had imagined not Della, but Chiara in the kitchen, cooking one of her favourite pastas or risottos, as he and Hunter practised their skills on the tennis court. Stefano had pictured the three of them eating outside on the terrace, as they had time and time again in years gone by, Chiara's laughter rumpling the stiff cloth of Hunter's many moods, her lightness making the tension between father and son bearable.

But Chiara is gone, of course. This stranger has replaced her; this woman who is looking at him so intently, as if it really mattered to her if he stayed or left.

Stefano says, 'I'm afraid I only like risotto the way my mother cooks it.' He knows as he says it that he's being ridiculous, churlish and childish, but he can't seem to help himself. Suddenly he wants to hurt, to wound, as he, as Chiara have been hurt.

Hunter sets his face carefully again, tightening it so that his displeasure is under control. But Della is beginning to understand Stefano. She says lightly, almost flirtatiously, 'Then you'd better go back to your mother for dinner.'

Hunter is pleased with this reply, with its flippancy,

its almost scornful amusement. It is more like the Della he knows, the Della he's in love with. He increases the pressure of the palm of his hand on the warm skin of her thigh, saying, 'Perhaps you should grow up, Stef. There's more to life than your mother's cooking. Perhaps you should at least sample Della's risotto before passing judgement.'

The two men lock eyes for a few moments. Then Stefano looks down at Hunter's hand, which is still on Della's thigh, the fingers half hidden under the material of her skirt. Her legs are pale and muscular. They are not unshapely, but they are hard, assertive, as if stating that their owner is not to be trifled with.

Stefano turns his eyes to Della's, who stands up to face him, leaving Hunter's hand to drop awkwardly on the vacated chair. Stefano is surprised at the darkness in her eyes, the deep blue turning into a sky just before nightfall. Watching, fascinated, he sees them change as they stare into his own, becoming blurred, hot and soft. As he looks the irises dilate, becoming deep black tunnels, daring him to go through them.

'Shit,' he says softly. Very, very softly.

'I beg your pardon?' Hunter says. He did not quite hear Stefano. He wasn't intended to.

Della heard. She understands Stefano's exclamation exactly: a sudden shocked recognition of what has been puzzling him since his arrival.

She doesn't lower her eyes but lets him see for himself. It's all there, in those navy-blue eyes, waiting for Stefano. He cannot quite believe it. He shakes his head slightly, as if trying to shake this thing between them away, then half smiles, half groans at her.

'Yes,' she says, smiling slightly herself. 'It's *deep* shit, isn't it.'

Hunter, thinking this all has to do with the risotto and the sparring remarks he and Stefano have been making to each other, says, 'Now, now, we're all getting a bit tensed up here.' He suddenly feels buoyant. Della has stood up to Stefano, has stopped being so hesitant, so apparently in awe of him, and is beginning to take Stefano in hand. Good for her. The boy won't stand a chance, Hunter thinks with amusement. Della will teach him to have a bit of healthy respect and admiration for his father. Any man who can still pull a woman like Della is not a man to be trifled with.

'No more bickering; it's been too good a day,' Hunter cries expansively, standing up between them. He places one hand on Della's shoulder, the other on Stefano's arm, bringing the only two people in the world that he loves together through him. Feeling generous, he decides that it's time to praise. 'We've had a successful day at the school, a record number of students. Stef, you've not done too badly on your first day, not at all. I'm sure the students will love you, especially the young college girls, the ones here to pad out their English before going on to jobs or university.' He winks conspiratorially at Stefano, man to man. Stefano notices his fingers tightening on Della's bare shoulder.

'And we had a hell of a good workout on the tennis court,' Hunter goes on. 'You don't mind my always beating you, do you, Stef? You wouldn't want me to throw the match, give away points to you as I did when you were a kid, would you?'

'Did you? I don't remember that.'

'There's a lot you don't remember, obviously. Still, I'll go easier the next time we play, if you like.'

'Oh no,' Stefano says easily. 'When I get round to beating you, I'll do it fairly.'

Hunter, relieved, laughs. This is all going so much better than he'd expected. He has to admit, now, that despite his intense desire to have Stefano back here, working for him at the school, he did have some misgivings. The boy was always headstrong, so like his mother. But, despite the little hiccups every now and again, things couldn't be going smoother.

When he says goodbye to Stefano, Hunter is effusive. He knows that from now on, it will all be smooth sailing.

*   *   *

When Stefano is gone, Hunter says, 'I'm actually glad he didn't stay for dinner. Mustn't rush things. He's coming around, don't you think?'

Della says softly, 'Oh yes. He's definitely coming round.'

Stefano has no intention of going back to Siena, to his mother. Though he isn't moving into Marco's apartment until the weekend, he will be staying there overnight tonight. Not knowing how long he would be in Florence on this his first day at work, he'd told Chiara he would stay overnight at Marco's.

This time he's riding on his scooter rather than walking down the Via San Leonardo in the early-evening light, but he's still assailed by the lime and olive trees; the stone walls, crumbling here and there; the deep mustards and pinks of the houses and villas glimpsed behind their gates, the red poppies growing in the fields, which can only occasionally be seen through gaps in the iron gates.

He is still stunned by the frank and inviting sensuality in Della's eyes as they rested on his. They have kindled an answering call in himself, but not as clear-cut as Della's own. She wants *him*; she has made that obvious. He curses himself for his stupidity in not recognizing it sooner. Women have let him know before, in ways both subtle and bold, that they would like to go to bed with him; he should have seen the signs.

But this is different. Della is not only quite a bit older, and presumably more experienced, than the other young women in his life, but she's also his father's lover. 'Shit,' he says aloud as he zooms down the narrow road on his Vespa, nearly running down two old men walking in the centre of the street, who turn and shout at him as he goes by.

He waves an apology at the men and smiles wryly as he thinks again, Shit. He realizes his vocabulary has become sadly limited just lately, but *Dio*, what a situation. He doesn't know whether to laugh or cry. Della, wants *him*, Stefano, and has let him know it too; so baldly, so boldly. '*Mannaggia!*' he swears again softly to himself. Who'd have thought it?

A whiff of lime flower, heady and strong, attacks his senses as he heads to the bottom of the hill towards Forte Belvedere, and suddenly he, like Della, is also filled by an erotic desire so strong he feels shaken by it. It is not, however, for Della; it is merely desire, pure and lustful, for a woman, *any* woman. This is not surprising, he thinks. Late spring and early summer is too sensual in this country not to *want*, and want badly.

And it's a long time since he has been to bed with a woman. After his last relationship ended, quite a few months ago now, he had felt too low, too drifting, to think about other women. The winter in London had been long and wet, his mother downcast, his erratic students uninspiring. He had felt too dispirited after his own split-up to care much about anything.

But now he thinks of Della, of the invitation in her navy-blue eyes. But superimposed on those eyes are the bold brown ones of Bettina. Why couldn't it have been *her* eyes issuing such a frank invitation? He remembers Hunter's hand on Della's thigh, but it is Bettina's thigh he'd like to feel his own hand against; that lush gold-brown skin showing so tantalizingly under her black miniskirt.

Stefano manoeuvres down the narrow streets of the city to the Piazza Santo Spirito, passing the grim fortress-like home of the Medici family, the Palazzo Pitti, before turning right towards the piazza. He parks his bike outside Marco's apartment and knocks on the door, but no-one is home yet.

Stefano turns into the piazza, hedged in with greenery, a fountain filled with bathing pigeons and sparrows. A dishevelled couple with rucksacks, heavy boots and dirty shorts sit under the fountain, consulting a map of the city. The stone benches dotted around the piazza are filled, some with old men reading newspapers, their wives inside preparing the evening pasta; some with young teenagers. The few small shops around the square are still open, one selling hand-crafted leather goods, another a few pieces of finely restored furniture. On the opposite side of the piazza from the row of houses where Marco's place is, a busy café spills its tables, chairs and customers out into the street. Two or three late stallholders from the daily fruit and vegetable market still ply their dwindling supply of fresh cherries, peaches and strawberries. There is the buzzing sound of a dozen cheery con-versations mingled with the muffled sounds of motorbikes and scooters whizzing through the narrow streets leading into the square. A ginger tom-cat wanders insolently across the piazza, ignoring the few dogs on leads, meowing now and then, as if to add to the hubbub.

Stefano saunters past the fountain, past the splash-ing pigeons. A couple of girls in their late teens stop him brashly and ask if he'd like to go out with them tonight. Good-humouredly he refuses, though he is tempted, tempted. But the rush of feeling earlier, which had set off a momentary craving for a woman, *any* woman, has focused into a craving for one specific person. With a bit of luck she'll be here, waiting for him as she had hinted she would be.

The evening is once again warm, perfumed, diffused with that soft Italian light, not quite day any longer, but not yet night; something mysterious and warm, pink and golden and turquoise. And then he sees her on the vast wide steps of the church of Santo Spirito. There are at least a dozen or so people, mostly young, spread out along the steps, sitting and lounging and indulging in that favourite pastime of Italians, both young and old, talking animatedly to each other.

'*Stefano! Eccolo! Come va?*'

'*Va bene.*'

Bettina pulls him down by her side, squeezing out the young man next to her, a thin lad with pale yellow hair, who shrugs and says he has to go anyway.

'I've been hanging around here for ages,' Bettina says, pouting slightly. Stefano notes that she has pencilled the outline of her lips again and lightly shaded the rest, the way it was when he first talked to her. Was it only this morning? During the day he had watched, fascinated, as the colour wore off, revealing the natural colour of her lips, a kind of pinky-brown, naked and gorgeous. But now they are pencilled in again, outlined like the precise, definite shape of a hothouse orchid. He has noticed quite a few of the Italian girls painting their lips in this peculiar way this summer and he wonders idly if it's the influence of all this Florentine art, the infusion of all that painting and colour over the centuries.

Bettina says, 'I thought you'd get here earlier; I had some friends I wanted to introduce you to.'

'I didn't know that. And you didn't say that you'd definitely be waiting for me. In fact you said you weren't at all sure whether you could make it.'

Bettina tosses her long hair and shrugs her shoulders. Underneath her shiny red T-shirt her breasts move like plump puppies in a litter. 'C'mon, I said I'd probably be hanging out with my friends at Santo Spirito later this evening. I didn't know you English need things to be carved on stone, like one of Michelangelo's sculptures.'

Stefano grins. 'This morning you said I was Italian. Make up your mind.'

A tall man, taller even than Stefano, with a shaven head and a gold earring, looms over them. '*Porca miseria!* So this is what happens when I leave my girl alone for five minutes. She gets herself tangled up with a foreigner.'

Stefano, startled, looks up quickly to see where this torrent of Italian is coming from. 'Marco, *ciao*,' he says, recognizing his old friend. 'I knocked on your door, but there wasn't anyone there.'

Marco is slapping Stefano playfully on the shoulders

and at the same time pulling Bettina up to a standing position. She is not very tall, and so he lifts her to kiss her soundly. Stefano catches a glimpse of thigh and black panties as her skirt pulls up under Marco's embrace, and a pang of regret goes through him. 'You didn't tell me Bettina was your girlfriend, Marco,' Stefano says, standing up too. He should have realized, he knows now. He remembers their names being linked once or twice by Sadie at the villa today, and by Marco the other evening, but Stefano had thought it was all in jest.

Marco grins. 'You didn't know? I'm surprised my mother didn't blurt it out. She tells everyone in sight. She seems to like Bettina, for some reason.' He kisses her again, on the top of her head this time.

'I thought you knew,' Bettina says, her arms wrapped around Marco's waist. She smiles kindly at Stefano. For a moment, seeing his downcast face, so handsome even when gloomy, she too feels a touch of regret. Then she looks up at Marco and the regret is gone. She's crazy about him.

They go around the corner to a bar filled with Marco's and Bettina's friends. One or two Stefano remembers from his earlier summers in Florence, and they greet him enthusiastically. There are others too – young women like Bettina, his own age group and mostly unattached. Some eye him keenly, with definite interest. But Bettina has spoiled him, at least for a time. He finds he is not responding to anyone else.

A few hours later the three of them, and four or five friends, walk idly back to the steps of the church of Santo Spirito and settle themselves down. It's dark now, but the night is still warm, the piazza lively. The wide steps are even more crowded with groups of young people. Two have guitars and are strumming softly. The tables of the café are filled with late diners. Everywhere there's the sound of people laughing, talking, sometimes singing, now that night has come.

Stefano has long since stopped feeling regret for the loss of Bettina, whom he'd never had anyway, through his pleasure at being with her and Marco and their friends. It's a long time since he has belonged to a group like this. In London, after finishing university, he'd become involved in an on-off relationship, too intense to leave room for easy friendships, easy nights like this one; and when it ended six, eight months ago, he was too lethargic to look up old friends and start his life again. His father's sudden offer of a job had come at just the right time; he'd been more than ready to leave England.

'Do you miss London?' Bettina says, as if reading his thoughts.

'I've only been away a week. I had a few days in Siena with my mother and then started work. How would I have had time to miss it?'

'You won't,' Bettina cries. 'We won't let you, will we, Marco! You belong here in Italy. With us.'

'A few hours ago you said I was an Englishman.'

'*Gesù benedetto*,' Marco exclaims. 'Women are so contrary.'

'No, no,' Bettina cries, 'it's not women, but men who are changeable.'

'Never. We are as steady, as loyal, as—'

'Hah, as what? As Hunter?'

As soon as she says this Bettina realizes what she has done. Hunter's relationship with Della, so obvious to everyone as soon as Della arrived at the school – everyone except Chiara, of course – had been remarked on and talked about for so long now that the word Hunter has become a joke word, synonymous with fickleness, disloyalty.

'I'm sorry, Stefano. I shouldn't have said that.'

'It's all right.'

'No, it isn't. I didn't think; I spoke thoughtlessly.' She puts her hand through his arm in a gesture of friendliness and apology. Then goes on, 'But since we're talking now, maybe you should know that we all

65

love Chiara. Sadie and I, all the students, all the temporary and part-time teachers that come to the school – we all got on so well with her, even though she wasn't working at the school by then, but had her own job outside.'

'Bettina's right,' Marco says. 'My mother was devastated when Chiara left, and so was I, you know. I was in love with her, when I was a teenager. Madly and crazily. I thought she was every man's dream.'

Stefano is touched by this. He likes to think of his mother as loved, adored and cherished, not sitting alone in her small apartment, not even her own place but her sister's old home, struggling to find work, new friends, a new life.

Bettina, aware of this, says, 'It had nothing to do with your mother, what happened. They seemed fine, she and your father, until Della came along. But then he went crazy. Followed that woman around everywhere, pretending she needed help with this and that, buying her little treats, like fresh strawberries and special cakes from the bakery. He thought none of us at the school noticed what he was up to, but we all did.'

'My mother never noticed,' Stefano says quietly.

Bettina makes a contemptuous gesture, directed not at Stefano's mother but at his father. 'She was too trusting, your mother. Besides, she wasn't around like we were, all day long. Della was teaching at the school, with Hunter right there, all day, every day. Your mother didn't have a hope.'

Stefano is silent. The guitar-players are strumming a ballad in Italian, obviously a well-known one, for many of the crowd are beginning to sing along. A drunk in a crumpled suit with a dirty white beard begins going up the steps and trips, falling down one or two. Several people go to help, but he waves them off angrily. In a few moments he's sound asleep and snoring.

Bettina says, 'It was a bad time for all of us at the

school, when your mother left. Tell her that, Stefano. Tell her how much we missed her. We still do, too. It's not the same there any more.'

Bettina makes him promise to pass on these messages. There is much that she could add, but Bettina wisely doesn't go on, though she remembers exactly how it was. Hunter's behaviour was inexcusable. The staff at the school could have forgiven him for taking another woman – the Blessed Madonna knows it happens all the time – but they could not forgive the way he gloated over it. Acting all lovey-dovey around her, the two of them kissing each other in the corridor, wrapping their arms together like octopuses during breaktime, touching each other up over their coffee. It was as if Chiara didn't exist and never had. She had fled to England when Hunter moved into Della's apartment for those first few days, and she was barely on the plane when Hunter started carrying on as if he and Della were Romeo and Juliet. Ridiculous anyway at their age, Bettina thought, and worse because it was so insensitive, rushing from one woman to another without breath in between. The others at the school still sorely missed Chiara, and Hunter continued to carry on like a demented adolescent. He showed no respect, and because of that he lost the respect of everyone.

But Bettina does not say these things. She wishes she hadn't mentioned Hunter's name so carelessly. Stefano is silent, dispirited. They stop talking and listen to the singing, which is getting louder as the song nears the end. It is almost operatic in its dramatic proclamation of love and loss, of heartbreak and sorrow. The crowd love it and belt it out merrily.

Bettina says, 'Don't be sad, Stefano. Now that you're here, everything will get better. I'm sure of it. You'll change the school, make it a happy one again.'

Her hand is still tucked through Stefano's arm. Marco looks at Stefano's troubled face and decides it's time to change the subject. He does this by suddenly belting out the final verse of the song being sung on the steps. His voice is deep, rich, quite good, and others stop their own singing to listen to him.

When it finishes he gets a round of applause, and someone hands him a can of beer, which he shares with Stefano. Finally Bettina says, 'I have to go; it's getting late.'

'Stay here tonight,' Marco protests. 'You don't want to go all the way back to Galluzzo now.'

Galluzzo is the small town that borders Florence, on the Siena road. 'You live there?' he asks.

'Yes, with my parents.'

It's not unusual for unmarried sons and daughters to live with their parents well into their twenties and thirties in Italy. Marco is the odd one out, having moved away from Sadie's home six months ago at the relatively young age of twenty-five.

'Phone them,' Marco urges. 'Tell them you're staying in Florence.' He runs his hand lightly through her hair.

She does, and the three of them finally go to Marco's apartment to the right of the church steps.

'We'll have time for a few hours' sleep before work tomorrow,' Marco says, disappearing with Bettina into his bedroom.

It is barely a few hours. Stefano, alone in the spare room, cannot hear Marco and Bettina making love in Marco's bedroom, but imagines he can.

To quell those images he thinks of his father and Della. He remembers Hunter's hand on her thigh and wonders what their lovemaking is like. He cannot imagine it. It would be an exercise in skill and precision, and Hunter would, of course, have to win.

Suddenly Stefano is angry again. It's arrogant to insist on being a winner every time. It's the way the old gods acted, Stefano thinks, remembering his Greek and Roman mythology: cavorting around on Olympus, not caring what havoc they caused, what lives they wrecked. Hunter sees himself as a god these days: young, immortal and beyond human laws.

But his father is none of these things. He is flesh and blood, and he should remember this. If not, someone, someday, will remind him.

7

Chiara feels sadness sticking to her like fine invisible cobwebs when Stefano packs his rucksack and moves to Florence the following weekend. Then she gets cross with herself. She knows she is lucky he has chosen to live in Italy, at least for a time. So she's careful not to let him see the depression clinging to her as he throws his gear into the car – Sadie's car actually, lent to him for the move.

But he sees, he knows, and says gently, '*Vieni, Mamma*. Come on, let's go have some lunch before I go. I'll treat you. I'm a full-time working man now.'

When they're seated at a trattoria on a narrow back road leading away from the great piazza of the Campo, Stefano says gently, 'Are you sure you'll be all right, *Mamma*? Here in Siena on your own?'

'Of course I'm sure. *Mamma mia*, I was born here.'

'I know, I know. I don't want you to be . . .' He hesitates.

A bearded man in jeans and T-shirt comes to take their orders. The place is full of students, for the food has a reputation for being not only cheap and tasty, but plentiful. They order spaghetti and ragù, the speciality of the trattoria, and a half-bottle of wine. It's midday on Saturday. Outside the tourists are crowding the narrow medieval streets, but none would venture inside this place; it looks too dingy, sordid even from the outside, with its faded plastic curtains and peeling wooden door.

Inside it's another world, clean and fragrant, with the smell of garlic and olive oil and sage. Stefano is fidgeting with the salt shaker on the table, then with his napkin, so Chiara knows he wants to continue their conversation. Helping him out, she says, 'Will I be lonely? Is that what you wanted to say, Stefano? I promise you, no. I won't be a bit lonely.' She smiles reassuringly at him as she lies blithely. 'I've looked up old friends since I've been here, and I've already made one or two new friends at work.'

This much is true. Through old contacts Chiara has found a job in a workshop doing restoration work: old furniture, antique framed paintings and sculptures. This is her profession; she works with wood. In Florence, after she'd helped Hunter set up the language school, she had worked freelance in little-known churches on the outskirts of the city, restoring seventeenth-century wooden statues of the apostles or sixteenth-century panelling. Occasionally there was a job in a palatial villa belonging to the odd contessa, or a very distant descendant of one of the Medicis. In London she had worked mostly on furniture, and though that is what she's doing now, she hopes it will lead to other things. All in all, she is lucky, and says so aloud.

Stefano is relieved and it shows in his face. Chiara is glad she has told a small white lie for his sake. Yes, she has seen old school friends, but they have their own lives now and she has little in common with them. Yes, she is pleased to be in her own country, but it's not as easy as she makes out to Stefano, to begin a new life, a life alone. Not in London, not here in Italy, not anywhere. And especially not at her age.

Stefano says, 'It's good you're back in Italy, *Mamma*. You weren't that happy all those years in England, were you.'

This time Chiara can be truthful. She remembers going to England with Hunter soon after their marriage in Italy, after they had met through a mutual friend when Hunter was visiting his parents at the Villa Tiglio. He was a trainee teacher and she had just finished her art training in Florence and was eager to pursue her career and far from ready to fall in love. But Hunter had been so different from the Italian men she'd known until then. What he lacked in effusive flattery and sophistication he more than made up for in stubborn persuasiveness, all the more effective for being passive. Instead of words, he used his eyes, those unique grey opalescent eyes, which followed her around silently and eloquently, beaming his love and passion so intensely that she hadn't a chance. He wanted her, and though she suspected a great deal of this was because he was in love with Italy at that time, it didn't take her long to begin to love him back.

Stefano is watching her closely as these thoughts flash like sheet lightning through her head – fleeting, illuminating and useless. How he watches her these days, this son of hers, with such worry and care.

She lifts her chin and lightens her face to take the worry from his. 'It's not true that I was unhappy in England, Stefano. Yes, I missed Italy very much, and it was hard, especially at first. But I was happy because I was with my family. With you, of course, and yes, with your father. I loved him, and I would have gone any-where with him.'

'Do you still love him?' Stefano asks. He is appalled by his own question. He didn't intend to say anything like that; words seem to fly out of his mouth like racing pigeons these past few days. He seems to remember asking Della the very same question only a short time ago. She never answered him.

For a few moments it looks as if Chiara won't answer either. She's staring down at her hands – workman's hands, she thinks distractedly; hands that do not create, but clean and repair what others have created. Finally she says, 'Can you love and hate someone at the same time? Can you miss someone, yet be so angry with them that there are long nights when you dream of their death and wake up glad of it?'

Stefano is quiet. He desperately wishes he hadn't begun this conversation. But the silence is too heavy with ghosts for him to let it go on, so he says, 'Maybe being angry is a good thing. Maybe it will finally kill your love for him. How can you love him after what he did?'

'The years, Stefano.' Her voice softens. 'You. How can I stop loving the father of someone so dear to me?'

'But he's a moody, pompous bastard.' Stefano's voice is harsher than intended. He realizes that he stopped loving his father years before Della came along.

'He's not all that. He can be sweet, and—' She suddenly breaks off, unable to speak, remembering how Hunter was at the beginning, and yes, even near the end. Especially at the end, when he was falling in love with Della and wanted to keep it from his wife. Oh yes, when Hunter chose, he knew how to be loving. For him it was like everything else, a game he was determined to excel at. And he did it well. He could be kind and considerate and treat a woman like a goddess – when he chose to. It was just that, as the years went on, he chose to be that way less and less.

The wine has come and both Stefano and Chiara begin to drink, not waiting for their food. They're too deep to get out now, Stefano thinks, and says, 'Do you know, we've never talked about this. When you left Florence and ran to London, all you said was that Dad had found someone else and you wanted to get as far away from both of them as you could.'

'I couldn't talk about it then. And I didn't want to turn you against your father; it was bad enough that you saw me so distraught and tearful.' She frowns slightly. When she goes on she looks troubled. 'Stefano, I hope that I'm not talking out of turn now, telling you these things. You asked and I wanted to be honest with you. But I don't want to set you against your father and Della.'

Stefano shakes his head. 'I can see for myself, you know – how things are, what he's like. But I wish you could forget him, *Mamma*. Both the love and the anger. He's not worth either.'

73

The bearded waiter brings the steaming food. It looks well cooked and succulent but neither of them touch it. Chiara says, so softly that Stefano can hardly hear, 'It takes time, Stefano. You cannot rush these things.'

'The anger, then. Let it go, if you can't let go of the love. It's not good for you to be angry. Think about yourself, not about *him*.' Stefano feels out of his depth saying these things, but he cannot stop. Who is he to give such advice? What does he know?

But Chiara appears to be thinking this over seriously. She says, 'Do you know why I'm still angry? Not because Hunter wanted Della; these things happen. But because he lied to me for so long and made such a fool of me. Everyone knew but me; the whole language school, students and staff.'

'Maybe someone should have told you.'

Chiara stares at her cooling pasta, then looks sadly at Stefano. 'Someone did. Sadie. It was so hard for her. She didn't know what to do; she wanted only to do what was best for me.'

'And that's when it ended?'

'Oh no. If it had I wouldn't be so angry now. He lied, you see. I asked him about Della and he lied. He said he found her unattractive, cold even, not his type at all. He said Sadie was a gossip, imagining things.'

'You believed him?'

'Oh yes. I trusted him, you see. And he could be very . . . persuasive.'

The silence now is damp with grief, and neither of them can, for the moment, break it. Stefano wants more than anything to end this conversation, but Chiara says softly, 'He wasn't quite sure of Della then, you see. He wanted to be sure of her before he . . .' She shrugs. The gesture is more eloquent than any words could be.

Before he dumped you, Stefano thinks. He wanted to be sure of his new woman, before he got rid of the old and was left with no-one.

Chiara has picked up her fork and is attacking the

food ferociously. '*Allora*,' she says briskly. 'After all this time you have my side of the story. To be fair, you should talk to Hunter. No doubt it would sound different coming from him.'

No doubt it would, Stefano thinks. No doubt it would.

Hunter is well pleased with himself. The first week of the new session has gone smoothly, with a record number of students. At the start of each term Hunter lives on his nerves, hoping the enrolment will live up to its promise and the school will continue to grow, year after year, as it has since he began it. Hunter intends to make it the best foreign-language school in Italy.

It's not easy running such an establishment in Florence. The city is overrun with them, though, of course, they are mostly schools teaching the Italian language and culture, its art and history. Nonetheless the competition is fierce, cut-throat. Hunter doesn't mind this, not when he's winning.

And he *is* ahead, by streaks. Hunter is proud of his school, and rightly so. He's proud of its emerging reputation as one of the most respected English institutes in Florence.

Hunter has worked for this. Years of being under the thumb of others, idiots who didn't have a clue about running language schools, or even teaching in them, had made him determined to be an administrator of his own one day. His ambition and hard work have paid off. Not long ago there was a write-up, a very favourable one, in a prestigious professional journal, praising Hunter's school and recommending it highly to all serious students of English.

Hunter has other things to be pleased about. His son is at last recognizing the fact that his father has a lot to teach him, settling in at the Villa Tiglio fairly smoothly after those first prickly outbursts. There have not been any more; indeed, after that initial show of petulance, Stefano seems quiet, subdued even. Hunter congratulates himself on the way he has handled the boy. He is pleased too that Stefano can see first-hand the success of the language school, *Hunter's* school.

All in all the week has gone well, and now it's Saturday. He and Della are playing tennis with Sadie and her husband, Marino, at the public tennis courts in Galluzzo. It's handy for both couples, for Galluzzo isn't far from either the Villa Tiglio or Sadie and Marino's home outside Due Strade on the Via Martellini.

It's an easy win for Della and Hunter. Sadie and Marino, though younger than Hunter, are not nearly as fit, he thinks with both satisfaction and scorn. Sadie, only in her mid-forties, is plump and flabby, and Marino, more or less the same age, plays tennis like he writes his novels: casually, sometimes distractedly, sometimes excitedly, as if it's all no more than a bit of fun. What a waste, Hunter often thinks, for they both have natural skill and could be quite good players if they made more of an effort. He is annoyed when people don't make an effort. Sadie and Marino don't take their tennis seriously enough, and it shows in their game.

Hunter is delighted with the effort Della makes today. She's not a natural tennis player, and hadn't played for years, not since she was just out of college and still living in England. But Hunter cajoled her into taking it up again, and with his help she has picked up enough technique to be an adequate partner for him, though she has her lapses. Chiara had played tennis too, but erratically, like Sadie and Marino. Hunter often had to chide her for her lack of concentration.

The game over, they get in their separate cars to go to the house on the Via Martellini, a lush, sprawling old place of rounded archways and windows, of wood and marble and terracotta tiles, set in pleasantly overgrown grounds and gardens. Sadie and Marino have been there less than two years. They bought it when Marino's detective novels became unaccountably popular in America and they suddenly found themselves rich. Marino still finds the whole thing vastly amusing. He simply cannot take his novels seriously.

The two cars arrive at the same time, driving up the elegant gravel drive to the front of the house. Before Marino gets out of the car he mutters an oath under his breath, softly and with long-suffering resignation. '*Maledizione!* Sadie, *cara*, did you have to do this? Ask them back for dinner?'

'Yes,' Sadie hisses. 'He's my boss after all.'

Marino shrugs. 'So quit. We can afford it now.'

Sadie doesn't bother to answer this. She loves teaching. 'You like company, remember? You didn't used to mind.'

'*È vero*, I didn't mind when it was Chiara who came with Hunter. We had some nice evenings with Chiara. It's not the same any more.'

Sadie shushes him as the two couples get out of their cars and go into the large kitchen. It's hard to focus at first, because every single shelf and counter, and the long oak table, is filled with *things*: pots of basil, sage, oregano, parsley; dried flowers; ceramic bowls and jugs and vases; fresh lilies and roses; terracotta pots, crammed with wooden kitchen utensils; shelves full of books, both cookery books and novels; piles of magazines.

Marino gets out a large bottle of a very good classic Chianti from Greve and pours four large glasses. Sadie begins chopping onions, garlic, tomatoes and basil. 'Give it to me. I'll do that,' Della cries, taking the knife from Sadie's hand. 'Hunter, open that bottle of olive oil for Sadie and get out her iron skillet. You know we're not to be treated as guests.' She begins chopping furiously. 'Do you have any dried chilli peppers?' she asks Sadie. 'I always put chillies in my pasta sauces. Just a bit, to give them a bit of spice. They're so bland without it.'

'*I* don't,' Sadie says shortly. 'Ever. I never knew you thought my sauces were bland.'

Della chuckles. 'Oh dear, have I put my foot in it

again? Hunter, I've done it again, darling! You'll have to punish me when we get home.'

Hunter, pouring olive oil into the frying pan, rolls his eyes at her indulgently, as if to a naughty but appealing child. He loves her when she's like this, loud and brash, yet still so quintessentially English; her accent perfect, her manner confident and bold. He's also relieved that she seems back to normal now, for he has been slightly worried about her this past week. She has seemed subdued, preoccupied. Dull, actually, if he were being honest.

Marino is savouring his Chianti, which is, he thinks, superb. Hunter, however, is sniffing his suspiciously, then begins a lengthy dialogue, or rather monologue, since he doesn't wait for Marino to reply, on why this particular classic is found wanting. Sadie winks sympathetically at her husband. He looks like a recalcitrant schoolboy as he sits listening to Hunter, his short, squat body fidgeting on the kitchen chair as if he cannot wait to get away. He keeps running his fingers through his fringe of dark hair on the back of his balding head as he always does when he's bored. Sadie blows a kiss at him behind Hunter's back, to show how his patience is appreciated.

To Marino's great relief, when the pasta sauce is cooking they all leave the kitchen and go through the huge living room, which is low, with old wooden beams, a terracotta floor and shuttered windows, to the garden. Marino puts the wine and glasses on an outdoor table, set squarely on a small stone terrace. Della says, 'I see you still haven't done anything about the garden, Marino. I thought you bought this place because you liked gardening. It still looks like a fucking jungle.' She takes his arm playfully and begins walking him around the garden, pointing out what needs doing.

'I like fucking jungles,' Marino says in English, which he hates speaking because he does it badly. He and Sadie always talk in Italian, and why not, he asks.

78

After all, they are living in Italy; if he lived in England, God forbid, he would speak English.

Hunter and Sadie follow them into the rambling garden, full of rough green lawn, olive trees and umbrella pines and massive, cracked terracotta pots big enough to hide a human being. A few old-fashioned statues of nymphs and satyrs, left over from the previous owners of the house, perch like voyeurs amongst the shrubbery. Jasmine bushes grow prolifically in corners and over rockeries. Their scent is thick and white, like cream.

'Marino, darling, you need *me* here for a week. I'd take care of your garden,' Della cries. 'How about it, hmm? Could you handle me for a week, or does it take an Englishman to do that?'

Sadie says mildly, 'Lay off, Della, he's mine.' Marino disengages himself from Della as Hunter begins talking to him, and Della helps Sadie put plates and cutlery on the table outside.

Sadie has made some *crostini*, with a chicken liver pâté to spread on them. They eat this and drink some more Chianti. Della, on her third glass, feels her world focusing again, balanced. The past week it had tilted beyond all recognition, days filled with nothing but the heavy scent of lime flowers and the presence of Stefano.

He was always there, like the fragrance of the lime trees: inescapable. He seemed to be watching her, following her, not only with his eyes but with his body, which filled up the Villa Tiglio like fresh air in a closed-up room.

Today, however, he is not around, and she can think once again. Or rather, force herself to think clearly and rationally. She has been ruthless with herself all day, while she and Hunter had their morning run, while she made salad for lunch, while Hunter swore at the traffic in Due Strade on the way to Galluzzo.

Sadie is saying something to Della, but she doesn't catch it at first. Hunter has gone down to the bottom of the garden with Marino to look at an ailing walnut tree, so the two women are alone. Sadie says again, 'You're miles away. What's up with you lately?'

Della says, 'I was thinking of Hunter.' Indeed this is true. She has been making herself think of Hunter all day. She voices her thoughts out loud, as if they are a chant, a prayer, a mantra, warding off what Bettina calls the *malocchio*, the evil eye. 'I was thinking about how happy he is, with Stefano here. He feels our little family is complete now.'

Sadie refrains from saying, And what about Stefano's mother? She pours herself another glass of Chianti. Her cheeks have gone rosy with the wine, clashing haphazardly with her wiry crest of orange hair. She has changed from her tennis shorts to a long sarong of lurid brightness. Sitting perched in the garden chairs she looks like a plump parrot.

The men are slowly walking up the garden. Hunter is pontificating about something to Marino, who is frowning slightly. Sadie knows that look; it is because Hunter is speaking to him in English. Hunter knows that he's uncomfortable speaking English, but he still persists in talking to Marino in the language. Sometimes Sadie feels Hunter is trying to bulldoze all of Tuscany into speaking English, no doubt to get them to learn it properly at his school.

Sadie says to Della, 'And you? How do you feel about this cosy family? Are you getting on with your stepson?' The word is steeped in irony.

Della looks at her sharply. 'He's not my bloody stepson, Sadie; I'm not married to Hunter. And I'm not *that* much older than he is. Actually, he's closer to my age than I am to Hunter's.'

Sadie thinks, Maybe. If you say so. But only by a year or two, sweetie, surely.

Once again she holds her tongue. She sighs, wishing she had ended these regular get-togethers when Chiara left. She has nothing against Della, except the fact that she took the place of Chiara, but that is enough. Della can be abrasive, but that doesn't bother Sadie, who can give as good in return if she chooses. It's just the fact that it doesn't work, this new foursome, not like the other one did. The vibes are all wrong. Sadie hadn't wanted to go on with it, but Hunter had persisted, rolling up one day with Della, shortly after discarding Chiara, as if nothing was different, as if he'd merely changed his shirt or traded in his car.

Della says, 'Stefano and I are getting on like a house on fire, since you asked. He seems a nice enough lad, but even if he wasn't, of course I'd be pleasant to him for Hunter's sake. I wouldn't do anything to disrupt the family.'

Sadie is outraged. 'Good grief, Della, get real. The family is, was, Chiara and Hunter and Stefano, and as a unit it's not only been disrupted, as you so euphemistically put it, but smashed beyond repair. Maybe it was necessary, maybe it couldn't be helped; that part is none of my business. But for heaven's sake, don't go on about not wanting to disrupt a family.'

Della is about to retort when Hunter, approaching the terrace with Marino, looks over her head and gives a shout of greeting, waving his hand. 'That must be Marco,' Sadie says. 'He said he'd be in later, with Bettina.'

Della turns to acknowledge the arrivals and finds herself looking at Stefano. He nods to her, smiling slightly.

Her mind and body freeze, and she becomes like one of the stone statues in the garden. She should speak, smile, greet him, but she can only stare at him as the terrace and haphazard garden, now darkening into deep-blue silk, fills with his presence and seems to expand with the glow of his skin, the hardness of his body and the scent of lime flowers, which she's sure she can smell in his presence.

Resigned, her body relaxes, her mind lets go and she smiles back at him. She refuses to look away, even when she knows Sadie is staring hard at her.

8

Stefano isn't surprised to see Della and Hunter at Marco's parents' house, for he saw Della's car as he arrived with Marco and Bettina.

Her reaction when she sees him, unmistakable in her face and eyes, confirms what he has known since the beginning of the week, but which he couldn't quite believe until she began to tell him so openly, without words, of course, but with every expression, every movement.

Until now he felt he must have been imagining things. She is his father's lover; she lives with him. She has taken the place of his mother; isn't that incest, for Christ's sake? Of course, not technically, but *still*. And so he has been watching her, making excuses to be near her. He wants to be absolutely certain he has got this right.

Now he knows he has. Her pale skin as she looks at him is luminous with longing and her eyes plead with him like the eyes of a woman going under.

So this, Stefano thinks scornfully, is the grand passion that broke my mother into fragments of her old self. He shakes his head at the banality of it all.

Hunter sees him and cries, 'Stef, I didn't know you'd be here! Have a seat; there's one right here. Have a glass of Chianti.' He is forgetting that he's not the host here, that this is not his house nor his wine.

'*Sì, sì, va bene,*' Marino says, not without irony. 'Go ahead, help yourself. Make yourself at home.' He points to the wine bottle, a new one now, and the glasses Marco has brought out from the kitchen.

There's a storm of Italian, with little prickly hailstones from Hunter in English, while the three newcomers greet the others and find more chairs to pull around the table.

Sadie goes inside to get more *crostini*, check the pasta sauce and put on a massive saucepan of water for the spaghetti. She returns just in time to see Della move, as if casually, from her chair to another empty one next to Stefano. Something feline and sly about this seemingly innocent movement captures Sadie's attention, and she stands surreptitiously in the darkened doorway leading to the house, watching. She has already noticed something earlier in the way Della looked at Stefano when he came in with the others.

Stefano is talking to Marco on his left, but Della, on his other side, cannot keep her eyes off him. Her face is both radiant and resigned. The longing there is as old as the Tuscan hills, yet there's no torment marring her serene expression. It's the tranquillity of resignation. She is no longer battling with herself; she's committed to the inevitable.

'Oh my,' Sadie says softly. 'Well, well, well.'

Marino, bringing out yet more wine, says, '*Cosa c'è?*'

'Look.' She nods towards Della and Stefano.

Stefano has now turned to Della, but they cannot see his face, only his heavy hair, curled just above the neck of his black T-shirt. They can see Della, though.

'*Gesù, Giuseppe e Maria!*' Marino exclaims. 'And the Holy *Santo Spirito* too. So that's the way it is.'

'It seems so. Poor Hunter.'

Marino shrugs. He feels no sympathy for Hunter, who has always managed, without saying so, to convey the feeling that Marino, and his less-than-literary detective novels, is not quite on the same intellectual mountaintop as Hunter, linguist and administrator of a prestigious school. 'Even gods get toppled,' Marino says philosophically. 'What hope do men have, who only *think* they are gods.'

Stefano, feeling the touch of Della's fingers on his

bare arm, finishes his conversation with Marco and turns to her. He is actually relieved to be distracted, for Bettina is perched on Marco's knee, showing a great deal of leg and looking deeply sexy in her short black dress. Stefano is resigned to the fact that he cannot have her, but is not yet able to cope with the regret he feels about it.

So Della's light touch is a welcome diversion. She says, 'Sorry to interrupt. But I wanted to ask you to come out to Fiesole with Hunter and me tomorrow morning. We're going to have a ramble around the hills and then a splendid lunch in the town; we know a super restaurant.' Her hand still rests on his arm, even though she now has his full attention. She knows she shouldn't do this, but she doesn't care. His arm feels as warm as summer under her hand.

She doesn't even pretend to herself any more that she is inviting him for Hunter's sake, who has no idea she's doing this. She just knows that she cannot bear to wait till Monday to see him again.

Stefano is tempted, out of curiosity. He's intrigued, despite himself, by the whole situation, heavy though it is. This is deep water and he should keep the hell out of it.

He glances away from her towards Bettina. He's going clubbing with her and Marco later tonight, to a disco next to the Cascine, Florence's public park. It will be a late night; it'll be light before they finally roll into the apartment on the Piazza Santo Spirito. He won't feel like waking up a couple of hours later to go on a hearty hike up the steep winding roads to Fiesole.

Della is waiting for an answer, still looking at him with that intensity that should warn him to run a mile. But he's not running, not yet. He would like to see exactly how far she's prepared to go.

But not tomorrow. Tomorrow he wants to sleep all morning, then hang out with friends his own age, the ones they are meeting tonight at the club. He wants to be young and free and irresponsible, not entwined in the twisted passions of his ageing father and his middle-aged lover.

'Thanks anyway,' he says to Della. 'But I've got a heavy night out tonight. I won't be up to trudging round Fiesole or anywhere else, tomorrow morning.'

Her hand moves from his arm and joins the other one in her lap. She looks like a child who has just been slapped. He feels a twinge of pity for her. 'I'm sorry,' he says, trying to soften the blow.

'What about the evening, then?' she says, eager again. 'Come to us for dinner. Or we can go out. There's a marvellous pizzeria by the Porta Romana.' Seeing the hesitation in his face she adds, simply, 'Please.'

He shakes his head, suddenly afraid. It's all getting a bit deep.

She cannot keep the pleading from her voice as she says, 'We've only seen you at work, really. Apart from the tennis matches you've had with Hunter you haven't been to the villa except during school hours.'

Stefano, remembering other, happier times at the Villa Tiglio, hardens his heart. 'Don't rush me, Della,' he says softly.

She misunderstands him, and it gives her the confidence to put her hand back on his arm as she says, 'I won't. But please come.'

In the end he agrees to meet her, and Hunter too of course, at the pizzeria tomorrow evening. He knows he's being led, but is curious to see exactly where. Or rather, exactly how far.

An hour or so later, when the pasta has been eaten and the sweet almond *cantuccini* have been put on the table to be dipped and soaked in the Vin Santo, Marco says, '*Papà*, can I use your car? I'll bring it back in the morning.' He grins. 'Well, maybe more like afternoon.'

Marino rolls his eyes. '*Madonna benedetta!* I have a choice?'

Marco, taking the keys, hugs his father easily, though he has to bend down in order to do so, as he's a good eight or nine inches taller than his father. He takes his height from Sadie, who comes from a family of king-sized men and women. Marino, when he is with them and his strapping son, feels as if he has climbed a magic beanstalk, but he doesn't mind in the slightest. He is proud of his son, who has even shaved his full, healthy head of hair. not because of fashion, as he jokingly tells Marino, but to be more like his father. Marino knows this is totally untrue, but is touched anyway.

Marco kisses the older man fondly on the cheek as he says, '*Grazie mille, Papà.*' Hunter, watching, feels a pang of resentment. Why can't Stefano be like that with him: warm and affectionate. He is like his mother, Hunter thinks. Spiteful and cold, both of them, when they cannot have their own way.

There is a flutter of movement as *ciao*'s are exchanged. Bettina kisses Sadie and Marino and waves goodbye to the others. Stefano lingers a moment to thank them for the dinner and the wine, and then he nods a goodbye to Hunter and Della. Hunter cries in English, 'Enjoy yourself, Stef! From what I remember of the Italian girls you certainly will.' He winks at him lasciviously. Hunter seems to have forgotten that he married one of those Italian girls himself years ago, then dropped her for an Englishwoman.

Stefano has not forgotten. He looks at Hunter angrily, adrenalin pumping, determined not to let his father get away with that remark. But Hunter has already forgotten him and turned towards Marino to comment on the Vin Santo. Stefano is about to interrupt when Della, standing next to him now, distracts him by saying, 'See you tomorrow, Stefano.' She leans towards him to kiss his cheek, deciding that she can get away with it, for he is, so to speak, family. Stefano, still glaring at his father's back, intercepts the kiss and redirects it from his cheek to his mouth, kissing her long and hard.

Only Marino sees, and Sadie. It is enough.

*　　*　　*

The morning air is thin, creamed with a frothy sky, as Hunter parks Della's car in the Piazza San Domenico on the outskirts of Fiesole. Though Hunter has his own car, they have somehow got into the habit of using hers. It's newer, more comfortable. And anyway, it's only fair, he sometimes thinks. They are, after all, living in his house – though Della contributes considerably towards household expenses – so why shouldn't they use her car?

They begin hiking up the Via Vecchia Fiesolana, the old road to the city. The morning is cool and fresh, the road empty; they have made an early start. On their left as they climb the hill are spectacular views of the Tuscan hills: tiled rooftops, old villas and olive groves. They don't go straight into Fiesole yet, but walk up and down the hills briskly, determined to work up an appetite before lunch.

Della doesn't talk much as they walk. Hunter doesn't appear to notice, for he is busy pointing out interesting objects to look at and admire: an old iron gate; the Villa Medici, built by Michelozzo for Cosimo il Vecchio; and some ancient stone terraces. Della looks but doesn't say anything.

It isn't until they are in Fiesole that she begins to make an effort. They are climbing the Via San Francesco, and have stopped on the terrace before the Gothic church to admire the fantastic view of Florence below them. Hunter has stopped talking, and Della, suddenly aware of the silence between them, says brightly, 'How grand it looks. Bloody amazing to think that sleepy little Fiesole was here first, long before Florence. The Etruscans, then the Romans, and even before that, the Bronze-Age settlers. All that history, still visible everywhere you look.'

Hunter stares at her and frowns. 'Do you know, that's the first thing you've said in the last hour? And you sound like you're reading from a guide-book.' His mouth is tight and controlled and his eyes determinedly fasten themselves on the rooftops and domes of Florence in the distance.

Della, on edge, decides to attack. 'What the fuck's the matter with you, Hunter? You look totally strung out. Loosen up, will you?'

'Me? You're asking what's the matter with *me*?'

'Oh, for fuck's sake. Yes, I'm asking you what's the matter. There's nothing bloody wrong with me. You're the one suddenly spoiling for a fight. I thought this was supposed to be a relaxing day walking in the hills. You're the most bloody unrelaxing man I've ever been with.'

Hunter tenses even more. His face is chiselled granite, his lips so stony he can hardly get the words out. 'You're the one itching for a fight. You started all this.'

'*Me?* Hunter, what in the name of sweet Jesus are you on about?' Even as she says this, Della has a moment of panic, wondering if Hunter witnessed the monumental thing that had happened between her and Stefano last night at Sadie and Marino's house. But no, she knows he didn't. When their kiss ended – and it was Stefano, not she, who finally pulled away and left the house to join Bettina and Marco, who were tooting the car horn out in the front – Della had turned to see Hunter's back to her, still engrossed in conversation with Marino.

Hunter doesn't look at her. His voice is as pinched as his body. 'You've been acting . . . odd.'

'Shit, Hunter. Spit it out. What do you mean, odd?'

What Hunter means is that she hasn't been all over him, as she usually is. She's acting as if he's not the man who, let's face it, saved her from spinsterhood, from a lonely existence in a foreign country, getting old and tired and fretful because young men no longer looked at her as boldly as they used to, no longer appreciated her short skirts, her sleek, streaked hair with the same intensity.

She had been so grateful, at first, after he'd pursued her so diligently. She had treated him like a king to begin with, and so she should. It was a fair exchange. Hunter had, after all, given up Chiara for her.

From the first, Della had been everything he wanted: sparky, good-looking, adoring. She had understood him too; she'd praised him, admired his energy, stamina and ambition. She, if no-one else, knew and appreciated what Hunter had done, creating and maintaining an English school that far outshone all its competitors.

Was it any wonder he had chosen to make their relationship permanent? He needed Della, needed her admiration and approval, and not only for the school. She saw him as he was: still young and powerful, in his prime, going places. Chiara seemed to see him as no more than a family man, if she ever saw him at all. She was always off doing her own work, or chatting over endless lunches with her Italian friends, none of whom seemed to pay much attention to him.

Yes, Della had made Hunter feel as if he owned the world, and he is missing that, he realizes. He says, slowly trying to articulate his thoughts, 'I don't feel you're really *here*. I haven't felt that all day, and even last week you were . . . preoccupied.'

'What you mean is that I haven't been making a fuss of you, as I normally do; that I've started to get a life instead of pampering you all day.'

Her words shock them both: Hunter, because this is exactly what he does mean; and Della, because she has stated the truth so starkly, or at least partially.

They are hampered from finishing this conversation by the arrival of two Dutch backpackers, who exclaim over the view and then try to engage Della and Hunter in conversation with their schoolbook English. The Dutch couple will for ever think the English cold and rude because all they get in return for their friendliness is a curt monosyllable or two; then Della and Hunter turn and walk away.

Neither now feels like going to the church of San Francesco on top of the hill, so they cut down into the woodland of the public park, which leads back down into the town. Hunter says, 'I didn't know it was such an effort for you; being with me, being . . . *nice* to me. I didn't realize it was such a chore.'

'God, just chill out, will you? I didn't say that. Stop twisting my words. I just wondered if maybe we were beginning to suffocate each other a bit.'

'Oh, I see. I'm suffocating you, am I? How odd. I thought I was, well, doing what you wanted. Being attentive. You know. A good lover, like you always wanted. You've never had any complaints before.'

Something about the complacent way he says this last sentence grates on Della. 'Look, Hunter, it's no big deal, being a good lover. Anyone can be if they put their mind to it.'

'Oh, I see. I *see.*'

Hunter has stopped walking and Della is forced to stop too. They are on a narrow path going through the shaded woods, and luckily they're quite alone. Hunter is looking at her so coldly that suddenly she feels uncertain. She remembers the relief she felt, the joy, when she realized that this man was really serious about leaving his wife. No more casual affairs that left her depleted, no more evenings and nights bored and alone with no-one to talk to, no more dinner parties where the hosts' kids called her auntie and made her feel a hundred years old. She didn't want kids, that wasn't a problem; but she did want someone to share the rest of her life with.

She reminds herself sternly of all the things she first loved about Hunter. The way he concentrated on her entirely at the beginning, as if she were all that mattered to him; the way he listened to her talk endlessly about her past, especially that last year in Rome, when she had been so unhappy, desperately trying to believe in the lies and promises of her married lover. Though Hunter was older than her, she had thought he was still nice looking, with that distinguished, coloured hair – sandy and white and grey all mixed – though now there is no trace of his younger light-brown colour. But his eyes have stayed the same, a pale grey flecked with other colours; opalescent eyes that still look at her with that open adoration and appeal. Sometimes, lately, she has noticed that he's able to switch off those eyes, as if switching off a computer, leaving them as empty as a grey screen, but then he has been busy. And, of course, there is the added worry of Stefano's arrival.

Stefano. She cannot let herself think of him. She would be mad to lose Hunter now. What is she doing, she asks herself, risking all this, all that she has at the Villa Tiglio? Hunter's frigid face unsettles her now, frightens her, and impulsively she puts her arms around him, running her hands down his backside, crying, 'Oh, Hunter, don't be so obtuse. You *are* a perfect lover, marvellous, and I appreciate it. In fact, that's the trouble; when you're around, I have a problem concentrating on other things, and I've got to, now. That advanced English course I've taken on is exhausting, full of bloody-minded know-it-alls who think they speak better English than we do. Then you've landed me with that English History class in the afternoon, and you know I'm flaky on history. I need all my wits about me to keep a step or two ahead of them.'

She wraps her arms tighter around him, leaning her head against his chest. 'Quite honestly, I'm whacked,' she says, 'and I have jolly good reason to be. And now here you are, accusing me of being preoccupied.'

Hunter is mollified, by both her words and her hands which are skilfully manipulating his buttocks and the base of his spine. He likes what she has said about her work: the language school is, after all, part of him; it's not as if there's an outside influence drawing Della away. He's pleased that she is taking her employment for him so seriously. It shows a commitment, not only to the school but to Hunter.

'Well, silly. Why didn't you say so?' he murmurs into her silky hair. 'Goodness, I didn't realize I was such a hard taskmaster. I'll have to make it up to you, hmm?'

'I'm just trying to do a good job and not let the school

down, Hunter, you know that. You mustn't distract me too much.' She pulls away from him gently. 'Now come on, I want my lunch. All that walking has made me starving.'

Nonetheless their lunch, though tasty, is not as relaxing as it should be. They're each too aware of the fact that they're being too nice to each other, far too loving, with their overt touches and deep looks and hand-holding across the table.

It smacks too much of trying to prove something.

9

Hunter is cheered after their rather flat lunch, by the prospect of meeting Stefano that evening for dinner. He admits that he has Della to thank for that, inviting the boy out for a meal like she did. It's the first time that Stefano is actually coming out for a social evening, unconnected with work.

Hunter wishes Chiara could be there too. He would like her to see just how he has tamed this son of hers, once so stubborn and rebellious, refusing to do anything his father wanted him to do. He would like Chiara to see how her poisons against her ex-husband have not worked, how she was unable, despite the way she must have tried in London, to turn father and son into enemies. He and Stefano are closer now than they ever have been and he would like Chiara to see it.

By the time they get home Hunter feels soothed and mellow, in the grounds of his glorious little kingdom on this hillside on the edge of Florence. The villa is cool, welcoming and shaded from the searing sun by the lime trees, fragrant with blossom. When Della decides she will go upstairs and rest before the evening, Hunter joins her. He will make love to her, remind her of what she has, remind her not to take it for granted.

But something goes wrong. Hunter's lovemaking is as careful and deliberate as always, taking care not to let himself go until Della has. But this afternoon she doesn't, no matter what he does, no matter how skilful he is. What puzzles him is that she acts as if nothing's wrong, makes no excuses or explanations, smiles at him in an abstracted way as if everything were the same. A flash of anger momentarily makes his heart pound. Does she think I'm a complete fool? he wonders.

But then, as the perfumed spring air blows gently in the open window and Della drifts into a deep sleep, Hunter's anger dissipates, and he decides that he too will act as if nothing's wrong. He remembers what Della had said, that she's wound up with work and the school; preoccupied, as she admitted. He will let her sleep, and hopefully she'll be more relaxed next time.

Della is not asleep but wide awake, though she's pretending not to be. Hunter's arms around her feel too angular, too sinewy; his body bony. She's no longer happy to be encased in them; she feels as if she's in a cage with narrow steel bars. When he's asleep she rolls away from him carefully and gets in the shower, taking care to scrub away every trace of him.

Stefano's late. Hunter and Della are already at the pizzeria at the Porta Romana, drinking *aperitivi* of Campari and soda when he arrives, making his way across the room full of chattering Italians to their corner table.

'Why, Stefano, you've decided to come after all,' Hunter says. 'We thought you'd forgotten us.'

Stefano has not forgotten. He has been thinking of Della all day, or rather, from midday onwards, when he and Marco got up and wandered aimlessly around the Piazza Santo Spirito. The Sunday-morning market crowded the piazza, with awnings covering stalls of fruit and vegetables, clothing and the once-a-month organic market, crammed with tables selling honey, cheeses, dried herbs, pulses and crafts. He had thought of her later that afternoon as he flirted with a pale, willowy young American who was trying to learn Italian. Stefano had idly wondered, as he bought her a beer with Marco and the others at the café, whether he should break the dinner engagement and take up the

American's offer of seeing her that evening. But in the end, he just wasn't that interested.

'Will you have a drink?' Hunter asks. 'And then we'd better order. It gets quite busy here, as you can see.'

Stefano asks for a beer. 'Well, cheers,' Hunter says when it arrives, raising his own half-filled glass.

Stefano says, '*Salute!*' He nods at Della, avoiding her eyes.

Next to them a family of five eat fresh pineapple noisily for their last course. The grandmother, or most likely great-grandmother, complains that it's not sweet enough and gives half hers to the youngest member of the party, a girl of about seventeen. She has lips painted like Bettina's, outlined in dark pencil and pale as lavender inside. Stefano watches the soft chunks of pineapple disappear into her pale-purple mouth.

'She's a bit of all right, eh, Stef?' Hunter says with a greedy smile.

Della has gone to the ladies' room. The waiter brings them each a pizza margherita, fragrant with melted mozzarella. Hunter goes on, 'Della is too, you know. Not obviously so, of course, like that little sexpot at the next table, but it's all there, all right, not far under the surface.' He winks broadly.

For a mad instant Stefano thinks his father is offering Della to him. Then, with another shock, he realizes that Hunter is indulging in a kind of macho changing-room repartee. He's bragging, for God's sake. Stefano feels a moment's pity for his father, then a cringing embarrassment.

Della comes back, her hair newly brushed, her lips touched up with a pale-pink glow. Hunter openly admires her, standing and putting his arm possessively round her shoulders as she prepares to take her seat again. He notices the father of the seventeen-year-old at the next table look at him with what he's sure is envy. Even Stefano seems to be staring in exactly the same way. Not for the first time, Hunter is aware of how having a young woman such as Della on his arm enhances him in the eyes of others.

The pizza is delicious, but only Hunter appreciates this. Stefano is caught in a crossfire of silent messages from Della, and from the teenage girl opposite, who is more than a little aware of his presence. She's precocious in her suggestive looks, shrugs and smiles. Della is more subtle, but the message is the same. Stefano has an insane urge to burst out laughing.

The family at the next table finally leave, the girl lingering until her father tells her to hurry up, they've paid the bill and are waiting. Stefano knows that she's hoping that he will speak to her, perhaps ask for her address or a phone number. He is half tempted, but only as some sort of a statement; he's not sure what. To stop Della? To remind her that he doesn't come with Hunter, is not hers to play with? He's not sure he wants to do this yet. He is still curious how far she's willing to go down the path she has hacked out.

Della suggests they all go back to the Villa Tiglio for coffee, but Stefano refuses, saying he wants to get back to the apartment. Hunter orders coffee for them there at the restaurant, then goes off to the men's room.

Neither Della nor Stefano speak. They have no actions with which to fill the silence: their food and wine have gone, their coffee not yet come. The silence widens and grows heavy. Neither choose to break it. By letting it linger they have suddenly become conspirators.

'Sorry to take so long,' Hunter says when he comes back. 'There was a queue for the loo. This place is really popular; lucky I booked a table. Did you two find plenty to talk about while I was gone?'

'Oh yes,' Della says. Stefano looks at her and smiles. They have not spoken a word to each other since Hunter left the table.

'Good, good.' The drink, the excellence of the pizza, the espresso – a tiny cup of pure caffeine which has just arrived – is making Hunter expansive. 'I'm so pleased you two seem to be getting on so well. I can tell you now, it was a worry for me, Stef. I knew you'd like Della as soon as you got to know her, but I also know how bloody-minded you can be, if you don't mind my saying so. I was afraid you wouldn't give her a chance.'

'Did you, Dad? Did you think that? Oh, I'm more than willing to give her a chance.' Stefano smiles openly, defiantly, at Della.

'I know you will, Stef. You already have.' Hunter turns to Della. 'And what do you think of my son? Is he just as I described him?'

'Not exactly.' Della looks at Stefano. 'No, I would say he's not at all as you described him.'

Hunter is slightly disappointed. He had painted quite a good portrait of Stefano, he thought, with vivid descriptions of the lad and anecdotes and old photographs.

Della smiles. 'You described a child, Hunter, a boy.' Her navy-blue eyes flicker slightly, but do not move from Stefano's face.

'Oh, right. Yes. Well, I suppose I did.' He gives a short laugh.

'But I'm not that, am I?' Stefano states laconically.

'No,' Della says. 'No.'

'Well then,' Hunter says. 'Have we all finished our coffee? Should we go?'

Stefano walks under the great medieval gate and tower of the Porta Romana, which once defended the main road to Florence from Siena and Rome. Now the piazza in front of it is attacked by traffic: armies of cars and scooters and motorbikes.

He walks down the Via Romana towards Piazza Santo Spirito, Marco's apartment and now Stefano's home. The small shops, greengrocers and bakeries, wine merchants and stores selling cheeses and meats, clothes and kitchenware, are all shut now, the street uncluttered, with only the odd couple strolling along, and an occasional cat or car streaking down the road.

Here and there clusters of parked scooters and *motorini* appear like a herd of steel animals, silently settling down for the night.

Turning left down the Via Mazzetta and then straight on to the Via Sant'Agostino, the streets become more lively. The Piazza Santo Spirito is again dotted with people enjoying the tranquil spring night, and the café and bar is still crowded inside and out.

Stefano is restless. He has no desire to go inside, despite what he'd told Della and Hunter. He had wanted to get away from them. He is finding his attitude towards them disturbingly unpredictable. Sometimes he is drawn to them; fascinated and obsessed, with a desire to find out exactly what's going on, what gods seem to be playing with the three of them, and to what purpose. Then, suddenly, the fascination goes and a strong distaste, even disgust, for the whole messy business floods him, like a tide of polluted water, and he finds he is frantically searching for a way out, a bridge over which he can run like hell away from it all.

Marco is at Bettina's parents' home in Galluzzo for the evening, and there's no-one in the piazza or on the steps of the church that Stefano knows. Sitting on the stone of the fountain are some of the people he recognizes from the club last night, and one of the young women is looking his way with a smile, indicating that he is familiar to her as well. But Stefano walks on, needing to move, needing the dark night air to cloak the confusion in his head.

On the bridge of Santa Trìnita, Stefano passes couples of all ages, arms knotted around each other like ivy on trees, looking out over the Arno towards the next bridge, the Ponte Vecchio, its arches lit and the illumination reflected on the dark river water. He stops for a moment, feeling alone and isolated as he stares out at the shadowy bridge, which seems to mirror the darkening shadows in his own life. Finally he turns and walks on down the Lungarno, and then left and right, and finally he finds himself in the Piazza della Signoria.

Tourists still linger here, though not the huge crowds that throb through the city centre in the daytime. Stefano passes the grey towers of the Palazzo Vecchio and stares moodily at the green water of the Neptune Fountain. Amannati's uninspiring statue of Neptune, which prompted Michelangelo to bluntly tell his fellow sculptor what a waste of good marble it was, seems to capture Stefano's dull spirits, which have been steadily going downhill since saying goodnight to Della and Hunter. But he's not really looking at it. He's not looking at anything, except the sordid mess he seems to have become embroiled in, the dangerous triangle he has become part of. Something has begun, been set in motion; something he cannot even begin to understand.

Stefano moves from the fountain across the piazza to the Loggia, with its restored Roman statues and, at the far right, Giambologna's *Rape of the Sabine Women*. He stares unseeingly at it for a few moments, just as he did at the Neptune, but gradually the clean fine lines and symmetry of this far better sculpture begin to slice through his preoccupation. As he looks at the three naked figures, the older man beaten and crushed between the strong thighs of the younger man, who carries the woman triumphantly in his arms, Stefano suddenly understands. He feels the power and strength of the sculpture, its image and meaning sink through his skin into his blood and bones, like the Eucharist.

Calmer now, he at last walks away. What has begun is as old as art, as old as history. Who is he to try to interfere with what is natural and right.

10

There is no time, the next day – Monday – to think of anything but the students. Stefano, to his surprise, is beginning to enjoy his work immensely; more, he finds it fulfilling, rewarding.

When he left university, the last thing he thought he would ever want was a job in a school, standing up in front of a class of students. He knew his father assumed he would follow him into the teaching profession, albeit not as successfully. The comment had been made more than once, during Stefano's years at college, that just because he was doing languages he shouldn't presume he would ever be able to teach them.

Perhaps because of Hunter, Stefano had refused to even consider teaching for a year or so in London, preferring to spend his first year out of university doing an assortment of odd jobs, purely for money. Then, wanting more time for himself, he began giving a few one-to-one lessons in Italian and French, and found he had a knack for it. From there he took a short course in teaching English as a foreign language and, to his surprise, his first proper job turned out to be at the Villa Tiglio School of English.

He was not at all sure he would like it. But it gives him a strange satisfaction seeing the students move from a kind of bewildered stupor, in their first struggles with the new language, to a gradual comprehension. With some the intricacy of grammar and accent seems to be revealed suddenly – an epiphany; with others it comes more slowly. Stefano likes it both ways; he likes sharing with his students that moment of clarity, when everything he says makes sense and has meaning to them.

Stefano, born to an Italian mother and an English father, had learned French quite easily at school, and has never gone through these agonies of language learning himself, but he can easily understand the difficulties of others. He remembers his mother's tales of learning to speak English. At school she'd done French, and when she met Hunter at a small party his parents were hosting at the Villa Tiglio, having been brought there by friends, her English, as she described it later, was *cattivo*. Because it was so dreadful, she was shy of using it. This had suited Hunter just fine, for his Italian, despite the fact that his parents had moved to Florence and he had already visited them several times, was non-existent, and he had decided it was time to learn.

At first Hunter refused to teach Chiara any English at all. Years later, when Stefano heard this story, he decided that it explained why Chiara fell in love with Hunter and married him: she could not have known what he was really like, with the language barrier between them. But besotted with Hunter and desperate to learn his language, Chiara had tried tapes and workbooks, to no avail. Finally Hunter, when he realized that he too was rather besotted and that he was going to marry this Italian, gave in to Chiara's pleas to help her learn his language. He sat her down, and within a month had taught her to speak fairly passable English. It was the beginning of his vocation as a language teacher, for although he'd embarked on a teacher-training course, he had been vague about which direction it would take him in.

Remembering this at the end of his own day's teaching, Stefano thinks guiltily of his mother; he has not been back to Siena in over a week. He decides he will go that evening, but as he prepares to leave the villa Hunter says, 'Fancy a game of tennis?' When Stefano hesitates, he adds, 'Or are you afraid of being beaten again?' He makes this last remark in the same bantering tone Stefano remembers from his childhood; the same tone Hunter used when chiding him not to be so clumsy when catching a ball, or so awkward when courting a girl, or so stupid when struggling with homework. Then, when Chiara frowned at Hunter, or when Stefano cried (when young) or sulked (when adolescent), Hunter would accuse them both of not being able to take a bit of fun, a bit of teasing.

Stefano says now, 'Sorry, I can't. I'm off to Siena. My mother is expecting me for dinner.'

Hunter resents this. It's the only nettle in the garden of his life now: Chiara's presence back in Italy. Why couldn't she have stayed in London, made a new life for herself there? When Hunter first heard that she was coming back he felt stifled, pressured, and the feeling is still there. He's sure that she has returned merely to annoy him.

Hunter resents too the way Stefano refers to Chiara as 'my mother', as if she were someone Hunter had never met. He says, 'And how is she? Your mother?' He hopes Stefano notes the heavy irony with which he says 'your mother'.

'Give it a rest, Dad. You don't really give a shit. You'd be much happier if she disappeared, moved to another planet so you wouldn't have to think about her.'

'That's not true,' Hunter lies.

'It's hard to pretend she doesn't exist when she's living in the next town, when I'm seeing her whenever I can. You don't like that, do you. Guilt, maybe? A few prickles of it, messing up the nice smooth surface of your life?'

Hunter sighs, a pointed sigh of long-suffering patience. How many times has he had to compose himself, set his lips tightly, control his anger at yet another one of Stefano's silly outbursts. Always unexpected too. Last night everything went so well, and then suddenly *this*.

They are in the library, a room at the end of the corridor, with bookcases full of English dictionaries, reference books, works on history, language and culture. The room overlooks the lime trees by the tennis court and their scent trickles in like a fine, thin mist.

'I think,' Hunter says carefully, 'that you are being unfair, Stefano.'

'Fine. I'm prepared to accept that. So why don't you convince me I am. Tell me exactly how I'm being unfair.' He sits down at one of the wooden desks and looks expectantly at Hunter.

Hunter is disconcerted. He feels at a disadvantage, standing there in front of Stefano, who looks to be patiently waiting for him to speak. Stefano's face is impassive, but his eyes are not kind.

Hunter decides that he had better sit down too. He does, in the chair opposite. The two sit facing each other warily.

Hunter begins. 'I didn't want to hurt Chiara. That was never my intention.'

'But you did.'

'But it wasn't premeditated.'

'No?'

'No! Stefano, you're a man now, you must know how it is.'

'No. Tell me.'

'Well. *You* know. Physical attraction, that sort of thing.'

'Oh? But I thought it was love. I thought you loved Della.'

'I did! I do. But . . . it was all those things. She – Della – made me feel happy, whole. A new man.'

'Young. You wanted to feel young again.' The scorn in Stefano's voice is obvious.

Hunter makes himself take a deep breath to keep control. Stefano's not making this any easier for either of them. 'Is that such a bad thing, Stef? Anyway, I *am* young; I'm not exactly doddering, you know. I didn't need Della to prove anything. I needed her for herself.'

'Go on. Tell me about it. You've never told me; I've never heard your side of it.'

'That's because you wouldn't listen. I did try to write.'

'I'm listening now. *Dimmi. Dimmi tutto.*'

The use of the Italian imperative shakes Hunter. He and Stefano always speak English to each other, but the Italian has rolled off his tongue naturally, easily. Hunter resents how foreign his son has become. This too is Chiara's fault.

'All right, I'll tell you everything, Stef. I didn't want to leave your mother, but I had no choice.'

'No choice? Of course you had a fucking choice.'

'You don't understand. Della was lonely, unhappy when she came here. I was her employer; she was grateful to me. Then . . . then she fell in love with me. It happens.'

'With no encouragement from you, of course.'

'No, none at all. I was married, I knew the rules. I didn't want to split up the family; the thought never entered my head at the beginning.'

Hunter looks at Stefano earnestly, appealingly. His pale-grey eyes look directly into the dark, perplexed ones of his son. Sincerity blazes from them like comets.

Stefano stares back. For a moment he's almost there, crossing the line over to the other side. The truth is, he *wants* to believe Hunter. It's emotionally tiring and sad to dislike your father. Stefano feels Hunter's deep pleading eyes tip into his soul like a tonic.

Hunter, sensing his advantage, presses closer, using his eyes to beg, to convey the sincerity of his feelings. Stefano wavers, but then he remembers. He has seen that look before, many times. He remembers it now from adolescence: Hunter's grey eyes fixed on Chiara, trying to tame her, win her over. And Stefano has seen it even more recently: Hunter looking at Della, soulfully, lovingly. The same look, used for different occasions. Exactly the same, Stefano thinks, even to the slight widening of the eyes as he tries to rip out your soul. Hunter should patent that look; he'd make a fortune.

Hunter begins to speak again, softly, confidentially. 'Yes, I was married. I was well aware of that, Stef. The last thing I wanted was to hurt Chiara. Believe me, I spent many a sleepless night agonizing over her.'

Stefano, noticing how blank Hunter's eyes look behind all the surface emotion, thinks, You old tosser. He says nothing.

'But then . . . well, do you blame me?' Hunter opens his palms in a gesture of innocence. 'You've seen Della; you know how attractive she is. And she was here every day, asking me for advice, following me around. She's a strong, formidable woman, you know, and in the end, quite frankly, she wore me down.' He looks beguilingly at Stefano, then repeats, 'Can you blame me, Stef?'

Stefano's silence is full of cynicism. Hunter's eyes go from soft to hard as he snaps, 'You're just being stubborn, aren't you. Won't give an inch. Come on, Stef, you've seen for yourself what a stunner Della is, and what a charmer she can be. You just can't admit it, can you.'

'It's hardly relevant, is it? What I think of Della? You were telling me how it happened.'

'Yes, well. To be frank, she wanted me. I admit it; it got to me in the end.' He leans conspiratorially towards Stefano and tries out a laddish smile. 'You can't tell me you don't know what it's like, Stef.'

'Why didn't you just screw her? Why did you break up your marriage and force Chiara to leave her home, her country—'

'I didn't force her to do anything. Chiara chose to go. And she's not penniless, you know. She had half the cash from the sale of our London house.'

'So that makes everything all right.'

Hunter sighs, long and audibly. 'No, I didn't say that. Look, Stef, it's done. I regret hurting Chiara, but I don't regret my life with Della. She needs me far more than Chiara does.'

'Oh? You just said she was a strong woman.'

'Jesus Christ. Will you stop twisting every single thing I say? And will you get that sarcastic tone out of your voice? Yes, I did say that, but she loves me; she's crazy about me. She says she doesn't know how she survived before she met me; says she has never been so happy, so in love.'

Hunter cannot keep the smugness from his voice, nor can he stop now. 'You wouldn't know what it's like, Stef, to have a woman like that in love with you. Maybe you will one day.' He deliberately leaves a note of doubt in the last sentence. He has had enough of his son for today.

Stefano looks at him steadily, without rancour. 'Oh, I will,' he says. 'I will.' And he thinks how ironic it is to find one's father so pathetic and yet to feel no pity for him.

'Your favourite,' Chiara says. 'Risotto. *Buon appetito.*'

Stefano tucks in. Chiara sits opposite him at the kitchen table, the oilskin cloth loaded with brightly coloured plates filled with salad, grated parmesan and bread. She says, 'It's good to have you here, Stefano. It's always great to see you.'

Stefano, his mouth full of rice, grins. 'Mm, great risotto, *Mamma*. So what's the *but*?'

'What?'

'I can always tell when there's a *but* coming. It's good; it's great to have me here – *but*. What's the *but*, *Mamma*? I know it's there; I can hear it.'

Chiara rolls her eyes at him and says in English, with a strong parody of her own accent, 'Ah, *mamma mia*, such a clever son I have.' Then, in Italian and this time seriously, she says, 'Yes, there is a *but*. I love seeing you, but I'd hate you to feel you had to come to Siena to make sure I was coping all right. No, no, listen to me,' she goes on as Stefano tries to protest. 'You've got

106

a lot on now: a new job, new apartment, new friends. I'm perfectly fine. Remember, I lived here for two months on my own when you were still in London. I'm happy just knowing you're in Italy and we can get together sometimes. You don't have to visit regularly, that's what I'm trying to say.'

Stefano, wolfing down the risotto, says, 'How about *you* coming to *me* next? To see our place? Marco wants to invite you for a meal; he swears he's a great cook, though I haven't seen any signs of it yet. How about Sunday? Come for lunch.'

Chiara hedges. 'How's the risotto?'

'*Squisito, Mamma*. As always. You know your risottos are the best in Italy, and I've already praised this one. Now stop changing the subject. You can't keep avoiding Florence. You've still got friends there who want to see you, so Marco and I are having them over on Sunday. It's all decided.'

'Who? Which friends are you having over exactly?' Chiara is unable to keep the panic from her voice.

'Marco's parents: Sadie and Marino. They're dying to see you again. Marco, of course, and Bettina. You know she's going out with him now.'

'That's all?'

'That's all. *Dio, Mamma*, give me some credit. You didn't think I was going to ask Hunter and Della, did you?'

'No, of course not.'

'So you'll come?'

Instead of dread, Chiara feels the thinness of new hope beginning to thread through her heart. Firenze, at last. To drive into the city, see the Arno again, walk along the Lungarno. Maybe in the afternoon she could go to the Convent of San Marco's to see her favourite frescoes again.

'*Mamma?* You look like a cat with cream. What are you thinking?'

'Of the Fra Angelicos.'

Stefano smiles with relief.

* * *

At one o'clock the next day Stefano leaves the Villa Tiglio as soon as his class ends, getting on his scooter and going down the Via San Leonardo quickly, then crossing over the Arno and going along the Lungarno to the Cascine Park. It's a Tuesday, market day at the Cascine, and he needs clothes: shoes, a new pair of jeans and some shirts for work. He knows from long-ago summers that some good buys can be found in this huge open-air market. He also wants to buy some kitchenware for the flat; Marco hasn't got round to it yet, and there's this lunch party on Sunday.

Though it's a morning market, most of the stalls are still set up, awnings flapping in the breeze coming off the Arno. There are hundreds of them, selling everything: rounds of *parmigiano*, prosciutto; spaghetti forks and underwear; Versace T-shirts in bins, with cheap cotton socks; work clothes and the trendy, shimmering clingy little tops that seem to be all the rage.

Stefano has just purchased a pair of trainers, and is waiting for his change when an English voice behind him says, 'Do you think we should be meeting like this?' He doesn't need to turn to know that it's Della.

The voice is light, teasing, but when Stefano finally faces her, having waited till his change arrived and his new trainers were put into a brown paper bag and given to him, she's looking at him steadily, unsmiling.

They move as there's a crowd around the shoe stall; Stefano continuing down the long line of stalls on his way to the end, Della at his side. Like the other evening at the pizzeria, the last time they were alone for a few minutes, neither of them speaks. On either side of them colour and noise blur their private thoughts; there are dozens, hundreds of tables and bins packed with goods, either in a jumble or neatly displayed. Music from small radios or stereos blares from some of the trendier stalls. It's windy, and the awnings covering the tables flap furiously every now and then when a sudden, heavier blast goes through the market.

They walk like this for about five, ten minutes. Stefano stops occasionally to look at a shirt, some shorts; Della too stops once to finger the material on a row of miniskirts. Each waits for the other. They've acknowledged that they are together.

Stefano speaks first. 'Where's Hunter?'

'Back at the villa, giving one of his private students some extra lunchtime tuition. A Japanese man, you've probably seen him around. Here in Florence on business and cramming up on his English before he moves on to London.'

A couple of young women stop them, students of Della's. They show off their purchases with much giggling and gesticulating: skimpy summer dresses, clunky platform shoes, cheap but tasteful jewellery. 'Speak English,' Della says imperiously. 'I let my class out an hour early today to come to the Cascine only on the condition that you speak English to each other.'

This dampens their enthusiasm and they soon go their own way. Stefano notices one of the girls making a face behind Della's back. The student sees Stefano watching, and winks at him, inviting his complicity. Stefano keeps his face bland and turns back to Della who is saying, 'They don't like it, but we have to keep at them. The only way to learn a language is to practise it. Speak it, listen to it, talk to yourself in it every moment you can.'

Stefano smiles. 'I'm not one of your students, Della. You don't need to lecture me.'

Della smiles back at him. 'No, I don't, do I,' she agrees sweetly.

As they continue the walk down the long passage of market stalls Della feels both elated and sure of herself. She has been in this state since Saturday night at Sadie and Marino's house, when Stefano had kissed her goodnight in such a fiery way. Sure now that Stefano is going through the same frenzy as she is, Della's convinced that it's all a matter of time, though she won't go further than that in her thoughts.

What Della will not, cannot do, is think about Hunter. She tried, last weekend, to remember him, to remember that he is her partner, the man she's supposed to be in love with. But always, there's the memory of Stefano's first week at the school, his presence filling the villa and every one of her senses like the warm early-spring weather. The scent of lime and jasmine, the vividness of the poppies, the feel of the hot breeze on her bare thighs in the garden – all these were mixed with Stefano. The fresh young scent of him, the feel of his breath on her cheek when he leaned over her desk to look at a workbook, the way in which her eyes filled with him, even when he was at the periphery of her vision.

She tried to think of Hunter even then, to make herself sane again. But every time Stefano appeared, Hunter seemed immaterial, unimportant.

Della has never, ever felt so helpless. Even with the man before Hunter, the one in Rome that she'd been so obsessed with; even then, there was never *this*, this feeling that she was gliding, crashing, jolting out of control. Since meeting Stefano, she has felt electrified, every inch of her skin suffused with nerve endings charged and waiting to be connected to him. Everything around her is intensified: the rich scents of earth and blossom, the colour of the poppies, the lime trees. Even sounds seem cleaner and clearer.

She knows, of course, how appalling this is; this longing, this craving, for Hunter's son. She knows it, admits it; but she cannot do anything about it. She would sell her soul, and Hunter's too, for a night in bed with him.

Thinking this as she walks beside him now, past a stall selling lacy black lingerie, she's disoriented to hear him say, without preamble, 'So, tell me about my father. What was it about him that made you want him so much?'

She stares at him but he's still walking, looking at a skimpy satin slip, then across the way at some garden

110

tools on the opposite stall; looking everywhere but at her. His question about Hunter seems so bizarre that she feels slightly hysterical. Want Hunter? She wants to scream. I didn't know what wanting was, until I met you. But she says, instead, 'Why are you bringing all this up now? Does it matter? It's over.'

'Over? Nothing's *over*. You're still together, you and Hunter.'

'I mean . . . I meant, all *that* is over. How it began, how it started. Why do you keep bringing it up?'

'I don't *keep* bringing it up. Let's just say I have this need to know exactly how it happened, how it is that you've taken over my mother's place at the Villa Tiglio while she sits in a small apartment in Siena on her own.'

Della is prevented from answering by the approach of an old, but still powerful, man, with peppery hair and a beard who walks between the stalls. He is carrying a big brown cardboard box with a sign on it: 'MONEY FOR GIANNI', and he's singing in a deep melodious voice.

The man is obviously blind, because he walks slowly yet surely as he sings. His voice is strong and pure. Customers stop buying and vendors stop selling to listen. He seems to be well known and liked by the market stallholders and they encourage him, calling, '*Bravo, Gianni. Bravissimo,*' and putting thousand-lire notes in his cardboard box.

Della and Stefano stand aside, as others do, to let him pass. He's singing a well-known Italian song, plaintive and sad, and when he gets to the chorus several of the vendors join in. Gianni stops his slow walk to sing the final verse and earns a burst of applause when he finishes. Stefano and Della join the others in putting a contribution in his cardboard box.

Stefano is oddly moved by this incident. There is something about the dignity of the blind man, and the respect he is given by those who obviously know him, which makes everything else not only unimportant,

111

but also slightly tawdry: Hunter and Della's unremarkable little liaison, Della's apparent infatuation with her lover's son, even his own prying into what, in the end, is really none of his business. Disgusted with it all, he turns to Della to make some excuse and leave her.

They are now at the top end of the market. On their left, the Arno looks ruffled with the wind, but much greener here than it does back down in the centre of the city. Della says, before he can speak, 'Shall we sit over in the park, by the pond? I bought some things for lunch from the food stalls before I saw you; there's plenty for us both.'

'Thanks, but I think I'll go back to the villa now. I've got some papers to look at, some work to do.'

Della looks stricken. Her lips move, tremble. He watches, fascinated. It's deliberate, surely, this quivering and confusion; this is Della, bossy and cocky; he has seen her at work, with Hunter and the others.

'Don't,' she says in a thin voice. 'Don't go, not yet. Please stay and share my lunch.' The dark sky of her eyes begins to fill with rain; in a moment, they will burst like clouds.

With a shock, Stefano sees that this isn't an act. The game has suddenly become real. It stuns Della herself: her own desperation; her own longing.

It makes Stefano fatalistic. He follows her to the wide square, where they find an empty bench and sit down, trying to ease themselves back into some kind of normal, civilized behaviour. In front of them tortoises of all sizes lie in the grass by a large pond, then ponderously trundle off into the water to dive clumsily in. Ducks and one black swan pick their way around the reptiles disdainfully. Two toddlers feed them while their mothers watch.

Della slowly begins to control herself again. Stefano has not, after all, left her; he's still here, sitting so close that she has a hard time not reaching out and touching him.

She takes rolls, *pecorino* cheese and prosciutto, from

112

several bags and places them on the stone bench between them. A sudden gust of wind blows one of the bags away. As Stefano retrieves it Della says, 'Shelley got the idea for his poem "Ode to the West Wind" walking through the Cascine Park. It must have been a blowy day, just like today.'

Stefano says, for the second time that day, 'I'm not one of your students, Della.'

Della carefully opens a brown bag of cherries and places them with the rest of the food. She's feeling confident again, euphoric. The sun, the hot wind and the proximity of the man next to her make her feel reckless. She turns to Stefano and says gaily, 'I know you're not one of my students. Thank God for that, I say! But then, Stefano, what exactly are you to me? Not a friend. Nor family. How would you define our relationship?' The words are light, but her expression is challenging.

As if his answer doesn't matter, she picks up the cheese and breaks it in half, takes a bit of it and indicates for Stefano to help himself. She's determined not to show him how important his answer is to her, determined not to lose the offensive. Last week, struck dumb and emotional by Stefano, she'd become a wimp, shaken and unable to think or act. Now she's herself, but more so. She is in love for the first time, for she sees now that what she had mistaken for love had been either a power struggle, as it was in Rome, or gratitude and relief, as it was with Hunter.

Stefano ignores the food and ignores her question. He has a sudden yearning for something simple, uncomplicated: the truth. He says, 'I'd like to know how it happened, OK? This thing between you and my father. You might think it's none of my business, and sometimes I think that too. But in the end, it's part of me, because both my mother and father are part of me.'

Della starts to speak, but Stefano hasn't quite finished. 'You probably wonder why I seem so obsessed about it, about finding out how it happened, about what went wrong between my father and mother.

113

I've wondered too, and I think it's because, well, I remember them as being happy, you know? I believed in their marriage? And so what happened, the thing between you and my father, seemed to make a mockery of my whole childhood, of everything I remember.'

Della stares at a tortoise, a massive creature who seems to be glaring back, trying to stare her out. For the first time, she's hit with guilt and it's not a very pleasant sensation. 'Stefano, I didn't know . . . I didn't realize. About your parents' marriage, that is. I only know what Hunter told me, what—'

'Look,' Stefano interrupts. 'That's past, that bit. But if I'm going to make sense of *now*, and of the future, I need to be clearer on how, and why, it all went wrong. I think it would help me to accept you and my father as a couple.'

Della doesn't want Stefano to accept her and Hunter as a couple, but he's looking determined, waiting for her to explain. She shrugs, decides to get it over with. 'I told you before. I didn't break up the marriage.'

'It broke by accident, eh? Like a dropped egg? Come on, Della. Let's start our relationship on an honest footing. Be straight with me, OK?'

Della has to close her eyes for a moment, so that Stefano cannot see the hope in her eyes. If he's talking about a relationship between them, then surely he's feeling the same emotions as she is.

'OK,' she says, when she can look at him again. She'll tell him about Hunter, get that bit out of the way so she and Stefano can start afresh, uncluttered by any mysteries of the past. 'There's nothing much to say about me and Hunter, but I suppose you deserve to know. When I first realized, after only a few weeks – days, actually – of working at the school, that he was . . . interested in me, I ran a mile.'

'Oh?' The disbelief in that one word annoys Della.

'Yes, I fucking did. Well, not ran – shit, I had a good job, I wasn't going to pack it all in just because the boss fancied me. Sure, I stayed. But he was married and I

114

honestly didn't want to know. Not at first, anyway. I was ready – to be quite honest I was desperate – to settle down, make a home in Florence. I thought I'd had one in Rome, after years of teaching in different countries because I was trying to get somewhere with my career, but—'

Della stops. Stefano says nothing, waiting for her to go on. 'I left Rome because of a man. I couldn't bear to be in the same city as him. So Hunter's attention took my mind off all that. And yes, I was lonely. I wanted a partner in my life, someone to share things with. What's wrong with that? But at first Hunter was nothing more than a good boss; sympathetic and caring. OK, so I confided in him, saw a lot of him, but it was friendship I wanted from him and he knew it. When you get to my age, you know about married men: they stay married, as a rule. But then Hunter did the unexpected. He told his wife he was in love with me and that was that.'

'So you're telling me you didn't have anything to do with him before he left Chiara?'

'I didn't say that. I'm just saying that at first I didn't want to know. I didn't find him at all physically attractive. He's not really my type, though he's in great shape for his age, and he's not bad looking. He's much older than me, of course. But he can be loving when he wants to be, and persuasive. And believe me, he wanted to be both. In the end he wore me down.'

She deliberately begins to eat again, putting slices of prosciutto between a couple of rolls and handing one to Stefano. 'That's it, agreed?' she says, but it isn't a question. 'That's all I'm going to say about it. I don't want to talk to you about Hunter again.'

Stefano nods. 'OK. Just one more thing. What about the little things that sometimes get to people, like, you know, guilt. Did you never feel that? Or regret maybe? All that suffering? Maybe not for you, but for others.'

Della puts down her *panino* and stares at him. She feels sick with longing for him and can no longer pretend she is eating, or that this is an ordinary picnic in the park. 'Guilt, no,' she says. 'Not then, anyway. If it hadn't been me it would have been someone else. Hunter was ready for it; he was bored with his marriage, terrified of getting old. Regret, yes. Not then, not when it happened, but now. Suddenly, in the past ten days, I've regretted this one fact more than anything: that Hunter is with me instead of with Chiara or someone else.'

She looks at him defiantly, as if daring him to pretend she means something other than what her words indicate. But Stefano is not into pretending. He searches her face thoughtfully, not sure exactly what he's looking for. Another gust of wind blows between them, tossing a blond streak of hair across her lips. Stefano reaches out his hand, and with his fingers gently removes it from her face. 'Eat your lunch,' he says softly. 'You haven't even touched the cherries.'

Then he's gone. He stands up and walks away across the park. Della watches him until he's obscured by the massive old chestnut trees beyond the square, and then, still looking at the spot where he disappeared, she slowly begins eating the cherries, keeping her eyes fixed on the dark, shady woodland beyond, as if he will eventually materialize from between the foliage.

11

The wind drops that afternoon, making the weather as sultry as a day in August. The poppies scattered in the field and meadows beyond the back garden of the Villa Tiglio blaze crimson in the sunlight and the cyprus trees on the hillsides break through air that is thick and heavy.

Stefano is late getting back from the Cascine. He has a large weekly intermediate class on Tuesday afternoons, and the students, many of whom take an hour off from their workplace one day a week to perfect their English, are already waiting in the classroom. Della, who has only just returned herself, notices that Stefano is not yet back and chooses not to tell Hunter, but to go in and begin the class herself, saying that Stefano has been delayed but will be arriving soon.

This is not quite true. At this moment Stefano is still at the Cascine, at the entrance to the market which has by now packed up; the trucks and caravans which brought the goods and stallholders taking everything away until next Tuesday. He's sitting on his stationary Vespa talking to Bettina, who is on her scooter. It's her afternoon off and they have just run into each other. Bettina is about to meet Marco, who works near by as an assistant trainee in a firm of lawyers. Stefano doesn't have a clue what he's going to do next.

After he'd left Della he walked under the trees through the deeper part of the park for some time, passing the children's playground and some playing fields. He cut back along the Arno, now unruffled and lazy in the afternoon heat, and walked back to his bike, avoiding the piazza where Della might still be waiting.

He's sick of Della and Hunter. Worse, he's sick of himself. He doesn't like what he's doing, though in truth he's not at all sure exactly what it is he's doing. He is digging, searching for something. But why? What, in the end, does it matter, this truth he is trying to find out? Nothing is going to change things, and in the end, are things so bad after all? His father is happy, his mother, if not happy, is at least beginning to find a life again. Stefano himself is now on polite terms with his father – more than they have been over the past year and a half – and this is also more than Stefano expected. What more, then, is he looking for?

He expected – and the realization hits him like the gusts of wind in the park earlier – to find his father changed. Softened, somehow, by the experience of Della. Stefano had expected, for the first time in his life, to begin to like his father.

He is sitting on his scooter, about to start it, when this thought does his head in. Yes, he had hated his father for leaving his mother; and yes, he had sympathized in every way not with Hunter, but with Chiara.

And yet . . . yet he had hoped that since what had happened was done, irrevocable, that some good would come of it. Some change in Hunter, some indication that for the first time in his life his father would see Stefano as an individual, rather than as a pallid reflection of himself. That he would, for once, be a father, not a lecturer or a coach, and a disapproving, critical one at that. That he would, for a change, stop asking for Stefano's admiration and applause and give some, ungrudgingly, to his son.

Bettina relieves him from the heaviness of his thoughts with her cheery, '*Ciao,* Stefano!' as she zooms in dangerously close to him on her scooter.

Stefano welcomes the diversion. '*Ciao,* Bettina. You'd better watch how you drive that thing, you nearly ran me down.'

'Now would I do that? I need you too much.'

Stefano feels a daft moment of hope until she goes on, 'If Marco has no-one to help him pay the rent on that place he'll have to move back to his parents, and then we'd never be on our own.'

'And here I was, feeling hopeful,' Stefano says wryly.

Bettina leans over to blow him a kiss somewhere in the vicinity of his face. 'Poor Stefano,' she teases, 'with no-one to love.'

Stefano grins. 'Fat lot of sympathy I get from you.'

She laughs, and Stefano watches her plump filled-in lips and strong, young teeth with fascination. Her clean olive skin is flushed with the sun, from her ride across town, and her long, polished legs gleam, one on the ground and the other propped on the pedal of her scooter. Stefano, not for the first time, wonders how she can manage the thing in the miniskirts she always wears.

'*Dai*, Stefano!' she exclaims. 'What nerve, wanting sympathy from me. With all the Italian girls pleading with me to put in a good word for them with you.'

'Name names, Bettina. Give me a list.'

'And swell your big head even more? No way. Anyway, I'm sure you know.'

Stefano does, for Bettina's friends are confident, not at all shy, but he's enjoying this game, this flirtation with her. Stefano knows that she adores Marco, but that doesn't keep her from testing her power over other men, lightly, innocently. Marco knows it too; she acts no differently when he's around, but luckily he understands her well and knows that she is fiercely loyal to him.

They banter for a few more minutes, then Bettina says suddenly, 'Stefano, do you know what time it is? You have that weekly intermediate class starting right now, this very minute. Go!'

Stefano, instead of rushing off on his scooter, remains where he is, looking away from her down at the ground. A *motorino* races by them and a friend of

119

Bettina's shouts greetings as he passes. Bettina waves, but doesn't take her eyes off Stefano. 'Is something wrong?'

Stefano hears the tenderness, the worry in her voice and looks up to see her eyes filled with concern for him. He is moved by it. 'I wasn't going to go back. To the school, to the villa. I've had enough.'

Bettina understands. 'It's too much, isn't it, seeing Della there with your father. I wondered if it would be. I would hate it, just hate it, to go home and see my mother gone and my father living in the same place with another woman. And in a house that was dear to me, a place that was part of my childhood, part of all my earliest memories. It takes the goodness, the sweet-ness, away from the memories.'

He nods, slightly startled, for this is just what he had been trying to explain to Della. Bettina doesn't know, of course, of that complication, but what she says is true. There is just much more to it than she has yet realized.

Bettina goes on, 'I wouldn't blame you if you walked out on all of them. I would if I were in the same situ-ation. But I wish you wouldn't, Stefano. The students love you; they've told me so. And not just the young women, either, though of course they adore you, silly empty-headed fools that they are.' She peers at Stefano to see if she has made him smile. She hasn't; he looks lost, miserable. She says, 'I'm teasing you, but I'm serious at how good you are with the students. It would be unfair on them to walk out like this. It's hard, starting again with a new teacher at this stage.'

Stefano stares ahead of him at the river, at a lone fisherman on its bank, slumping hopefully by the sludgy water. He knows he will go back, knows that the sudden impulse to pack up and leave Hunter and Della to stew in the unappetizing mess of their own relationship, has already left him.

'D'you know what I'm saying, Stefano? You'll go back?'

He is grateful for the endearing kindness of her words and realizes that he would like to press his face into the shimmering fabric of her deep-green T-shirt and feel her long fingers gently rake the thickness of his hair. He would like more, much more than that, of course, but it would do for a start.

'I'll go back.' Just saying these words lightens him up enormously. He grins ruefully at her. 'That is, if I'm not fired already. My class was to have begun five minutes ago.'

'*Va*', hurry. I'll see you tomorrow. And Stefano, remember I'm there. If it gets too bad with Della and Hunter, come see me.'

Stefano nods and waves and drives away. You bet I will, he is thinking. You bet I will.

Hunter sees Stefano arrive. 'I thought you were in your classroom,' he snaps. 'You're late.'

'Sorry. I got held up.'

'You should have phoned.'

'I'm not *that* late. By the time I found a phone and made the call, I'd have been a whole lot later.'

'Stef, just because you are my son doesn't mean you can take liberties. I'm not going to be any easier on you than I would be on the other staff members. Don't think you can take advantage of our relationship.'

'Dad, get a grip. I'm a few minutes late, it's not the end of the world. It's not happened before and it won't happen again. Now, can I please get to my class before you hold me up for another ten minutes?'

He walks quickly away from Hunter. When he goes into his classroom he's surprised to see Della standing in front of the students explaining something about nouns. 'Ah, there you are, Stefano,' she cries. 'I told your class you were unavoidably delayed. I'll leave you to it now that you're here.' She walks out and winks at him as he stands aside to let her pass. She has changed from the long summer skirt she was wearing at the Cascine Park into a miniskirt – not as short as the

121

ones Bettina wears but short enough to show her pale, muscular legs. They are not a patch on Bettina's, Stefano thinks, though not bad, then swears silently at himself for even noticing.

Della walks out of Stefano's classroom right into Hunter's line of vision. He had been left standing awkwardly after Stefano had walked away from him and didn't know quite what to do, for he was feeling too cross to do anything decisive. Letting his irritation pepper the first person he sees, he hisses, 'Della, what in the hell were *you* doing there? In Stefano's classroom? I thought you had your own student this afternoon for a private session.'

'Don't talk to me in that tone of voice. What the fuck are *you* doing? Spying on me?'

The door to Stefano's classroom is wide open and the sounds have carried in. Della's voice brays and carries like a stable of outraged horses and Stefano raises his own voice as he speaks to the students. He hopes they haven't yet learned English swear words.

'*Spying* on you? What kind of paranoia is that?'

'Well, what the fuck do you *think* I was doing in Stefano's classroom? I was covering for him until he got here.'

'*I* didn't know he was late. Why didn't you tell *me*? It's not up to you to decide who is going to cover where.'

'Jesus fucking Christ. You are such a stuffy old bore.' She walks disdainfully past him and then past Bettina, who has walked in unnoticed a few minutes earlier. 'What are *you* doing here? I thought it was your afternoon off.'

'Don't take that bossy tone with me,' Bettina cries in Italian. 'We all know you have Hunter under your thumb, but just because he's a fool, don't think you can get away with it with me.'

Inside Stefano's classroom the students prick up their ears. They understood *that* all right.

'Bettina!' Hunter exclaims. 'For goodness' sake lower your voice.

'Why you cheeky little bitch,' Della booms.

'Della, shut up!' Hunter shouts.

'*Me? Me* shut up? Did you just hear what that Italian cow said about us, about you and me?'

Stefano thinks about shutting the door of his classroom, but decides it would be too obvious. He goes on talking about nouns and adjectives.

'You just listen; I'll say it again, in case Hunter didn't hear,' Bettina cries, losing it completely. 'You are nothing but a bossy tart, trying to run this school the way you run Hunter. I would say it in English too, if I knew the words, because I'm not sure that you even understand Italian. You call yourselves language teachers! How long have you lived in this country and still you speak Italian like pigs.'

'You're fired,' Della shouts.

Hunter's mouth, open to say the same thing, snaps shut. Turning on Della in a fury, he forgets that he has just ordered everyone to keep their voices down and shouts, 'Who the hell do you think you are? What authority do you think you have to fire someone in *my* school?'

'*Your* school? After I gave a fucking year and a half of my life helping you build it up to become the success it is?'

'*Chiara* did that,' Hunter snarls. 'And it was a lot longer than a year and a half.'

There is a serious silence, which Bettina breaks by bursting into tears and rushing to her office in the alcove. Della says to Hunter, 'You're a bastard.' Then she too walks away.

Hunter is left exactly where he was five minutes or so ago when Stefano stormed past him into his classroom. He remembers the open door, the students inside, and groans out loud. Then he storms down the corridor and out the front door.

Stefano says, 'Now, I will once again explain the

rules of nouns and their modifying adjectives. I have a feeling you didn't listen carefully the first time.'

Stefano finds Bettina still in the office when his class finishes. There is no sign of either Della or Hunter.

'I heard all that,' Stefano says. 'You're an idiot, you know. Albeit a sweet one. Whatever possessed you to talk that way to Della?'

'It's true, all of it. She *does* boss Hunter around all the time, and everyone knows it.'

'I'm not doubting the truth of it. I'm doubting whether you should have said it to the two of them. What got into you?'

Bettina sniffs. She's no longer crying, but her eyes are red under her carefully reapplied make-up. 'I was cross with Della, cross with them both, after talking to you in the park. They have no right to take you for granted the way they do. Just because you've come back, they expect you to rush into their arms and be a happy family with them. It makes me so angry.' She sniffs again. 'Do you think I'm really fired?'

'No, of course not. Hunter can't let you go now, even if he wanted to; he'd lose face. It would look like Della really does run the school.'

'I wish I could quit. If I thought I could get another job near my home with such good hours I would quit. It's hateful working here.'

'Even with me?' Stefano teases, wanting to make those heather lips unfurl in a smile again.

It works. 'I suppose I can't leave you on your own here, can I, after lecturing you on coming back. I'll have to stay for your sake. Ah, *Madonna*, the sacrifices I make!'

'Just out of curiosity, what *were* you doing back here? You said you'd see me tomorrow.'

Bettina shrugs. 'I was worried about you. You seemed in such an odd mood when I saw you at the Cascine. I wondered if you really intended coming back. I thought if you hadn't I could make some excuse for you, at least give you time to decide if that was really what you wanted to do.'

Stefano is touched by this generous impulse. 'Ah, Bettina,' he says softly, taking her hand in the most chaste and brotherly manner, 'what a lucky man Marco is.'

He says it in the same light, teasing voice he always uses with her, but there's something deeper underlying it. She recognizes this and acknowledges it with a slight nod. 'Tell *him* that,' she says in the same playful voice. 'Maybe then he'll appreciate me.'

But she knows Marco does. And makes herself think of him, because it's oh so tempting to let herself think of Stefano.

12

Della drives out of the Villa Tiglio in a fury. Luckily she has no more classes. The way she feels now she would like never to return to the place again.

Except for Stefano. She would have liked to have seen him, waited for his class to be over, but she knew Hunter was lurking around and she didn't think she could bear to even look at him, let alone speak to him.

Della drives to the top of the Via San Leonardo and turns right towards the Piazzale Galileo, then left and straight down the busy streets to Due Strade. She finds a parking space down the side of the traffic-filled road and mindlessly begins to make purchases at the small shops comprising the Due Strade area. She doesn't know why she's doing this, but she has to do something, anything, to stop her mind chuntering crazily in her head.

She buys cherries – they are magnificent this year; large, succulent, the colour of the best Chianti – from Anna, the cheerful blond woman at the greengrocers, and tries to concentrate as Anna rhapsodizes over the cherry crop. Then Della buys some soap powder at the tiny general store. She buys bread and a selection of cold meats and exquisite salads from the *rosticceria*, taking so long over her choices that the man behind the counter, normally patient and good-humoured, sighs audibly and taps his fingers on the glass.

When she has finished, she stops at her favourite café to drink strong black coffee, which she normally hates, standing up at the counter as there are no tables here. She would rather have weak Earl Grey tea sitting in an English garden; she would rather be in Rome drinking in a bar with friends. She would rather be anywhere than here, she decides, anywhere but in this dusty old city with dusty old Hunter.

This last thought stops her dead. She orders another coffee and stares moodily out of the open doors of the café at the motorbikes and cars jamming the street, horns honking and drivers shouting at the odd pedestrian who scuttles into their paths. She turns back to the shiny grey-and-white speckled marble of the countertop and then to the rest of the shop which is filled with a lush display of cakes and sweets. Two elderly Italian men in smart suits eye her boldly, but instead of getting a lift, as she usually does, from their open appreciation, it depresses her. She's tired of elderly men fancying her; it's making her feel old, and she's not, she is still young. She thinks of Stefano's smooth, hard body, of his glossy black hair, and a sound like a sob catches in her throat. The men who had been staring at her turn away, glancing back at her oddly.

The two women behind the counter serve the customers with coffee and *pasticcini*, keeping up a constant stream of chatter as they do. One is seriously gorgeous, like Bettina, which reminds Della again of the events that led up to her fierce argument with Hunter. She's still cross at Bettina, but upset with herself for letting the silly girl rattle her.

She will sort it out with Bettina, but with Hunter there's a deeper rift. The realization in the park today, during that lunchtime picnic with Stefano, that she not only doesn't love Hunter but never really did, disturbs her.

She thought she did, naturally. When he told her he was leaving Chiara, that the love between him and his wife had been dead for a long time, for years, and that he couldn't take it any longer, Della had mistaken the euphoria she'd felt for love. Here, at last, was a married man ready to take the plunge, ready to begin again, with her. Here was a man crazy about her, ready to save her from all those relationship struggles that had gone on with every man in her life, from her brothers who she fought to dominate all through childhood, to stop them from dominating her, and all the others.

When Hunter told her all these things about his marriage, Della did not even consider the fact that Chiara might have something different to say about it. The two women barely saw each other at the Villa Tiglio. When Della first took the job there Chiara had been working in a church in one of the smaller surrounding towns and hadn't come home for lunch as she apparently used to do. But in those six months, the months before Chiara left, Della saw her occasionally, and she actually quite liked her, if she thought about it. But Della didn't really like to think about Chiara, which was understandable. She preferred to see her through Hunter, when he confided in her about how difficult his wife was, how their marriage had been a mistake from the beginning.

But now, with Stefano searching, questioning, prying, she is beginning to feel uneasy about it all. Worse, she is beginning to doubt Hunter, doubt, for the first time whether he has been entirely honest with her.

But at the time, there were no doubts. Hunter, when he chose to, could make a woman believe anything, and there he was, focusing on her like a spotlight, making her feel that she was indeed the only woman Hunter had ever felt deserving of such illumination. There was something addictive about it, about Hunter's craving for her. He couldn't get enough of her, it seemed; he not only loved her, he wanted her around all the time, not just in his bed but wherever he went – in the school, at meetings and social events. He loved showing her off, loved taking her to restaurants and bars, loved putting his arm around her, possessively, in front of the students and the staff members.

Della isn't stupid; she knows that Hunter is addicted too. Not so much to her, but to the idea of her: her relative youth compared to his fifty-odd years; her slimness; her vitality; her spark. The *newness* of her, compared, of course, with the oldness of his wife, the familiarity of Chiara.

This then, this mutual need, was what they'd thought was love. Della recognizes this not with regret, but with sadness. She'd really thought she loved Hunter, once. For a moment she wonders if she could make herself love him again. How simple it would all be. Della wants to love Hunter, not Hunter's son. But Stefano has made her see his father clearly, too clearly now for any more dissembling.

All this honest soul-searching pains Della and she hurriedly leaves the café. Once outside on the busy Due Strade she realizes she has nowhere to go. Returning to the villa, with her thoughts still turbulent, is unthinkable, and she gave up her own apartment just up the road on the Via del Gelsomino a year ago, to move finally and irrevocably in with Hunter. She realizes that what she needs is a friend, but she hasn't made any in Florence. Tied up with Hunter and the school from the moment she arrived, she neither wanted nor sought other relationships, friends or otherwise. She has plenty of old school chums back in England, but what good are they now, she thinks. Even if they were closer, they were too tied up with husbands and children – one even has a tiny grandchild, heaven forbid – to give her the attention and sympathy she's craving right now. She supposes she could go to Rome for a few days; she has friends there, quite a few of them. For the first time since coming to Florence two years ago, since meeting Hunter and the hectic life she has had with him, she's missing Rome.

She doesn't want to go back to Rome. Though she is at last over him, the memory of the man who jilted her so ignominiously, taking her to lunch first at their favourite restaurant in the Campo de'Fiori, still haunts and humiliates her when she returns there. She will never be able to walk through the old city again, remembering the stares of the fruit and vegetable vendors packing up their produce in the piazza as she stumbled tearfully from the restaurant, her eyes and face as watery as the fountain. She had looked back once to see the man who had just told her he was tired of their affair, tired of her, still sitting under the cool awning of the restaurant and already forgetting her, beginning to tuck into the plate of pasta in front of him with gusto.

No, not Rome.

Somewhere in her line of vision a woman with orange sherbert for hair, wearing a flowery flowing thing with billowy sleeves, is waving at her. Della stares and returns to the present. 'Sadie,' she says as the woman approaches. 'It's you.' Her voice is husky with relief.

Sadie looks at her sharply. 'What are you doing here? I saw you from across the road; you looked confused. Are you ill? Aren't you teaching this afternoon?'

'It was my one-to-one. He cancelled.'

'Oh. Well. So you're just doing some shopping?'

'Uh, yes. I suppose so. I don't know.'

Sadie's scrutiny intensifies. Della, usually so assured and in command, is strangely vague, uncertain, quiet.

'I'm just on my way home,' Sadie says. 'Want to come up for a bit? I could make iced tea; we could sit in the garden. It's so hot for this time of year. Heaven knows what summer will be like.'

Della, because she doesn't know what else to do, agrees. Sadie has walked down from her house, so the two get in Della's car and drive the short distance to the Via Martellini.

Marino, seeing them approach up the long gravel drive, under the umbrella pines, retreats into his study. He had come out to take a break from the convoluted intricacies of his latest plot and to gossip with Sadie after her return from Due Strade, but he has no wish to see Della. He finds her terrifying, as he does many English women, he decides; they are so bold, so assertive. Not for the first time, he thanks the Blessed Twelve Apostles for giving him Sadie, the rare, sweet exception.

Sadie makes iced tea, laces it with lime and sugar and brings a jug of it out onto the terrace, where Della is staring at nothing. The garden is still pleasantly scraggly, the bushes overgrown, the gardenias voluptuously blowsy, the grass slightly in need of a cut. An orange tree drips full, ripe fruits almost to the ground, its branches greenly weary with all that weight.

'So what's up?' Sadie asks bluntly.

Della considers a lie, but decides Sadie will soon find out anyway from Bettina. 'I had a row with Hunter at the school. Bettina too. I'm afraid we shrieked at each other. It was quite inexcusable, really.'

'What about?'

Della laughs, and the laugh seems to waft crazily in the still, hot air, like a lost butterfly. 'I wish I knew. Bettina said something about my wanting to boss everyone and then Hunter jumped in, so there we all were, rowing like fishwives right in the corridor, with a class going on a few feet away.'

'Was Stefano in on this?'

'Oh no, it had nothing to do with him. He was safely tucked away teaching.'

She sighs, shifts gears, moves far away from Sadie and on to another planet. Sadie knows she is thinking of Hunter's son. Della's face is unusually gentle; she looks, at this moment, far younger than her years.

'Well then,' Sadie says. 'It will blow over. Bettina's easy, doesn't hold grudges, and Hunter – well, surely you and Hunter have had tiffs before. Everyone does.'

Della shifts back from the clouds to look at Sadie. 'Actually, no. We haven't. Well, we didn't. Things seem to be changing.'

'Nothing to do with Stefano, is it?'

This rouses Della. The softness leaves her face and she frowns. 'What a bloody peculiar thing to say. Why should it have anything to do with him?'

'You tell me.'

Della chooses to ignore this. Though she is confused and distraught over her feelings for Hunter, she is suddenly terrified about letting anyone else see this. She's part of Hunter now, part of his life. She has invested too much in this grand love affair; she has no home other than his, no friends other than his friends and their colleagues at the school. Whatever she feels now, Della cannot let it fall apart. It's far too late for that.

Sadie takes a breath and decides to take the plunge. She has lived with Italians for too long; she's becoming as upfront as they are. She can't pretend she hasn't noticed Della and Stefano.

But then she remembers giving another warning once, to Chiara. About Hunter, and Della. Chiara didn't believe her, didn't want to believe her. Would Della be any different? Would she even listen, if Sadie tried to tell her that people will begin to notice? Already she and Marino know. It won't be long before others do too.

But Della has become prickly again. Sadie is paddling too near the truth and it frightens her. She says briskly, 'We're all touchy; it's the heat, so early on in the season. I wish I'd never mentioned my silly row with Hunter, it was nothing. We'll have both forgotten about it when I get back. I'll go now, I think. Thank you for the iced tea.'

'And Stefano?' Sadie is gently persistent.

Della, half standing, falls back into the garden chair as if a sickness has overcome her. A strong scent of gardenia hits her full in the face and she feels her head spin alarmingly. 'What do you mean? What about Stefano?'

'Oh for goodness' sake, Della. Please try not to treat me like a complete fool.'

'I don't know what you're talking about.' Della closes her eyes and feels herself wrapped in thick white gardenia petals, imagining Stefano brushing them away to get to her.

'You'll blow it, you know. You've got a man at last,

132

and he's all yours, to play with or boss around or to do what you please with. You've waited a long time for this; you thought you had it in Rome but it fell apart. This will too if you're not careful.'

Della sits so motionless, still with her eyes closed, that Sadie feels quite sorry for her. She is about to go to her and put a friendly arm around her shoulders when Della opens her eyes and says, 'I really think you've been playing amateur analyst for too long, Sadie. You really haven't got a clue.'

Before Sadie can decide whether to take offence or to laugh at this, someone else has come through the kitchen door and is standing behind them. 'Oh. Sorry. Am I interrupting? I thought Marco would be here.'

Della closes her eyes again and Sadie laughs, a loud, raucous snort that frightens the blackbird just beginning to sing in the cedar tree. 'What a sense of timing,' Sadie roars. 'We were just talking about you.'

Della opens her eyes. 'Were we?' she says. 'I don't think so.' She looks steadily at Sadie.

Sadie laughs again. Sod Della, she thinks. Sod Hunter too. She wouldn't give a stuff about either of them except for Stefano. She wonders if he can handle what he's getting embroiled in.

Stefano sits down opposite Della while Sadie goes inside to fill up the jug and get another glass. 'Thanks for taking my class when I was late today,' he says.

'That's OK. No problem.'

'Sorry if it caused you hassle with my father.'

Della shrugs.

'I couldn't help but overhear. None of you bothered to lower your voices. You should have seen my students struggling to understand the English.' He smiles.

It undoes her. She takes a deep breath and drowns in gardenia, in the smell and taste of Stefano as she leans into him and presses her hands onto the hot fabric of his shirt, burrowing her face in the golden space between his neck and shoulders, feeling his skin

133

against her lips as she says, 'Stefano. Oh God. I think I'm falling in love with you.'

'*Oh Dio*,' Sadie says softly, stopping so suddenly that Marino, right behind her, bumps into her and nearly drops the tray of glasses and biscuits he's holding. 'Not again.'

'*Porca miseria!*' Marino swears, but it's not at Sadie. He too has seen Stefano and Della through the open double doors in front of them. '*Non lo credo*,' he exclaims. 'They're doing it again! This is becoming a habit. Does Marco know? Do they always carry on like that, those two?'

'Nobody knows, just you and me. There must be something about our garden that sets them off.'

'Maybe we should bottle it, sell it as an aphrodisiac. It would make even more money than my novels.'

'Should we beat a retreat or just barge right in?'

But Stefano has seen them. Standing up quickly he unpeels Della from his skin and says, 'If Marco's not here I'll catch him back at the apartment. *Ciao*, everyone.' He nods to them all and is off.

No-one speaks after he's gone, not for some time. Marino decides that a strong *aperitivo* is in order and goes inside to fetch the Campari.

Sadie looks at Della, huddled like a wounded white bird in the garden chair, her streaked, pale hair dishevelled by the crush of Stefano's body as she pressed herself into him.

'You're a fool,' Sadie says.

Della says nothing. There's no need: the blaze of her face, the burning of her eyes, tell Sadie that Della is beyond words or warnings.

13

Hunter prowls around the villa. Everyone is gone: Bettina red-eyed and haughty; Stefano watchful and preoccupied; Della belligerent and angry. All have left the villa, along with the sniggering students, who will now tell all the others, tomorrow morning, that the staff have deteriorated into bellicose behaviour, bickering like siblings, only worse, far worse.

He is upstairs in the vast drawing room he once shared with Chiara, but which is now embellished with strong traces of Della. The furniture is modern, tasteful, English. Della, uncomfortable with Chiara's mixture of battered antiques left over from Hunter's father, complemented with restored pieces that she had worked on, spent a madcap week in London buying new furnishings and driving them back to Florence in a rented van with an old school friend. Now the room oozes sturdy fat armchairs with fine fabrics in pale lime greens and pastel yellows, with lamps and small streamlined tables in every space and corner, with newly framed prints of English country scenes to remind them both of their island roots.

Hunter roams the room like a locked-in beast. He tries music, putting on Bach, but finding no comfort there. His thoughts stick on Della and how she had lashed out at him, and in front of Bettina and within earshot of a classroom of students. He feels undermined, threatened. The blood is racing like waterfalls through his veins, and his heart is doing the same thing in his narrow chest. His whole world, the world in which he reigned like a minor god, is shifting. He finds his balance going, gone.

Trying to steady himself he begins to prowl around the room, having tried sitting in a lime-green armchair for several seconds only to find he felt slightly nauseous, as if he were on a long sea voyage. He tells himself that Della has always answered him back, playfully, cheekily, in that loud, cocky well-spoken voice of hers. It was her way, her manner, her style, but it was a game she played, a tease.

She hadn't been teasing today, nor had this been a game. Hunter stalks to the window and looks out over dark-green hills, vineyards and olive groves, cyprus trees and blazing poppies and sees nothing but his own cold anger. How dare she speak to him like that; how dare she insult him in front of Bettina, in front of his own son, who was surely listening through the open doorway of the classroom. Rage makes him dizzy, unhinged.

Turning from the window Hunter paces to the other side of the room and sees something dry, grey and crumbling, like a religious wafer no-one believes in any more. For a split second he looks at it with a familiar curiosity, until he realizes that he's looking at himself in the large mirror over the lime-green sofa. The growls of fury he's making change into a low, soft moan as he stares at the cracked and caved-in thing staring back at him.

Hunter runs from the house, down the gravel path between the lime trees and out through the iron gate into the Via San Leonardo. He doesn't have his running kit on, but he doesn't care; he runs down the hill, past the lilies in the church and the jasmine creeping behind stone borders; past the towering walls of the fort and through the city gate, and down, down the steep, rough road until he's in the city itself. It's thronged with tourists this thick, hot afternoon, who stare at the pale wafer of a man dressed in beige summer trousers and a white shirt, running as if from himself across the packed Ponte Vecchio. The crowds on the old bridge, clustering around the jewellery shops, looking for bargains in gold and silver or posing for photographs with the river behind them, split like the sea as Hunter runs Moses-like through them. Down the Via Santa Maria, parties of American tourists exclaim as he rushes past, not noticing or caring as he jostles a shoulder here, a camera there. A group of Japanese women stare, some French teenagers giggle. Hunter runs on, sliding in his smooth Italian leather shoes so unsuitable for running, but gaining his balance and cutting right down the Vacche Reccia. In his raging brain he has some idea of cutting through the Piazza della Signoria through the enclave of the Uffizi gallery and then down the Lungarno until he can exhaust himself, but as he bursts into the piazza his heart bursts too.

The pain is blade-sharp and unrelenting under his ribcage. For what seems like hours, but is only the briefest of seconds, the old, old landmarks of the Piazza della Signoria whirl round him like an ancient galaxy: the grim stone tower of the Palazzo Vecchio, the sea-green satyrs preening around the statue of Neptune, the dun-coloured arches and solemn sculptures of the Loggia.

'Hey, man, you all right?' A beefy hand reaches out to steady him. Hunter's world shifts back to some kind of balance as he looks into a young, bearded, sunburned face, turned kindly towards him.

'Fine,' Hunter says with difficulty.

'Man, you don't look fine. I'm gonna take you right over to those cops there, in that van at the other end of the square.'

Hunter shakes his head. The pain is gone, leaving only the slightest of dull aches. 'I'm really quite all right.'

'English, huh? C'mon, those cops are there to help tourists like us. Happens all the time, people passing out all over the place from too much of this culture stuff. It's the Florence flu, I guess. I felt kinda dizzy myself in the Cathedral the other day. All this art and stuff gets to you after a while.' He waves his arm at the statues in the Loggia. Hunter is still clutching on to the wire fence in front of the sculptures, which he'd grabbed when the pain hit, but he feels too weak to fully let go. 'I'm fine, truly,' he insists again, his voice stronger now. 'Just a touch of heatstroke. I need to stand quietly here for a bit and I'll be right as rain.'

Hunter pulls himself up straight to prove to the man and to himself that he is indeed perfectly well. The stranger hesitates, then shrugs. 'Suit yourself, man.'

'Thanks all the same.'

'You just keep clear of the art galleries and museums for a day or so. Get some fresh air, y'hear? Take care now.'

When he goes, Hunter, still clinging on to the fence, takes deep breaths to calm himself. Several people in the crowded piazza look at him curiously as they pass, so he turns to face the statues in the Loggia, pretending he's looking at them, until the colour begins to return to his skin.

At first he stares at the sculpture directly in front of him with unfocusing eyes, too concentrated on feeling life flowing into him once more to be aware of anything else. He takes another deep breath, closing his eyes as he does so. When he opens them he sees that he's looking up into the anguished, sculpted face of a grizzly old man as he's being vanquished by a younger, stronger one, who is triumphantly holding aloft his prize: a naked woman.

For a moment Hunter thinks he's hallucinating, for the older man seems to be *him*, the younger one Stefano. The statue looms like a warning from the gods, filling his vision, making his head twirl and his heart lurch.

Then the craziness goes and he recognizes Giambologna's sculpture of the *Rape of the Sabines*. He closes his eyes in relief for a second, then opens them again. Dismissing the statue, he walks across the

Piazza della Signoria, down a small side street to sit at the tiny round table by the counter in his favourite café to drink cold mineral water and an espresso. Finally he feels strong enough to walk slowly to the Piazza Santa Maria Novella, where he catches a number-eleven bus to the Via del Gelsomino, which lets him off only a short distance from the villa. There, feeling drained and exhausted, he lies on his bed fully clothed and falls fast asleep.

Della finds him in bed when she returns. It's only ten o'clock, but Hunter's reading last Sunday's English *Times*. He'd woken an hour ago, showered, eaten some fruit and gone back to bed, feeling much better but still slightly weak.

Della's absence had frightened him. He'd expected anger when he woke up, only to find she still hadn't returned from wherever she'd run off to after their squabble, but all he could drum up was a frustrated irritation, mixed with a deeply panicky fear. He feels too tired for rage.

She breezes into the room and hardly looks at Hunter, saying briskly, 'Well, there you are! I phoned you from Sadie and Marino's house, but there was no answer. They asked me to stay for dinner, and you too. But I couldn't get hold of you, so I stopped trying. Where the hell were you?' She tosses this off insouciantly, as if speaking to the wall, and Hunter's irritation hardens to a metallic coldness.

'Out running,' he says, not bothering to take off his reading glasses or put down the newspaper. 'I wondered where you'd got to. Rather ill-mannered, don't you think? Going off like that without warning?'

The frost in his voice is that nasty kind, Della thinks, which seems harmless but can cause fingers and toes to fall off without warning. It makes her uneasy. She has spent the whole evening at Sadie and Marino's house, accepting their invitation to dinner and waiting for Stefano to come back. She couldn't believe he wouldn't return after her declaration of love to him in the garden.

He'd never returned, yet when she finally left the house she had hoped he would be somewhere, waiting for her. Surely he too had felt it: the impact of their touch, the chemistry it created. If Sadie and Marino hadn't interrupted them, surely it would have happened, surely they would have made love at last, right there in the garden.

Even as Della drove home, she was sure Stefano would find her somewhere, either outside on the Via Martellini or waiting for her at the villa. The more she thought of this, the more she was sure he'd be there, talking to Hunter on some pretext or another, but waiting for *her,* needing to see her as she needed to see him.

Her disappointment when she returned home was so intense that she had to sit in the drawing room before she could face Hunter, upstairs in the bedroom. His coldness startles her. She has almost forgotten their earlier, heated argument at the school that afternoon, though obviously Hunter has not. She scarcely remembers what it was about now.

She tries again, friendlier this time, facing him directly. If he abandons her she'd be completely adrift, for Stefano didn't come back for her. She feels rejection facing her again, the old familiar feeling of being left out, pushed away. She can't cope with it any more; it seems she has fought against being left out by men for years. First with her brothers, pitting herself against them with both slyness and feistiness, and later with her male bosses, employers who couldn't cope with her bold assertiveness, her brash confidence in the workplace, and who tried to rid themselves of her. They never suceeded, of course; she was too good at her job and too tenacious.

And then there were the lovers. The one in Rome, who'd been so callous in his dismissal of her, had been the worst: toying with her, taking advantage of her neediness, her readiness to love and be loved, to settle

140

down with one man at last. He had played cruelly with her desperation, plying her with hope, with hints of a future together, then dropping her when the game grew tedious.

Della remembers now that one of the reasons she loved Hunter was because she knew he would never leave her, not once he'd left Chiara. He had sacrificed too much for Della to let it all go. She knew she was safe with him.

Hunter would never reject her, but Stefano has. She forces herself to think of this. Tonight she opened her heart to him, told him in words what her body language had been saying since he'd arrived. But he hasn't responded; indeed, almost immediately afterwards he left the house.

Suddenly she's angry at Stefano, angry at herself. She has been behaving like a fool; Sadie was right, and it will have to stop. Thinking of her behaviour during the past week, thinking of how brazenly she let Stefano, her lover's son, know she was falling for him, Della feels a deep flush of embarrassment burning her skin, her whole body. She has not only been a fool, she has been both crazy and selfish. But it will change from now on, she tells herself. From now on she'll see Stefano only at school, and then strictly as a colleague. During breaktimes she will remain working alone in her classroom, and when Hunter wants to see him at home she will be elsewhere.

The decision calms her anger. She has taken the initiative and has ended the whole affair.

Not for an instant does she let herself believe it is Stefano who has ended everything. And that this everything has been, sadly, nothing at all, a non-starter.

Now there is just one more thing to do. Going to Hunter, sitting on the edge of the bed beside him, she begins to cajole him out of his mood, out of his bad temper. This, at least, will be a great deal easier than putting Stefano out of her head completely.

* * *

141

The next day Hunter looks in the mirror while shaving and sees what he wants to see, what he has always seen since meeting Della: a man in the prime of his life; blooming, looking twenty years younger than his age.

There's no residue of the pain that racked him yesterday after his run into the city centre. After a good night's sleep he made love to Della like a twenty-year-old in the early hours of the morning, foregoing his morning run with her to prolong his performance.

'Coffee,' he says as he comes out of the bathroom, seeing her still sprawled naked on the sheets, her eyes closed. A warm wind coming through the open window ruffles the lighter blond streaks of her hair, so they flutter feebly for a few seconds, like dying butterflies. 'I'll put the coffee on, Della. You'd better hurry, the students will be arriving soon.'

He sits by her bed and nudges her gently, looking over her to the mirror on the opposite wall, double-checking that what he'd just seen wasn't a mirage. Yes, he thinks as he looks at himself again, his mind *was* playing tricks with his image in the mirror yesterday. He'd been tired, upset and distressed over the mindless row with Della and Bettina. And yesterday's trauma, the burning pain and weakness, was obviously no more than a touch of indigestion brought on by their stupid argument in the corridor. Today he both looks and feels vigorous and handsome, virile and youthful.

Della opens her eyes in a mist of confusion. She had dropped off while Hunter was in the shower and had dreamed Stefano was making love with her. She's still in the dream, and feels Stefano is even now pressing against her thigh with his hard, young body.

She looks up to see not Stefano but an old man, leering like a satyr at her, and nearly cries out aloud before she recognizes Hunter.

Stefano's early today, not for any reasons of guilt after being late yesterday, and certainly not to see Della.

He'd woken up after a restless night, longing to see Bettina, and is now sitting on her desk in the office.

Bettina is frisky and unrepentant today after the anger and tears of yesterday. 'I won't get fired; you're right about that,' she says cheerily. 'Hunter needs me too much. This morning there have already been two complaints from out-of-town students about their lodgings, which I've sorted out brilliantly and efficiently.' She laughs delightedly.

Stefano says, 'Tell me. How long does it take you to do that paint job on your lips in the morning?'

Bettina laughs again. 'Hours. Many, many hours. It's a work of art, my face.'

'Hm, too true,' Stefano murmurs. He wonders if any of the Renaissance painters could have done justice to Bettina's lovely, expressive face.

'I mean my make-up, silly.' She blushes, seeing how Stefano is looking at her.

Stefano sternly tells himself to get a grip. He fancies Bettina like crazy, and she knows it, but their light flirtation is beginning to get heavy in places, threatening to land them in trouble if they're not careful. Stefano knows Bettina and Marco are deeply in love, and have been for over a year. He knows too that they are good for each other; they are friends as well as lovers. He's not vain enough to think Bettina would leave Marco for a fling with him, but he's wise enough to know that if you fool around with naked flames something always gets singed. He likes Bettina and Marco too much to be responsible for any problems in their relationship.

Yet he cannot bring himself to leave the office, to stop *looking* at her. He would like to touch her, the way Della touched him last night, pressing her lips against his neck so hard that he could feel the tip of her tongue touching his skin. Her touch has made him hot, restless.

They are interrupted by Hunter. Both Bettina and Stefano tense, but for different reasons. Bettina

143

wonders if there will be words said about yesterday; Stefano thinks uneasily of Della.

But Hunter is relaxed now, easy and ebullient, restored to his usual self after the events of yesterday, which he has now chosen to eradicate completely from his head and heart. He greets Bettina pleasantly and compliments her on the problem she has just resolved. Bettina plays along, accepting the compliment graciously, but she winks mischievously at Stefano behind Hunter's back.

With Stefano he is comradely. 'Was nearly late myself coming down,' is his only referral to Stefano's tardiness the afternoon before. 'My own fault, being tied up with a woman like Della. Couldn't pry her off me this morning.'

His sly grin curdles something inside Stefano, and he has to turn away to keep from saying something he knows he'll regret later. But as he turns he finds he's face to face with Della.

'Your class is waiting, Stefano,' she says coolly.

He wonders if this frost is genuine or because Hunter's listening. He decides he doesn't care either way. 'Fine, let them wait. They're early; it's not quite nine o'clock yet.' He deliberately turns once more to chat to Bettina.

Hunter is delighted by this. It has been nagging him since yesterday, that there was some truth in what Bettina said: that Della was trying to run things, acting as if it were *her* school rather than Hunter's. He has noticed before how Della likes to have her hands firmly on the controls. It's not a bad thing for her to realize that she's not the pilot, not even a co-pilot, to be honest. She's only really one of the cabin crew.

And so he relishes the way Stefano turns his back on Della when she tries to order him into the classroom. Della can get out of hand sometimes, Hunter decides. He'll remember to make sure she knows her place at the Villa Tiglio.

Della is staring at Stefano's back and finds, rather

rather than becoming annoyed, that she has a dreamy, surreal urge to touch it. Her hand seems to move of its own accord; there is no way, even if she wanted to, that she can stop it. Underneath the cotton of his sky-blue shirt she can feel hard flesh, muscles, skin.

He turns, surprised. Her hands slide like silk off his back as words tumble out of her mouth, words she had determined never to say. 'I just wondered. About, er, us. I mean, working together, you know? I, um, I have a beginner's class too, and I wondered whether we could compare notes sometimes, see how they're progressing. Perhaps we could team teach one morning, put the two classes together. We'd have to get together and prepare it, of course.'

He looks at her curiously, then shakes his head slowly. 'God, you're keen, aren't you?'

Hunter listens, though his back is turned to them, as he rifles through some letters, and says complacently, 'I told you she's my best teacher, Stef.' He emphasizes the word teacher, to make it clear that is exactly what Della is. Only a *teacher* in this school, like Sadie and Stefano. Nothing more.

Having made the point, Hunter adds generously, 'Hiring Della was the best thing I ever did. Her work for the school is tireless. We should all take note.' Bettina, staring at her computer screen in the alcove, snorts to herself but holds her tongue.

Stefano, looking at Della, says, 'Oh, I am. I am taking note – of everything.'

Della, face blazing, looks back at him defiantly. 'Good,' she says.

They stare at each other for a moment, challengingly. Then Della breaks away and walks off, leaving the challenge hanging, like the scent of lime trees in the cool morning air.

14

The rest of the week moves quickly and erratically, the weather turning cooler for a couple of days and then unseasonably hot once again. The students at the school come to the villa in shorts and sandals, the men in light T-shirts, the women, especially the younger ones, in skimpy tops, sunning themselves at breaktime on the back terrace, the hills hazy in the distance.

Bettina, relieved to be still in a job, becomes so preoccupied at the beginning of the week with being indispensable to Hunter that she rarely has a free moment to chat with Stefano between his classes. This bothers him, for he realizes he is becoming far more drawn to her than is wise. He's jittery, on edge. He's not used to the heat; he hasn't been in Italy for several summers. It's not even summer now, but it feels like it.

He's not used to the female students in his class either, to all that naked flesh displayed so carelessly as they struggle over the conjugation of verbs. One or two of them have suggested he meet them for a cappuccino, a beer, whatever, but he stays clear of that. He just wishes the hot spell would end.

Della seems unnaturally calm. Stefano watches her as if he were watching a big cat; blinking in the sunlight, as if he were waiting for it to spring. She has taken to wearing wrap-around skirts to work during the heatwave, sarongs of bright colours tied loosly around her waist. They flap about as she walks and fly open sometimes to reveal smooth white legs. Stefano finds himself watching the material roll away from her body as she sits or changes positions, exposing parts of

146

her flesh that flash momentarily and then disappear. Sometimes their eyes meet. Stefano's are perplexed, but not Della's. Hers are both watchful and fatalistic.

Della is in a strange mood this week. Her resolve of the weekend, to keep clear of Stefano, collapsed as soon as she saw him on Monday morning walking down the corridor and into Hunter's office, filling up the vast, airy spaces as if they'd been created just for him. The gold of his skin has become even darker with the sun, burnished and rich. She'd been in the office when he had arrived, and could almost hear the air prickling with the vibrancy of his presence, inhaling his heady young essence with the scent of the morning blossom from the garden. She could no more walk away from him than she could walk away from her own body.

Yet she hasn't forgotten Hunter, hasn't let herself forget what her life was before him. Unfortunately she cannot reconcile this with her feelings for Stefano, but it's too hot, and her emotions are too strong to try and sort it out now. And so this week she does nothing but wait, and watch.

Hunter is in fine form now. He and Della have had their morning run twice since that strange day when he'd felt so weak and ill, and he has suffered no pain, no weakness. For a few days, he is more than usually careful about what he eats, so that the excruciating attack of indigestion isn't repeated.

On Thursday morning Bettina and Stefano arrive far earlier than usual at the Villa Tiglio; Stefano because he woke early, restless again and unable to sleep, and Bettina because she'd had a slight row with Marco on the telephone the night before and she too woke early and irritable. The quarrel was trifling, unimportant; Bettina knew it was she who began it, nagging Marco about their weekend plans, being in an odd mood and then lashing out at him when he asked what was wrong.

It's the tense atmosphere around the Villa Tiglio, she decides as she goes into the empty villa and down the corridor towards the office. Della and Hunter are out running; she'd passed them just as she was turning into the drive on her scooter. There should be a good half-hour before anyone comes to disturb her, so Bettina decides to spend the time looking at the list of next term's students to make sure she has found the right accommodation for all of them.

She walks past Hunter's desk and through to her alcove. A shock goes through her as she sees someone sitting at her desk, his back towards her. '*Meno male!*' Bettina exclaims softly as she sees who it is. 'Stefano, it's you! You frightened me to death, sitting there like that; I thought I was alone.'

Stefano turns guiltily, leaping up from the desk. 'Sorry, I didn't hear you come in.'

'No, I see that. You were miles away. What are you doing at my desk?'

Stefano hesitates. Bettina's question is not accusatory, only lightly curious, yet he doesn't answer it. The truth is he had gone into the office to do some photocopying, but had seen a new framed photo on Bettina's desk and had gone over to look at it. It was one of Bettina and Marco, and Stefano had slumped down into the chair to stare at it, or rather to stare at the image of Bettina with longing and frustration.

Bettina is looking at him oddly, quizzically. She's wearing pale beige trousers today and a tight sleeveless jersey top, cropped short at the waist. He can see a hint of smooth brown midriff quiver slightly as she takes a deep breath. The breath gives him courage, or makes him reckless – later he will try to sort out which it was. But now he takes a step over to her and takes her in his arms, kissing her as he has wanted to do since he first set eyes on her.

There is a moment, the merest split second, when Bettina has to make a decision. Stefano hadn't misinterpreted that deep breath he'd seen her take; she'd seen his face as he looked at her and her body was responding to it.

As she begins to return the kiss, she realizes this is what has been making her edgy and sleepless: Stefano. Wanting to do what she's doing now, wanting to taste what it's like. Wanting Stefano, and having him too, at least for a moment.

But in that split second before they can go further, Bettina thinks of Marco and makes her decision. As her body pulls back, so does Stefano's.

They stand for a moment, inches apart, staring at each other. Bettina speaks first. She says simply, 'Marco.'

Stefano shakes his head and walks away from her, safely keeping his distance. 'I know, I know. I was out of line. Way out of line. I'm sorry.'

Bettina takes another deep breath and once again Stefano sees the movement of taut smooth skin. She says, 'Don't be sorry. I haven't exactly discouraged you. I think . . . I think maybe I've wanted this to happen.'

Stefano tries out a smile. 'Well,' he says, 'it has.'

Bettina smiles too. 'And if I tell you that I was starting to enjoy it, will you promise not to tell anyone?'

Stefano holds his hand over his heart. 'I promise.'

Then Bettina becomes sombre again. 'But no more, Stefano. This will be our secret. Maybe it had to happen, who knows. But you and I are friends, and what we have is too good to spoil by wanting more.'

Stefano nods. 'And what you and Marco have is too good too.'

'Yes, it is.' As Bettina says this she knows it to be true. And she knows how ironic it is that, as she stands there thinking of how she could have loved Stefano if she'd met him first, she is aware of the depth of her feelings for Marco. Suddenly she cannot wait to see him, to sort out the silly quarrel they had last night, to apologize for her touchiness, to simply be with him.

'I'm sorry too,' she says to Stefano, touching his arm lightly. He knows what she means and lets himself

149

indulge in a moment of imagining what it could have been like, if it weren't for Marco. Then he reaches over, hugs her quickly and goes out into the garden.

In the shadows of the lime trees Stefano, hidden from both the heat of the early-morning sunlight and the sight of the staff and students beginning to arrive, walks aimlessly, trying to get a handle on his scrambled thoughts and emotions. The feel of Bettina in his arms was even sweeter than he'd imagined, yet he's appalled at himself for what, in the end, was a selfish pass at his best friend's girlfriend. The whole incident has made him realize how screwed up he is these days, what with his father and Della, the unrelenting heat, Bettina, Italy itself like a gaudy Aladdin's cave of colour, scent and sensation.

When he finally composes himself enough to go back into the classroom he's a few minutes late. As he walks through the corridor he looks out for Hunter, almost wishing his father would appear and start criticizing and harping at him. Stefano could quit there and then, and either go back to Siena to stay with his mother while he tries to find another job there, or return to England. But there's no-one about, and Stefano goes in to face his class with relief, knowing that for the next couple of hours he can forget himself as he gets immersed in his teaching.

On Friday afternoon, when the students are gone and the week finished, Hunter asks Stefano to stay for a game of tennis. Stefano, feeling lethargic and unfit, agrees. He hasn't settled down to any kind of exercise since coming to Florence and decides that a tennis game is as good a keep-fit exercise as anything.

The past two days have, to Stefano's surprise, not been at all bad. After Thursday morning's incident with Bettina he was relieved to find that for the rest of the day, and the next, she treated him with the same warm, insouciant friendliness that she has always done, and he responded in the same way. In some ways it seems almost easier between them, as if the air has been cleared, as if an expected disaster has been somehow averted, and permanently at that.

Stefano has also become more and more involved with his teaching. He gets a buzz every time the students catch on to yet another intricacy of the English language, and he realizes how much he would miss this job should he not be able to tolerate his father. This is another reason why he agrees to play tennis with Hunter that afternoon: he really would like things to run more smoothly between them.

The match doesn't take long. Hunter is in good form and Stefano is not, so the older man wins in straight sets. *'Bravo!'* Della cries, sipping a gin and tonic on the sidelines. *'Bravissimo!'*

Stefano thinks wryly that Hunter doesn't mind when Della uses Italian to praise him. She has stood up and Hunter goes to her, caressing her intimately, but she is looking past him at Stefano. 'So are my performances still up to scratch, darling?' Hunter murmurs teasingly, looking slyly from the corner of his eye to see if Stefano is watching. Stefano is, and the expression on his face is unlike any Hunter has seen on him before. Hunter wonders if perhaps there's a touch of jealousy there. After all, Stefano doesn't have a woman of his own, not now, not here in Italy. 'Pity you don't have a girlfriend, Stef. We could set up regular doubles matches. Well, maybe one day. It's bound to happen eventually, I suppose.' He tosses this off condescendingly. 'At least you've got plenty of time,' he adds, insinuating that Stefano needs it.

Stefano looks at Della and nods slightly. 'Yup, you're right, Dad. I've got lots of time.'

Hunter offers a drink and Della invites him to dinner, but Stefano declines both and leaves right after the match. 'Well, what should we do?' Hunter asks, his mood hearty. 'Let's go out to that new restaurant we've wanted to try, in Greve, shall we?'

Della agrees, to pass the time. Stefano has been out of her sight for ten minutes and it seems a lifetime. Just as it has every night this week, just as it will continue to be until something happens.

She has been waiting, patiently, for something to happen all week now, but nothing has. She could feel Stefano's troubled eyes on her during the days as she wandered in a hot, somnolent state between classroom and office and garden; she could feel her skin prickling in response to his gaze. But after the day's classes he was gone. She hasn't talked to him alone since that time at Sadie and Marino's.

'How about it?' Hunter's asking. 'Should we eat out?'

'Fine by me.'

As she showers and then dries herself, she glances at the full-length mirror behind the door and catches a glimpse of her breasts, soft and floppy and unappealing as she bends down to dry her legs. She straightens up quickly and stares at her naked body. Her breasts, now that she's standing straight, still look full and firm and pretty good, as does the rest of her body. Nonetheless, a sudden chill goes through her and she shivers. Having been used to feeling so young, practically a child, around Hunter, she now remembers how much older she is than Stefano.

She looks at her body again, feeling relieved and happy at what she sees. But so is Hunter, she remembers. *He* is happy about *his* body, always staring at it in the mirror, admiring his slight but wiry slimness, his still-hard belly, his fitness. Yet lately, Hunter's body has looked old and scraggly to her; its colour grey and unhealthy, its texture dry and parched. She's sure it wasn't this way before, when they first met and first touched.

She shivers again. The words of an old song suddenly go through her head, something about time being on my side. But it isn't, of course. Time is not on Hunter's side, nor hers either, if she's being honest.

If time is on anyone's side, it's on Stefano's. The

thought strikes Della that she would be a fool to waste a moment of it.

Stefano returns to the apartment on the Piazza Santo Spirito to find Bettina there with Marco. They are planning a trip to the sea tomorrow, phoning around to friends who would like to come. 'We have two carloads already,' Bettina cries. 'I'm borrowing my mother's car. Marco, go and telephone your father to borrow his. We'll need a big car, like Marino's, to fit everyone in. I think we should leave early, don't you? Nine o'clock? Then we can have all day, and dinner too, by the sea.'

Marco says, 'You *are* coming, aren't you, Stefano?'

Stefano looks doubtful. 'You haven't forgotten that my mother is coming here for this big lunch on Sunday? I should spend tomorrow getting things ready.'

'*Madonna*, what do you think we are?' Bettina is indignant. 'Marco and I have already made a huge list, and as soon as he phones his father we'll all go shopping for the food.' She consults a list on a pad of paper and recites, 'We'll clean the apartment, lay the table, make a salad dressing, prepare a tiramisu—'

Stefano and Marco both groan at this. Bettina goes on, 'Relax, I'll make the dessert, I know you two are hopeless at anything more complicated than a pasta sauce. We'll get everything as ready as we can for Sunday, then tomorrow we can play.'

Marco phones Marino and is lent the car for the next day.

Sadie phones the Villa Tiglio. Hunter answers, as Della is still in the shower. Sadie asks Hunter if she can borrow his car to sort out a problem that a homesick student from Palermo is having with his landlady. 'Bettina usually deals with the accommodation problems, of course, but she and Marco and Stefano, plus dozens of others, from what I can gather, are off to the sea tomorrow, and I said I'd do it for her. The thing is,

Marco has borrowed Marino's car and mine is in the garage.'

Hunter, pleased that his staff are willing to work on a Saturday, says that it will be no problem. He offers to deal with the student and landlady himself, but Sadie says that since the student is one of hers she would prefer to do it.

Five minutes later, Della phones Sadie. Marino answers, and Della rambles for a few moments about arranging another doubles match in the next few weeks. When a date is set, she says, 'I'd better write it down straight away. I have to write down everything for Hunter these days; he's become so forgetful. We're off for the day to the coast tomorrow, and he'd forgotten all about it.'

'That's a coincidence,' Marino says. 'The kids are off to the beach too. That's why we're carless.'

'Well, that *is* a coincidence. Where exactly are they going?' Della tries to sound casual while holding her breath.

'Baratti, the beach down from the harbour.'

Della lets out her breath and smiles into the telephone. Hunter likes Baratti and can easily be convinced that it was his idea to go there.

Sadie grabs the telephone from Marino. 'Don't,' she says to Della. 'Don't even think it.'

But Della is crazed. Somehow she manages to make Hunter think he remembers planning this trip ages ago, though of course it was conceived in Della's mind the minute she heard Stefano would be there. The dreamy, patient waiting of the past week has turned into a determination not to squander time as if it can be replenished at the market.

Saturday morning is warm but not quite so hot, and as unruffled as a bed no-one sleeps in. The sky is blue with foamy white streaks; the ground green and red with wild grass, lush leaves and poppies. The *auto-strada* is thick with cars and noise and the suffocating smell of petrol fumes, for everyone else seems to have had the same idea of a day out at the seaside.

Hunter, driving Della's car, is not patient in traffic, but for once Della doesn't chide him. She puts on the radio, trying to get the news, but instead fills the car with a loud burst of rock music.

'Good grief,' Hunter says. 'All this stress and pollution and now *this*? Can't you put on a tape of Mozart or something?'

'It's Casino Royale.' She leaves the music on.

'Never heard of them.'

'Well, you should; they're quite popular in Italy. I'm sure Stefano has one of their CDs.' As a matter of fact, she'd seen Stefano buy one in the Cascine market last Tuesday. And she cannot help it; she needs to say his name.

Hunter, luckily, is pleased to talk about his son now that he has knuckled under and become one of his team. 'What do you think, Della? Is Stef coping all right with the work?' he asks, honking a Fiat who has suddenly and for no apparent reason slowed down.

'He seems to be getting on fine. He has a knack for teaching, I think, and he's good with the students. A couple of them told me that they're staying on in Florence and doing the intermediate course, just in the hope of having Stefano again as their teacher.'

This is going too far. Hunter honks his horn again and then swerves into the next lane to overtake the Fiat. The driver he has cut in front of blares his horn angrily. 'Bloody Italians. So impatient,' Hunter mutters.

'Might not be a bad idea,' Della muses, 'letting Stefano go up with the classes. I know that usually we like to let the students have a change of teacher, but—'

'Stefano will go where I put him.' Hunter, interrupting, overtakes a Lancia and cruises at a dangerously high speed in the fast lane. 'He's got a lot to learn, Della. I'm surprised you can't see that.'

Della leans back in her seat and smiles. 'Oh, but I can, Hunter. I can see that quite clearly. That's why I've offered to help him all I can.'

Hunter takes his hand off the wheel to fondle her knee. 'I think that's a good idea. Let's face it, Stef may be doing all right so far, but he doesn't have the experience and dedication that we have. In fact, between us, I sometimes doubt whether he ever will. But as long as he does a decent job I'm happy to keep him on. So long as he doesn't get too cocky and start feeling that there's no room for improvement.'

'No.'

'Maybe you can take him in hand, point out to him that just because he's my son it doesn't mean he should rest on his laurels. We need to keep him on his toes.'

Della looks out of the window at the motorway traffic and wishes Hunter would go even faster. She can't wait to get to the coast.

'I'll take him in hand, Hunter. Don't worry, I'll try to talk to him.'

Hunter looks down at her gratefully, narrowly avoiding a collision with a motorbike and a lorry.

The beach at Baratti isn't crowded, it's too early in the season for that, despite the recent hot weather. Della and Hunter walk, with towels and a beach blanket and a basket of food, down under the cluster of tall umbrella pines onto the sand. Hunter likes this beach because it's not the usual Italian beach, with lines of deckchairs side by side; there's room to spread out, move and get away from people, not only now in May, but even in the crowded month of August. There are no deckchair sellers here, or beach huts, or cafés selling *gelato* and beach balls, not at this time of year anyway. The stretch of sand is in the midst of a protected nature reserve, an area of wooded hills going down to the sea. It's a jagged coastline, with the remains of Etruscan settlements scattered up and down the once marshy area.

The sea is calm today and as green as grass. While Hunter spreads a blanket, Della looks around. Farther down the beach she can see a party of about eight or nine people, spread over the warm sand on beach towels. Stefano is one of them. She holds the knowledge to herself, her own secret.

Hunter, peeling off his shorts to reveal blue swimming trunks, stretches out his thin, tough legs on the sand as he flops on the blanket. He tosses back a long strand of white hair from his face like a preening young girl and taps his stomach to feel its firmness. 'I love trips to the seaside, don't you?' He wriggles his toes in the sand, feeling boyish and well pleased with himself. Then, looking along the beach, he suddenly exclaims, 'Goodness, is that Stefano and his gang?'

Della looks in the direction that Hunter is pointing, but she has already registered Stefano's bronzed skin, white shorts and black hair tumbling off the red towel onto the sand as he rolls over languidly from his front to his back. She has even noticed that he has his green headband on, the one he sometimes wears to keep his hair out of his face when he's playing tennis. 'I think it is,' she says, looking away. 'What a coincidence.'

'I knew they were going to the coast somewhere today. Marino mentioned it when he phoned, as I told you. But I didn't know where. How odd that we all ended up in the same place.'

'Hmm,' Della says, rubbing suntan cream into her pastel skin. She closes her eyes, as if it weren't important. The sun burns like fire on her face.

'They haven't noticed us yet. Should we walk down and say hello?'

'Oh, eventually. Plenty of time.' Della lies down on her stomach, so that she can watch Stefano. She rests her head on her arms, her eyes nearly level with the sand. Across those millions of hot grains is Stefano. She can almost feel the heat of his body running like an electric current along the beach.

*   *   *

Stefano also feels the current running like white lightning from his body across the sand, but it's not directed at Della. The magnet is Bettina, olive and brown and golden in her black bikini, her hair like a shiny mahogany tabletop as it rakes her back, shoulders and breasts.

Marco cannot keep his hands off her, she is so ripe and lush. His eyes brim with love and lust and proud, joyful affection as they follow her every movement. Stefano notes with a fatalistic melancholy that her eyes seek out no-one but Marco.

Last night, or sometime in the early hours of this morning, Marco had asked Bettina to marry him, and Bettina, without a moment's hesitation, had burst into tears and said it was the happiest moment of her life. From then on sleep had been impossible. They'd spent what was left of the night discussing plans for a wedding in the autumn, the number of children they would have and the house they hoped to live in.

This morning, shyly and joyfully, they had told Stefano. Drinking their coffee before setting off on the beach trip, Marco and Bettina had held hands tightly, eyes blazing with excitement and happiness, as they shared their plans with him. Marco hugged him like a member of the family, and Bettina showered him with brotherly kisses, all vestiges of their past attraction and of that kiss in the empty offices of the Villa Tiglio, gone and forgotten in her new role as bride-to-be and future mother of Marco's children.

Stefano was not, after the first few moments, overly surprised, nor even devastated. He'd had no hopes anyway, no expectations, nor did he ever intend to come between them, despite that early-morning incident. They are both his cherished friends and he can tell them honestly that he's pleased for them.

Nonetheless he feels downcast today, his life force is low, uncharged even by this golden blue-green day. Closing his eyes he lets himself drift on the lazy, warm spring air, deciding to float a bit, go with the flow, whatever that flow turns out to be.

It turns out to be Della. She has waited for her moment; Stefano is alone amidst the cluster of towels, bags, discarded sandals and clothing. His party has disbanded for a while, some going for a walk along the curved shoreline of the bay, a few intrepid souls swimming in the cold spring sea and the rest eating their packed lunches under the shade of the parasol pines.

Stefano sits solitarily under a scruffy beach umbrella someone brought with them, reading a paperback, a Calvino novel. He isn't hungry, nor does he want to swim, and he certainly can't face going for a walk with the newly engaged couple, who so obviously, today at any rate, need some time on their own.

'My, you *are* fluent, reading Calvino in the original. He's tough going, even in English.'

Stefano looks up to see that the shadow passing over the pages of his book is Della. Somehow he isn't surprised.

'You forget I'm half Italian. My mother, remember? Chiara?'

She sits down beside him. Close, too close. The rays emanating from his skin threaten to burn her. 'Touché,' she says with a slight smile. 'You're never going to let me forget it, are you?'

Stefano shrugs. 'Where's my father?'

'Off exploring somewhere among the pines.'

'Did you know I – we – would be here?'

'Does it matter?'

Stefano shrugs again. He realizes that it doesn't.

Behind them in the sand, under the heavy pine trees, some of the others have finished their *panini* of prosciutto cheese and *rucola* leaves and are standing up, stretching. Soon they will wander back to their towels to doze in the sunshine on this first seaside visit after the cold wet winter.

Della says quickly, 'You said the other day that you

159

were translating an article into English for your weekly intermediate class, about the ancient Etruscan civilization. I know of one of their tombs hidden away in a nearby forest; do you want me to show you? We can be there and back within an hour and a half.'

'I've seen most of the Etruscan ruins around here; the big sites anyway.'

'You won't have seen this one, I promise you.'

Stefano is about to refuse when he sees Bettina and Marco approaching, arms wrapped around each other, limbs touching, sleek and bare, like two wonderful sea creatures who can never be parted. Soon he'll find his ease with them again and be able to share in their delight with each other, but not yet, not today. The loss of something he never had is still too fresh.

'Right, I'm on,' he says, standing up and pulling on a blue T-shirt, grabbing his trainers, pulling off his green headband and shaking the sand from his hair. 'We'd better find Hunter.'

As they walk along the toasted sand Della says, 'Hunter's not coming; he wants to stay near the sea. I told him I'd see if you'd like to go exploring with me. He was quite pleased about it. He thinks that as an experienced teacher I can clue you in on a few things.'

Stefano glances at her to see if the irony in her voice is reflected in her face, but she's looking straight ahead, her expression inscrutable. Over her swimsuit, she has put on one of her long sea-green sarongs, made out of a fine, see-through fabric. Her shoulders and arms are bare. They are athletic, well-shaped. She seems healthy and rosy, fit and blond and very English, walking so boldly and stridently at his side, as if she belongs there, with Stefano not Hunter.

It's only a short drive to the wooded mountainside where the Etruscan tomb is hidden. Della parks her car at the side of the road and leads Stefano up a narrow but well-worn dirt track, through the tightly packed trees. They walk for ten minutes, fifteen, twenty. The track isn't wide enough for the two of them to walk side by side, so Della leads, with Stefano close behind. Once she trips – the path is fraught with heavy, gnarled tree roots and great sharp stones. It winds up and down and around and about the mountain, maze-like and ancient. Once or twice they meet other walkers, but not often. The trees are dense and the sky is canopied from view by a heavy curtain of velvet green foliage.

Della veers sharply off the track and up a steep slope, which is slippery with rotting leaves and fallen branches. The path is barely discernible under their feet. Above them there's nothing but the deep blackness of the tent of branches. Somewhere there is sun and the blue of a spring sky, but not here, not in this forest heavy with the breaths of a long-dead civilization.

'There,' Della says softly. 'There.'

Stefano sees, amongst the scrub and foliage and ancient tree roots, wide stone steps leading deep into the earth. It's an Etruscan burial site, all right; he can feel it in the trees and leaves and in the damp smell of stone and ritual that permeates the woodland.

Della walks slowly down the steps, her head erect, her back straight, as if the fact that she and Stefano are there is a ritual as ancient as the Etruscans themselves.

She turns to find him smiling at her. 'What do you find funny?' she asks, slightly annoyed at his amusement. To her this is a sacred moment. She is hoping that some pagan magic in the place will charm Stefano, binding him to her as she feels bound to him.

'You,' he says. 'You're not exactly subtle, are you.'

They are at the bottom of the stone steps, deep in the dank earth. The mouth of the tomb gapes like the mouth of a womb in front of them.

'No,' Della says, 'subtlety isn't my style.'

She steps closer to him. He knows she's going to touch him. He knows he should retreat, go back up the stone steps and out of the tomb, into the sunlight.

But something holds him there. For a moment

neither of them move, then she's in his arms, reaching for his face to pull it towards hers, pulling them both down so that they're sitting on the stone steps, then falling backwards onto them as the need in Della becomes his need too. Della's hands are all over him, and his hands respond, like birds answering a mating call, flying all over her body.

As he kisses her again and again he's sure he can hear the laughter of some long-dead Etruscan, amused beyond the grave at how little life changes in the wide sweeping arc of time.

15

It takes Stefano a few moments to fully comprehend exactly what it is he's doing, or about to do: make love to his father's lover.

Della senses the moment. Stefano is pulling away, holding back, going from her. Gone now. Frantically she tries to regain her control, guiding his hands again to the warmth of her breasts and thighs, seeking his face with her pleading eyes, her mouth still warm from his.

When she realizes that it's no use, she slumps back against the hardness of the stone steps and groans aloud. 'Don't,' she whispers. 'Don't do this to me.'

'I'm sorry.' He's sitting as far away from her as possible, but he reaches across the stone to take her hand. 'I'm truly sorry,' he repeats, thinking, not without a touch of irony, that this is the second time he has apologized to a woman in the past few days: the first time for initiating a kiss and an embrace, the second for resisting.

He shakes his head slightly as she moves towards him, encouraged by his hand on hers. He pats it avuncularly and lets it go.

Della cries, 'Why? Why did you stop? You want to as much as I do.'

Stefano doesn't contradict her. For a moment he did; for a moment her warm female flesh was a consolation for the loss of Bettina.

Della, distraught, plunges her head into her hands. 'If you don't want me, why did you kiss me that night at Sadie and Marino's? And why didn't you run like hell when you realized how I felt?'

Again Stefano is silent. There are no answers, or those he has are complicated beyond his understanding.

Or, he thinks suddenly, as simple as life, as simple as art, as simple as the echo of laughter from long-dead Etruscans. Giambologna's glorious sculpture forms in his head, with the revolving lines of his three forms: the older man, down and defeated; the younger man, victorious; and always, in the middle, the woman. Yes, Stefano thinks, the answers are as old as these mountains, as old as the most primitive of civilizations.

He looks at Della kindly, trying to make it easy for her. 'We can't. You know that. There are taboos, certain rules it would be dangerous to break. You don't want the Etruscans pelting us with curses, do you, if we commit incest on their ancient burial site?'

While he talks he is pulling her up, helping her to her feet, his voice light and teasing, affectionate. He doesn't want to hurt her; he would like to see her come out of this without embarrassment or pain.

She understands that he is giving her back some tatters of her torn pride and she covers herself with them gratefully. 'Is that why you won't make love to me, because of Hunter? And if I weren't your father's partner, his live-in girlfriend, then what? If he'd never left your mother, and I'd never got involved with him, and you met me at the school, what then?'

He touches her face briefly, warmly. 'We'll never know, will we.' He turns and begins walking up the steps of the tomb, with Della following.

'But what do you *think* would happen?' she persists.

Stefano is silent. Della takes his silence as a spoonful of hope and swallows it eagerly, finding in it some relief from the sickness of despair and frustration.

Hunter, tired but exhilarated by his power walk along the beach, is sitting on the blanket, drinking mineral

164

water from the cooler, when he sees Della and Stefano walking towards him through the parasol pines and down the sand. 'Ah, there you are. I thought you'd fallen into the tomb! What do you think of it, Stef? Great to find a ruin like that stuck right on the hillside. Spooky place too, don't you think? It makes one's imagination run riot.'

'Oh yes,' Stefano says, glinting mischievously at Della. 'Mine ran riot all over the place.' He's determined to make light of the incident and treat it as an unimportant secret between himself and Della, to keep the heaviness out of their relationship. From now on he will always treat her this way: affectionately but teasingly, casually amicable, careful to avoid any situations in which they might be alone together. He hopes she will do the same. It's the only way.

It rains on Sunday. Dull, insistent rain, not letting you forget it's there, insinuating itself under jacket collars, sliding meaningfully down umbrellas.

The awnings of the Sunday market in Piazza Santo Spirito weep copiously onto the heads of the shoppers, down the rucksacks of the few brave tourists who find their way to Oltrarno, on the other side of the Arno. The pigeons in the fountain look sadly drowned and sorry for themselves. Stefano, in bed, hears the rain and the muted calls of the vendors, and he puts his head back under the pillow.

He's not allowed to stay there long. 'Come on, wake up,' Marco shouts as he glides into the room and closes Stefano's window to stop the rain pouring into the bedroom. 'We've got too much to do today for you to stay in bed.'

Stefano rolls over and opens his eyes. Marco grins maniacally at him.

'*Dai*, Marco! Just because you're going to marry the most beautiful woman in Italy there's no reason to be so cheerful. It's wet, it's raining, I'm hungover and my mother will be here soon.'

'Stop being so pathetic and get up. We've got work to do.'

Stefano moans theatrically, but finally gets out of bed. For the next hour they chop vegetables, grate parmesan cheese and tidy up the beer bottles from the night before. Last night, when they returned to Florence long after midnight, after a meal of fish stew in Baratti, Bettina dropped the others off and returned to her parents' home in Impruneta to break the news of her engagement to Marco. Marco himself celebrated by getting spectacularly drunk with Stefano when the two were alone in the apartment, but he looks as fresh and healthy as summer dew this morning.

Stefano doesn't. His eyes are deeply ringed in black and his skin is slightly greenish in the rain-soaked morning light. As Marco, who is making the salsa for the pasta, orders him to chop garlic, red peppers, onions and aubergine, Stefano goes over the events of yesterday in his head and wishes to Christ he'd never got out of bed.

Hunter and Della had left shortly after the visit to the tomb, Hunter deciding that it was time for an *aperitivo* and then a meal at his favourite fish restaurant in Livorno. He'd asked Stefano to join them, omitting to ask the rest of Stefano's party. Stefano declined, of course, but graciously, trying not to show his great relief at their departure.

The onions are stinging Stefano's eyes. '*Santo Cielo*, isn't that enough? I've done hundreds.'

'And we have hundreds coming to lunch. Your mother, my parents, Bettina, you and me. Six. Hundreds, you see? Keep chopping.'

By one o'clock everything is ready. The pasta sauce is simmering in a huge iron skillet borrowed from Sadie, and the water is on the cooker in readiness for the pasta. A salad of rocket leaves and other greenery waits to be dressed in olive oil and garlic, with a touch of balsamic vinegar. The table, moved from the kitchen

166

into the living room for this occasion, is laid with borrowed plates and cutlery.

Bettina arrives first with masses of pink and white roses, which she has plucked from her parents' garden. She searches the kitchen for a vase and, not finding any, makes do with bowls, in which she floats the roses like lilies on a pond. She has also brought a spare table lamp with a fine salmon-coloured shade, which she plugs into a socket near the table. Marco's bachelor pad is miraculously transformed into a charming space of soft light with a welcoming table. The delicate fragrance of roses mixes with the happy smells of fresh vegetables burbling in olive oil. It suddenly doesn't matter that it's still pouring with rain outside.

'*Ecco! È perfetto*,' she says, surveying her work. 'You see, Marco, how you need a wife?'

'What about me? Don't I need one too?' Stefano says.

'A woman, yes. A wife, not yet. You're far too unsettled.'

Sadie and Marino are the next to arrive, in a flurry of umbrellas, wet raincoats and boisterous greetings. Sadie's hair, dampened by the rain, has gone haywire, rushing away from her face and scalp as if it cannot get away fast enough. She's wearing a dress of red-and-white stripes, turning her into a candy cane. The colours clash viciously with her orange hair, but Sadie is oblivious. She has no sense of style and fashion, but is blessed with the fact that she doesn't realize this. Marino, fed up with the excessive compulsion of his countrymen and women to look classy and beautiful at all times, finds Sadie's complete lack of fashion sense one of the most endearing things about her. Her Italian friends and acquaintances think she's being superbly British and eccentric when she comes out with her outlandish outfits, and Marino encourages this. He is vastly proud of her.

'How nice everything looks,' Sadie cries. 'How clean and tidy. Stefano, you must be a good influence on

Marco. When he lived alone the place was a tip.'

'I think the credit goes to Bettina,' Stefano says.

Bettina, stunning in a plain black dress, pinches Marco's elbow. 'Tell them,' she whispers.

Marco does, and Sadie and Marino are joyful and congratulatory. They've been hoping for months that Marco would settle down with Bettina, and now they welcome her into the family with warm enthusiasm. Bottles of prosecco are opened, and toasts are being made as the doorbell rings and Chiara arrives.

The reunion is made less awkward because of Marco and Bettina's wedding announcement. A glass of the sparkling wine is poured for Chiara and she too drinks to the couple.

'What wonderful news!' Chiara exclaims when Bettina, Marco and Stefano rush off to the kitchen to see to lunch. 'I'm so happy for you all. I don't know Bettina very well – she was at the school only a few months before I left – but I liked her even in that short time. And Marco, such a fine young man he's become. Just think, I've known him since you first came to work at the school, Sadie, at the very beginning. How long ago was that? Seven, eight years?'

'A long time, Chiara. And a long time since we've seen you.'

'Too long,' Marco says.

Chiara's face loses the animation it had a few moments ago, and she looks older, more fragile. Despite the new becoming fullness in her cheeks, she nonetheless seems thinner, less substantial. Something is gone from her, some solidity, foundation. She looks wispy, like the petals of a flower.

Marino says, 'Welcome back to Italy. To home.'

'I never thought you'd come,' Sadie says. 'I thought we'd lost you to England.'

'I'm sorry I didn't write, or phone. But . . . you know.'

'But it's all right now?' Sadie says. 'Seeing us, I mean. Being in touch again.'

'Oh yes.'

And it is, *grazie a Dio*, Chiara thinks. How I've missed these people. Sadie. Dear comfortable Sadie. And funny, sweet Marino.

Enboldened by their meeting and the wine, she says, 'And how is the school? And Hunter, and Della?'

Marino frowns, making a fierce gesture of dismissal.

Sadie says, 'Let's just say that things aren't the same since you've been gone. We play tennis with them occasionally, and have the odd meal together, but it's not the same.'

'Not at all the same,' Marino says. 'I wish we could drop this pretence that we're all friends.'

'It's hard. I work with Hunter. But it's not like it was with the four of us, Chiara.'

Sadie stops there, for there is more, so much more that she could say. Not just about Hunter and Della, but about Stefano. The knowledge gives her heartburn at night just thinking about it, wondering what will come of Stefano and Della. But she keeps quiet, hoping their infatuation will burn itself out, and that no-one but she and Marino will be any the wiser.

The conversation stops as they all think of the years before Della: dinners together every weekend, Christmas and holiday gatherings. Marco and Stefano, more or less the same age, getting to know each other and becoming friends. Chiara and Sadie, worrying about them together as the boys went through the whacky, tormenting time of adolescence.

For a moment Chiara's face, usually so alive with colour, becomes white with sadness. Sadie and Marino notice and start talking simultaneously: 'But you're back now, and so close, in Siena. You'll have to come and see our new home. Stay for a weekend or longer.'

Chiara says she will, but knows it won't be the same, will never be the same.

Sadie and Marino know this too. Luckily the younger people return with great plates of steaming spaghetti and salsa and two bottles of Chianti, ready to pour. The past is put away as the present is filled with eating and the future is toasted with promises. What has been is gone, and Chiara makes herself shut the doors on it and turn away.

And then Hunter and Della arrive.

16

They arrive just as lunch is over – the pasta eaten, the Chianti drunk, the guests glutted on bowlfuls of cherries. They are still sitting around the table, which is strewn with empty wine glasses and espresso cups and small plates filled with cherry pips. Everyone is merry, despite the unseasonable darkness of late afternoon: rain and black cloud still cluster over Florence. Outside, in the piazza, the church steps are slick and slippery, and the pigeons in the fountain are long gone. The market stallholders in Campo Santo Stefano have also given up. The square from the window looks bleak and tired.

The lunch party has been a success. Chiara, holding on to her determination to lock up the past, finds that she's beginning to let pleasure into her life again. She's enjoying Sadie and Marino and Marco, and Bettina too, without remembering every minute that they are associated with Hunter and the past.

Stefano, seeing his mother relax and listening to her inviting Sadie and Marino to her place in Siena, stops worrying about her for the first time since he has returned to Italy.

He stops worrying about other things too. Even yesterday, Stefano thinks as he watches his mother, her face rosy with wine, her skin losing its paleness and beginning to regain its natural glow – even yesterday was necessary: the confrontation between himself and Della. Like the moment with Bettina a few days earlier, he feels a catalyst was reached, a decision made. The air has been cleared between them, and he'll be able to breathe around her again.

When the apartment bell rings, Marco assumes it's some of his mates and buzzes the front door open. 'Come in, it's open,' he shouts to the knock on the apartment door.

Chiara, facing the door, sees them first.

Stefano sees his mother's face fill with distress, her eyes dilating with emotion. He turns to see what she's looking at. 'Oh shit,' he says under his breath, and the other four turn to look too.

There's a beat, a moment when Della and Hunter could have turned and run, *should* have turned and run, pretended they'd never come, made excuses, any excuse, and fled.

But Della, who has either not seen Chiara or else not recognized her, says, 'May we come in?'

Again, a beat. Marco, who will later kick himself for not saying, No, sorry, we're having a private party; being well brought up, he says politely, 'Why, uh, yes, of course.'

The door shuts behind them and it's too late. Only then does Della recognize Chiara. She turns away in shock and embarrassment.

Hunter, who has seen Chiara but will not look at her, brazens it out by adopting a breezy, businesslike manner. 'Sorry to interrupt your party. We didn't know anyone was here. I was looking for Stefano.'

Stefano says curtly. 'What is it?'

'Oh, not important, not if you're busy, which, uh, you obviously are. It's to do with the school, just a small problem that one of the students is having with the work. We'll sort it out tomorrow. I just thought, er, we just thought that on a rainy day like today you might be free and, you know, we could have discussed it.' Hunter is feeling seriously awkward. He looks it too, as if he's disrupting the smooth space around him with unnecessary angles and sharpness. Damn Della, he thinks; this is all her fault. It was she who suggested that they might be able to have a brief word with

172

Stefano at the apartment before classes on Monday.

Chiara is suddenly angry. This awkwardness is because of her and they're all acting as if she's not there. Hunter and Della haven't even looked at her, except for that first shocked glance. They're both looking at Stefano.

'Hello, Hunter,' she says softly but quite clearly.

'Chiara!' Hunter cries, as if he has only just spotted her there.

'Hello, Della.' She nods at the other woman, regally. Stefano's proud of her.

'Chiara, what a super surprise,' Della cries. The discomfort she's feeling is painful, and a flood of compassion for Chiara, for how she must be feeling right now, takes her by surprise. She hides this in a rush of words. 'Hunter and I knew you were in Siena, but we didn't know you were coming to Florence. Stefano, why didn't you tell us? You could have come to the villa for a drink beforehand. Well, another time.' She's babbling and knows it.

'How are you, Chiara?' Hunter says.

Marco, deciding that everyone is being civilized and so there's no need to worry, relaxes, finds two more chairs and offers them coffee. Sadie curses herself for teaching her son such good manners and waits for Hunter and Della to refuse and go home. Marino scowls at the cherry pips on his plate and Bettina scowls at Marco, whose sweet innocence she could crucify at this moment.

'I'd love a coffee, Marco,' Della says. 'A nice big English cup, please, and weak, if you don't mind. Not one of your little Italian mind-blowing shots of caffeine.'

The others look in horror as Della settles into one of the chairs Marco has brought out. Mistakenly, she has decided that it would be much more embarrassing for everyone if she and Hunter left, rather than try to act civilized and stay. She realizes her mistake by the heavy silence, broken only by the scuffle of chairs as

Hunter sits down as well, but it's too late now.

Marco and Bettina escape to the kitchen to make more coffee while Marino brings out a bottle of Limoncello, a very good, very special bottle of lemon liqueur which he'd planned to give to Marco and Stefano later, as a kind of house-warming present. He has a strong need for a shot of alcohol now, despite the wine they drank with lunch.

Everyone else seems to feel the same need, for the others eagerly accept a drink and more glasses are found. Chiara gratefully lets the bittersweet taste linger in her mouth before swallowing it. The warmth seeping into her blood is comforting. She drinks it quickly, far too quickly, and Marino pours her another.

Again, there's a long silence which nobody can seem to fill, not even Della, who can't take her eyes off Chiara. She has a mad desire to throw herself at Chiara's feet and ask her to help her out of the emotional disaster area she's in with Hunter and Stefano.

The silence goes on and on, pungent with embarrassment. Then Chiara says evenly, 'Stefano tells me that everything is going well at the school.'

Hunter seizes on this with great relief. 'Oh yes.' He launches into an account of the Villa Tiglio School of English: the number of pupils, the new courses he has introduced.

Della stirs herself. She got them into this mess, coming here today, so she feels obliged to keep the conversation going. 'We're priming Stefano for one of our new courses: business conversation. We've only just set it up, actually. It's a difficult course, one that could be rather dry, but Hunter and I are working hard on the syllabus, to make it more interesting.'

Chiara notices the royal we, and so does Hunter. It upsets both of them, for different reasons. Della realizes her tactlessness too late. She looks to Stefano for help, but he's staring stonily at the table.

Sadie says, 'Why don't we stop talking shop? After

all, it's Sunday.' Then she wonders what the hell they *can* talk about safely, and wishes she'd kept her mouth shut.

Marino mentions the engagement and Hunter and Della make the proper cries of delight, which fills up a few more minutes, much to everyone's relief. More toasts are made and more Limoncello poured. Bettina and Marco come out with the coffee, which everyone drinks noisily, making inane comments on how good it is, and asking what brand it is.

Sadie thinks, Now. Now they will leave.

But no. Della seems paralysed, frozen in her seat beside Stefano, who is as coiled and tense as a roll of wire. Hunter, on the other side of Della and opposite Chiara, is oddly at ease now that the first few moments of awkwardness are over. After the initial tension he has relaxed and seems even to be enjoying himself. He's the only one who is.

Sadie watches Hunter closely. He is, she decides with a shock, strutting, *preening*. As she watches, he flicks back his hair – an irritating habit he has only recently picked up, now that his hair is longer than it has ever been. He has one arm around Della's shoulders, possessively; it's quite obvious that this is the embrace of a lover. Yet his body is leaning towards Chiara, and his eyes are trying to make contact with her; his face is lit up, open, radiating interest and yes, even love and concern, as he asks her about herself. My God, Sadie thinks, he's trying to charm Chiara all over again.

Sadie has seen him do this before, just as Stefano has. She'd watched for months while Hunter looked at Della in the same way, while at the same time keeping his arms lovingly around his wife, frightened to lose her until he was sure of Della.

'You bastard,' she says softly, so that only Marino can hear. And then, 'Poor Chiara.'

But Chiara is wiser now than she was two years ago. She too recognizes Hunter's loving look, the pale-grey

175

eyes both limpid and intense, the face eager to convey warmth and understanding. Like Sadie, Chiara realizes with a shock that Hunter is trying to win her over, to regain her sympathy, love even, with his compelling, sincere eyes and loving attention, just as he has always done, just as he did when rumours about him and Della ran like herds through the school and he wanted to stop Chiara from believing the truth.

She thinks, How transparent you are. And how stupid I was for not seeing it, for letting myself believe those opal eyes, those shadowy words you used to make a fool of me.

The thought hovers in her head like a sad old ghost, then lands on her heart, breaking the last bit of love she had for Hunter into invisible fragments which vanish as she examines them. Then she looks again into his eyes, and sees, like Stefano, the emptiness behind them. For Hunter doesn't care for her any more, not in the slightest. He's looking at her this way, with the old charm and affection, only because he cannot bear to see her no longer adoring him.

'Don't,' she says softly across the half-full glasses of Limoncello and empty coffee cups and the bowl of pink and white roses, still floating innocently on the table. 'Don't, Hunter.'

For a moment they look at each other with honesty; for the first time in a very long time.

It's too much for him. Hunter has lied to himself for so long that he no longer recognizes the truth, even when it stares at him from a face as familiar as his own reflection in the mirror. 'What do you mean?' he bristles. His face hardens unpleasantly.

Chiara speaks softly. 'You know exactly what I mean. Let's stop playing games, Hunter. There's no point; it's all over.'

Hunter's aware that the whole table, including Stefano and Della, are listening. He knows he should simply ignore Chiara, pretend he didn't hear, or else make a joke of it and turn to begin a conversation with

Della or Sadie or anyone. Or else just get up and leave; that would be the best thing. But he's afraid of losing face, of walking out as if he is beaten. He cannot let Stefano, or anyone else, see him beaten.

'Well,' he says haughtily, tightening his hand on Della's shoulder and then caressing her arm defiantly as he talks, 'I think it's you who's the one playing games, Chiara. Della and I have tried to be civilized about all this, have tried to contact you, but you've ignored letters, refused to answer phone calls. Then you come to Siena, so near to Florence, when you could have gone anywhere in Italy, and still refuse to see us. And you say that *I'm* playing games?'

Stefano says warningly, 'Give it a rest, Dad.' His voice is hard, dangerous.

But this admonishment from his son, in front of Della, as if he were indeed a doddering old man, turns Hunter into dry white ice, both hot and cold; deadly. Ignoring Stefano, he goes on, 'But you've always played games, haven't you, Chiara. When Della and I first fell in love, you refused to believe it. You ran off to London like a madwoman, to Stefano, to turn my son against me.'

'Dad, for fuck's sake, get a grip.'

'Hunter, that's enough.' Della stands up and tries to nudge Hunter up too. 'Time for us to go.'

He doesn't budge, but stares at Chiara with hatred. 'You think I'm an idiot, don't you. You think I don't know how you've tried to keep Stefano away from me. Well, you've lost, haven't you, Chiara. Stefano is here with me, and at least *he* knows what Della and I mean to each other, even though you refuse to recognize it.'

Stefano rises from his seat. 'Jesus Christ, are you mad? You haven't a clue—'

'No, Stefano!' Chiara's voice is stronger than his as she interrupts. 'Leave it, and sit down, please. Let me deal with this.' Anger is striking her body like flashes of lightning, electrifying her spine. 'Hunter, despite your evil words, you know that I have never, would

177

never, turn my son against his father. As for this other thing you accuse me of, it was I who tried to find out the truth about you and Della months before I left Italy. Weeks after Della arrived, I begged you to be honest with me, but you lied. Right up to the end you lied.'

'Now wait a minute, Chiara. I told you about Della. And you ran off, instead of sitting down to talk about it – the three of us, in a civilized manner.'

'No, *you* wait, Hunter. I can't believe you're saying these things. Have you gone crazy? Have you forgotten how you told me about Della? You made love to me all night, that's how. Oh, don't look so shocked. You remember, I know you do. *Allora*, you shake your head at me, so let me remind you. It was hot, Hunter, very hot that night; we laughed because we were so sweaty and slippery we kept sliding off each other. *Mio Dio*, I was happy that night. We were going away the next day, down south to the sea, and I was afraid we'd be too tired to drive because we'd been making love all night. But you reassured me, Hunter. *Hai dimenticato?* Well, I'll remind you, then. You said I wasn't to worry. We would take our time, the next day; we had all the time in the world. *È vero*, your very words: all the time in the world! Do you know how those words haunted me, Hunter? How they killed me, later, when I woke and you were gone?' Her voice breaks, and she looks away from Hunter to Della. 'With *you*,' she finishes, her voice so low now that the others can barely hear her. 'He was with you. Only, even then, he never bothered to tell me.'

There's a silence as shocking as Chiara's words. It's filled only with the sound of the rain and the erratic breathing of the people in the room. Hunter's head feels as if it's expanding like a balloon, ready to burst, explode. He cannot believe Chiara is saying these things, these secret, intimate things. He knows he should say something, refute her quickly, but his tongue seems to be swelling and he cannot speak.

It's Della who breaks the silence. 'Hunter, you are unspeakable. You appeared at my flat that morning, early, saying you weren't going on holiday with Chiara because you and she were finished. You said you'd told her the night before, that you'd spent all night discussing it, and that she'd accepted the marriage had broken down. You stayed in my flat all day and all night. It was hot that night too, Hunter, remember? We kept sliding off each other too.'

'Jesus.' Stefano starts to rise again, but Chiara reaches over the table and restrains him with her hand. Stefano lets himself be restrained. He's afraid he'll kill Hunter if he moves.

Chiara is speaking to Della. 'I am frantic when I see this note,' she says softly, forgetting what English tense she should be using in the emotion of the moment. 'I wake at nine and Hunter is gone. There's only a note, saying he's confused, our vacation is cancelled, and he needs to go away and think about things. I don't know where he has gone, or why. I am *pazza*, out of my head with worry for him. Then, late that night, he phones, to say he's with you and our marriage is over.'

Della is appalled. 'I didn't know this. I knew nothing about this. I thought he'd talked it all over with you, that you'd accepted.'

Chiara shakes her head. 'He wouldn't talk. Not at the end, not at the beginning. Everything was ending and he wouldn't talk to me about it.'

Della says, 'Look, I'm . . . I'm sorry.' It sounds as lame and pathetic to her own ears as it does to everyone else.

'It makes no difference now. It's finished.'

But it's not quite finished. Hunter, his head still woolly, but his mouth beginning to work again, cries, 'Now look here, Chiara, none of this is strictly true—'

But Chiara isn't having any more. 'No, *you* look, just look at yourself. Yes? Take a long, deep look, with honesty, for once. Yes, *veramente*, my heart was broke, broken, when you left me, but marriages end, *da sempre*, for whatever reasons. This I would have understood, finally, if you had been honest with me. What I will never get over, never forgive you for, is that betrayal at the end.'

'Listen—'

'I've listened to you enough, I'm not listening any more. Do you know what's so sad, so tragic, Hunter? That it was so unnecessary, that last betrayal. Do you think I didn't suspect your feelings for her by then? Yet you took such care to lie and convince me it wasn't so. And it was all for yourself, Hunter. Not one time did you think of me, after all our many years together. You didn't love me enough even for that.'

Chiara, her voice quavering as she says those last few words, lays her head on the empty plates and glasses and cherry pips and begins to cry. Stefano, deciding it's time now to kill his father, springs up from the table, but Hunter's already at the door. 'I see you're becoming hysterical,' he accuses her as he scuttles out. 'I'll leave so that you can calm down.'

He is out of the door without looking to see if Della is following. As he runs down the stairs, Stefano runs after him, shaking off first Marino and then Marco, who both try to stop him. Chiara lifts her head and cries, 'No, leave him, Stefano.'

But Stefano doesn't hear, or doesn't want to hear. He runs out of the apartment and down the stairs, into the early-evening rain and onto the wet stones of the Piazza Santo Spirito, but Hunter isn't there. The piazza is empty in the dreary rain and Stefano stands frustrated and furious as he tries to guess which of the many streets Hunter would have parked his car down.

He'll go to the villa, he decides. He'll meet Hunter there.

But first he will see to Chiara. As he goes up the steps to the apartment he meets Della coming down. 'Hunter's gone,' Stefano says. 'He doesn't seem to have waited for you.'

'He'll be walking,' Della says. 'I have the car keys.

180

Serves him right. I hope he gets soaked.'

'Tell him', Stefano says, 'that I'm coming up to see him tonight. I'll make sure my mother is all right and then I'm coming to the villa. Tell him that.' He runs upstairs before she can answer.

Half an hour later Stefano walks out into the rain again. Sadie and Marino are taking Chiara home with them, where she'll spend the night. She's shaken and tearful, but calmer now.

Stefano leaves the piazza to walk to the villa, but a car pulls up beside him before he gets far. 'I've been waiting for you,' Della says. 'I'll give you a lift.'

Stefano climbs in beside her. Neither of them say a word as she drives the short distance through the city and up the hill of the Via San Leonardo to the villa. Della has much she would like to say, to lessen the guilt and misery mixing like bile inside her, but she knows this isn't the right time. Stefano's mood is black, ominous.

'His car's gone,' Della says. 'He must have grabbed the keys when he got home and left. I wonder what he's up to. Let's see if there's a note.'

Stefano follows her through the archways into the house, straight up the stairs into the living room. She switches on lamps against the dank darkness of the rain, and finds the note on the coffee table.

'He's gone to Fiesole, he says. To have a quiet, civilized dinner at our favourite restaurant there. He says I can join him if I want.'

'Christ,' Stefano says, reading the note she hands to him. 'Is he completely inhuman? After all that, he's gone out for a meal?' Stefano reads the note again. 'I can't believe it.'

'He does that when he can't cope with things. He shuts them out, pretends they haven't happened. He knows I'll be fuming at all that stuff that came out today with Chiara. Remember, he lied to me too.'

'Are you going? To the restaurant?'

'Hell no. Let him stew. The way I feel now I never want to see him again.'

'When do you think he'll be back?'

'Not for hours. His pride won't let him. When I don't show up he'll have to pretend he was having such a good time without me he nearly forgot to come home.'

'*Porca puttana,*' Stefano swears with an explosion of anger and frustration. '*Cazzo!*' His voice is thick, bitter with rage.

The rain beats down on the lime trees outside with a dull, repetitive drumming, but the air inside is like treacle. 'Don't go,' Della says, as Stefano makes a move towards the door.

'I can't wait here all night for him.'

'No, please.' She's in front of him, blocking his exit. She feels as if she's stopped breathing in the thick, syrupy air. Stefano's rage and frustration pump furiously in the small space between them and she presses herself on him to rid the room of it. 'Stay, please? For whatever reason. To wait for Hunter, to rage, to keep out of the rain, whatever. I don't care why. I don't care about the past, or the future. Just now, Stefano. Let's have *now*. There's nothing to stop us.'

For a few moments Stefano doesn't move; he lets her arms wrap around him, her mouth find his skin. He's not sure when rage turns to lust, or whether it even does, nor does he care which of the two takes him through another doorway and tumbles him with Della onto her bed, Hunter's bed, where he makes love to her long and hard and falls asleep soon after, released, guiltless and exhausted.

17

An hour later Stefano wakes beside Della and waits for despair.

Nothing. He is jellied, filleted of emotion.

Staring at the ceiling of his father's bedroom he begins to feel an easy lightness, as if some god or demon inside him has been released and is floating far out of reach above him. He waits for guilt, dismay, anger. But there's nothing but this sweet peace.

Della, awake in the cradle of his arms, is feeling much the same. She would like to lie there for ever in the solid, soft circle of Stefano.

She makes herself stir, feeling him wake. 'Stefano, you've got to go.' She kisses the words into his neck, his throat.

Stefano doesn't want to go. He feels strong and young and triumphant: a god, a king. Tentatively, he explores this feeling. The clear lightness in his head and heart is related to the absence of shadows, of ghosts. No more hauntings of the shady past, or the murky present. Or, more precisely, no more ghosts of his father, prickling him into unrest and turmoil. His father, the father who has goaded him and put him down since childhood, is dead at last. Stefano won't have to kill him now.

He wraps his limbs more securely round Della's warm body, nestling into her gratefully, tenderly. Regretfully, she says softly, 'No, please. Later, tomorrow, but now you must go. Hunter will be back soon.'

'Sod Hunter. I don't care if he does come back.

Anyway, I thought you never wanted to see him again.'

'I didn't, I don't. But I think it's best, for now, if I do.'

'Let him find us. What the hell.' Stefano is amazed at the calm and contentment he's feeling.

For a moment Della is tempted to agree. But the thought of Hunter arriving and the horrific scene that would follow, destroying this moment, this longed-for moment with Stefano, brings her to her senses. Eventually Hunter will have to know, but not now. It will be ugly, telling Hunter, and she can't cope with anything sordid and ugly now. She is still too full of Stefano and what has just happened between them to be able to deal with Hunter, to let a confrontation between them take away from what has just occurred.

'It's been so good, so perfect, tonight,' she says, pulling herself away from him and sitting up. 'I don't want it spoiled by Hunter, or anyone. I want to remember this evening as it was, as it is now.' She looks down at Stefano, at his luminous skin and beautiful body, the stunning nakedness of him, and smiles.

Stefano, still wrapped in a feathered sheet of peace and calm, sees the point of this. He doesn't want to see his father. It's not because he's afraid, or even ashamed of what he has done with Della. He realizes that he has nothing to say to Hunter any more. As far as he's concerned, Hunter no longer exists.

Stefano and Hunter meet under the archways of the front of the house. The rain has stopped at last and the sky bristles with stars. The lime trees smell wet and leafy and cast prickly shadows from the light of a nearly full moon. Wafts of blossom scent, blown out by the rain, drift like will-o'-the-wisps across the light-and-dark pathway.

'Stefano. What are you doing here?' Hunter's voice is guarded.

Stefano looks at his father and feels nothing: no guilt, no gloating, no revenge, no anger. It's a sweetly

184

intense nothingness and it fills him with a quiet euphoria.

'I was looking for you.'

'Why? Is anything wrong?'

Stefano thinks, You can ask that? You can stand there so coldly after nearly destroying my mother a second time with your outburst; you can lie to us both, and you don't know what's wrong?

He looks at his father with something that could be pity, if Hunter wasn't looking at him with that concerned, innocent, perplexed expression, as if he doesn't know what is wrong, as if the scene of a few hours ago had never occurred. Manipulating the truth even now, Stefano thinks; adjusting it to suit himself and his own needs. He turns and walks away.

But not before Hunter has seen the contempt in his son's face. Hunter shouts at his back, 'Stefano, you come back here and tell me what you're up to, coming here in the middle of the night. Were you looking for me?'

Stefano turns. 'Yes. Yes, I was.'

'Why?'

'I wanted to talk to you.'

'Well, I'm here. Talk now. Come back inside, if you want to.'

Stefano shakes his head. 'There's nothing I want to say now.'

Relief passes through Hunter. The only thing he regrets about the scene today with Chiara was that Stefano heard it. He had been driven into a corner by her goading and had perhaps spoken to her more angrily than he would have liked to in front of Stefano.

But the boy seems to hold no hard feelings, seems to have cooled down. 'See you tomorrow, then?' Hunter says hopefully.

'Tomorrow? Oh, at the school, you mean. Yes. Yes, I suppose you will.'

As Stefano walks away Hunter finds he's trembling with the relief of a disaster averted. He had been afraid,

185

very afraid, that Stefano, in one of his impetuous tempers, would walk away from the Villa Tiglio and his job and never come back. Quite frankly, he needs Stefano at the school. To call in another teacher now would be disruptive for the students.

Now there's only Della to deal with, Hunter thinks as he walks into the house. She'll be in a rage about that little lie he told her all that time ago. But he can woo her all over again; he's done it before. And she'll realize that he only lied to make it easier for everyone.

Hunter feels a great deal happier now. He didn't enjoy his solitary meal this evening one bit; he can feel his indigestion beginning again. But thinking about today, he decides that he didn't, after all, handle himself badly. It was Chiara, not him, who made a scene; Chiara who embarrassed everyone there by her pitiful accusations and revelations.

They would realize it too. All of them: Sadie and Marino, Marco, Bettina, even Della. They would realize it was just Chiara being overly Italian again, needing scenes and drama, to justify the fact that she has been passed over for someone else. But Hunter has won after all. Stefano is still with him.

And the boy seems to understand. Hunter thinks of how mature and accommodating Stefano was just now, considering what had happened. Everything will be all right, he tells himself with relief. There's just Della to win over now.

Della's in the shower when Hunter enters their bedroom. The three double windows of the large room are open, letting the stone-washed air clean every crevice with its scent of scrubbed earth and blossom. Hunter goes through the open doors leading to the balcony to see the moon swelling like a balloon in a birthday sky. After the stress of the afternoon and the evening, when he waited for hours for Della to turn up at the restaurant, he feels serene and confident.

Della appears at his side in the silky deep-blue

pyjamas he loves, the ones that match her eyes. She smells of soap and lime flowers. 'Did you see Stefano?' she asks. Her face is glowing, drowning in moonlight.

'Yes. I met him as he was leaving the house. He said he was looking for me, wanted to talk to me.'

'Yes.'

'I assume you put him off, persuaded him to leave. He certainly didn't feel like talking when we met, though I gave him every chance.'

'I told him he'd better go, yes. I didn't want the two of you to meet, not tonight.'

'Well, whatever you said, it worked. He must have been in quite a temper to come here so late, looking for me. I suppose Chiara gave him an earful after I left the apartment, probably sobbed on his shoulder all evening. I suppose we can't blame the boy for wanting to charge up here like that and give me hell. Chiara can make anyone act unreasonably.'

Della is silent. In the distance, cyprus trees make shadows in the moonlight. Hunter decides not to mention Della's absence at the restaurant in Fiesole tonight. She too must have been stewing over some of the things Chiara had revealed. He had planned to go over that, to show Della where Chiara had been lying, but Della seems to have forgotten it already. He'll let it be, since it has all worked out so nicely.

'Well, I suppose I should thank you,' he says, putting an arm around her silky shoulders. 'You obviously calmed Stefano down, talked him out of murdering his father.' He chuckles.

'Yes,' Della says. 'I think I did.'

'Poor darling.' He pulls her into the wiry branches of his arms. 'It's been an exhausting day. Shall we go to bed?'

Della is already moving away. 'I just want to sleep. To sleep and sleep and sleep.'

In minutes she's in bed, eyes closed and curled tightly like a vine around a string. Hunter tries again, caressing her shoulder, but she already seems to be in a deep slumber.

He's disappointed. But acknowledging that this dreadful day has ended far better than he expected, he lets her be, saying only, 'You sleep, darling. I suspect you need to forget this day, just as I do.'

But Della, eyes closed, is wide awake, remembering.

To the surprise of everyone the school carries on the next day, and the next week, as if Sunday had never happened.

Bettina says to Stefano, 'I nearly broke off my engagement to Marco that evening, after everyone left at last and we were finally alone. I told him, if this is what marriage is like, forget it.'

'I know what you mean.'

'Luckily Marco has the example of his parents. Marino and Sadie are still crazy about each other. Not like mine, who seem to be surprised when they're in the same room together. No passion there, I think. But at least they don't growl and spit at each other like animals. At least my father doesn't leave my mother for other women.'

'Lucky you.'

Bettina looks around the office and through the open doors down the corridor. No-one is around so she whispers, 'Did you follow Hunter and have it out with him after you left us? I know Chiara told you not to, but did you?' Her face glints with innocent eagerness.

'I couldn't be bothered. By the time we met up I'd lost my anger.'

'Oh.' Bettina's disappointed. She decides that this is the English side of Stefano coming out. An Italian man would have bellowed and raged at Hunter for making such a scene; an Italian man would have sought vengeance on another man who treated his mother so badly. She decides that as attractive and sexy as Stefano is she's glad she's marrying Marco.

*   *   *

Sadie is polite, but cool and distant with Hunter, when the staff meet in the front courtyard during the Monday-morning break. This is fine by Hunter. She'll come round; women always do. He surveys his little kingdom smugly. From the back terrace there are bursts of laughter from the students as they eat their bananas and *panini* and other snacks they've brought. Della, Stefano and Sadie talk quietly about the problems of one of the students, the same problem that Hunter and Della had intended to discuss on Sunday with Stefano. Hunter offers advice about which books would be useful to the student. This done, he gives them a little pep talk on keeping up the morale of the school, keeping up the good team spirit. He doesn't mention Sunday. No-one does.

Sadie looks out over the front lawn at the wetness of the lime trees lining the long gravel drive, and keeps her lips pressed tightly together.

Della too looks at the lime trees, remembering the scent of them when she saw Stefano for the first time. They look glossy and welcoming now. She wishes she could pull Stefano behind them and make love to him again in the shade of their full branches.

Stefano is staring at Hunter, his face neutral. But he doesn't even see Hunter, let alone hear him. He's as untouched by his father as he is by the soft breeze gently stirring the leaves of the lime trees and wafting their scent over all of them.

Bettina's eyes are closed. As she feels the welcoming sunlight on her face after yesterday's rain, she murmurs silent thanks to all the saints of her childhood for seeing to it that she is neither a teacher nor an Englishwoman, but a soon-to-be-married Italian *fidanzata*, engaged to the most wonderful man in Italy. Before Hunter has finished talking, she has dozed off.

It's not until the afternoon that Della gets a chance to talk to Stefano alone. She finds him in his classroom after his last students have gone, going through some papers. 'Tonight, Stefano? Can we meet somewhere tonight?'

Stefano glances at the open doorway, where at any moment a stray student or a staff member could appear. He shakes his head. 'Look, this isn't the right time—'

'It's all the time we have. Hunter and I are going for a run in a minute and then you'll be gone. I've been racking my brains to think where we could go—'

'We can't go anywhere. As soon as I leave here I'm going up to Sadie and Marino's. My mother's still there. She took a few days off work and I've promised to go up for a meal.'

'Later, then. Please.' She puts her strong hand on his smooth cheek and strokes it slowly. 'Please,' she says again.

He looks at her warmly, remembering last night and how she exorcized his demons with her skilled love-making, her passion and intensity, which awakened the same urgency in him. Suddenly he can't wait to be alone with her again. 'All right, later. Where?'

'I don't know, I can't think. I'll wait for you just up from Due Strade. I'll be in the car, parked in the road leading to the Via Martellini.'

Stefano nods as a voice in the doorway says, 'Do either of you have that big English/Italian dictionary? I've been looking everywhere for it. I hope one of the students hasn't nicked it.'

'No, Sadie. It's not in here.'

'Oh. Right.' She pauses for a moment and looks thoughtfully at the two of them. Something has changed here. She can feel the new tension between them; it's on a different voltage now.

Della stands up. 'I'd better go and get ready for my run; I'm meeting Hunter in a few minutes' time.' She walks from the classroom. 'See you later, Sadie, Stefano.' She doesn't even look back at him.

But Sadie isn't fooled. 'What's up, Stefano?' When

he doesn't answer, she says bluntly, 'Something's changed between the two of you.'

'Changed? Nothing, Sadie. Nothing at all.'

He tries to keep his face impassive, but his eyes are charged. He seems years older than he did yesterday.

Sadie shakes her head. 'Just be careful, OK? Just watch yourself. You're too nice a bloke to get involved in this.'

'In what, Sadie?' Stefano's face looks innocent and young, but also self-aware and self-contained. Assured. It's his time, Sadie thinks. It's his turn now.

She sighs. 'I suppose it was inevitable.'

She isn't sure, and Stefano doesn't ask, what was inevitable. His affair with Della? Or something older than that, something timeless?

Who is she to know or to make judgements. She says again, fruitlessly, 'Just be careful.' She knows she might as well tell a young lion to take care as he prowls his newly conquered kingdom.

18

Chiara walks out of Sadie and Marino's house on the Via Martellini and into the Florentine sunshine. Sadie is teaching at the Villa Tiglio, and Marino is locked in the scruffy little room he calls his office, working on his latest thriller. The rain-washed jasmine fills the road into Due Strade with air as fresh and scented as a childhood memory. As she walks past the tumbling white flowers growing over a stone wall, Chiara remembers not Hunter or the Villa Tiglio, but her earlier times in Italy, and she's exhilarated to be back.

Not only is the city cleansed and freshened by Sunday's downpour. Chiara's face is olive-smooth after yesterday's tears. She knows they are the last tears she will cry for Hunter, and that even those weren't for Hunter as he is, but the Hunter of their younger selves.

Marino and Sadie had taken her back to their comfortable, relaxing house, where they had opened more Chianti, letting Chiara cry and reminisce, offering her affection and support after the horrendous scene with Hunter. Then, when she was worn out with emotion, they began talking slowly, easily, of other things, filling each other in on the past two years, gossiping about old friends and acquaintances, as they all got slightly drunk. She'd woken this morning with a headache, but with the heaviness of the last months – of nearly two years – gone.

At Due Strade she catches a number-eleven bus, which goes down the Via del Gelsomino and then left down the wide street and through the Porta Romana into the city.

Florence, and in the sunlight. Ahead are her beloved Fra Angelicos, which she hasn't seen for so long. There is the Ponte Vecchio, which she has crossed countless times since childhood, and which she will be crossing again shortly when she gets off the bus. She will stop there and look out over the river, admire the graceful arcs of the other bridges, clear and shadowless under the high sun. From there she will walk to the Duomo, its pink and green and white marzipan marble façade rising with Brunelleschi's dome and Giotto's bell tower just around the corner. And then — there is so much! There is Botticelli in the Uffizi, and the chapel of Masaccio's frescoes, and all her other favourites which she grew up with; they are like family, old friends, welcoming her back.

All this is ahead of her today, and in the sunshine.

And all her life too is ahead of her now.

'And I finished in the church of Santa Felicità,' Chiara says in Sadie and Marino's kitchen, while helping Sadie dip skinned chicken breasts in flour, then sauté them in olive oil and put them in a casserole with chickpeas and thyme. 'I stood in front of this marvellous sixteenth-century painting, looking at this luminous light which seemed to shine from the figures, and I thought, I feel like that: as if a strange light is glowing inside me. Do you think it's being back in Florence again?' She laughs. 'Or do you think it's all the drink we had yesterday?'

Marino, making his beloved pesto sauce, with basil from the two great pots on the window sill, and garlic, olive oil and pine nuts, says, 'I think it's the baggage you've just got rid of.'

'You mean Hunter? But he got rid of me, ages ago.'

'And now you are rid of him.' He takes a huge chunk of parmesan and begins grating it finely.

Sadie wipes the flour from her hands and says, 'If he didn't make me so angry I could almost feel sorry for Hunter. All that self-delusion.' She puts the rest of the chicken in the heated olive oil, where it sizzles tanta-lizingly.

'Do you know what?' Chiara says. 'I do. Feel sorry for him.'

To her amazement she does. But that is all.

Stefano arrives soon afterwards, and the four of them once again eat outside. The food and talk is as light and fresh as the air around them, pricked with sunlight through the olive tree, clean and wholesome. No-one drinks much, except for a small glass of red wine with the meal and a great deal of mineral water. They feel scrubbed and new after yesterday.

Stefano feels this way too, oddly. He knows it's odd because he shouldn't be. He is involved in God knows what: something clandestine, dangerous, sordid even, if you looked at it dispassionately. But it doesn't feel like this. It feels right and satisfying, though he knows that this feeling too will pass as the next stage unfolds. He does not know what the next stage is; he does not think about it: he does not care.

Stefano leaves early from Sadie and Marino's house. Light still washes the deep watercolour sky as he walks down to meet Della. The days are already long, and will get longer still before sliding back to darkness and winter.

Della is in her car, parked in front of the closed, shut-tered doorway of the greengrocer's. She too, like Stefano, has lost all her agitation; she's as serene as an earth goddess, her desperate passion for Stefano now satisfied and metamorphosed into dazzling content-ment. Again like Stefano, she accepts that it cannot last. But whatever the future brings she has now. She has Stefano.

Wordlessly he gets in and she drives away, turning right down the Via del Gelsomino, then left again onto the wide street leading to the Piazzale Michelangelo. She pulls into the vast parking area, crowded with cars, caravans, sellers of plastic statues of David, tatty 'I Love Florence' stickers, cards and ice creams.

They get out and walk beside the low wall protecting the piazza from the slope of the hill. Together they stare at the panoramic view of the city at night, along with the tourists: teenagers giggling and preening, more conscious of their own young beauty than that of the city's; Florentine families strolling to see the lights of their beloved city in this favourite spot overlooking it.

'I used to come here with my first girlfriend on hot August nights,' Stefano says. 'There was a gang of us.' He remembers the groping and grappling in the parked cars of the piazza later, the heat and sweat of young bodies, the lust and longing, the frustration and craziness of it all.

They stand for a while, staring at the lit dome of the cathedral and the bridges over the Arno. It is all simply beautiful. Without thinking about it they have put their arms around each other, as if they were one of the many other couples romantically entwined and looking at the view.

Stefano is aware that this is crazy too, standing here with Della. Anyone could drive by, stop, see them together. Any one of their students could be here, wondering what Hunter's son is doing with Hunter's girlfriend.

He says, 'Does Hunter know you're with me?' He is mildly curious as to whether Della has told his father about him, but only mildly. What Della tells Hunter is her own affair.

'I told him I was going to see a friend.' She turns to him and smiles. 'You *are* a friend, aren't you?' Her hands slide around him even tighter, and she tips her head to kiss him lightly on the lips. An old woman, out with her children and grown grandchildren, looks at them softly, remembering.

Her boldness catches him. 'Come on,' he says, pulling her towards the car.

In the car he keeps his hand on her thigh as she drives, far too fast, out of the town and into the countryside. There, in the car, parked by an isolated vineyard, he makes love to her a second time. Neither of them notice in the full moonlight how the vines are beginning to grow, making their way, snakelike, up the taut cord of the grapevine.

By some silent, mutual agreement, Della and Stefano continue to keep their relationship secret, clandestine. When Stefano thinks about this he realizes that he doesn't care one way or another what Della does, whether she tells Hunter or not, leaves him or not. Hunter no longer matters, but for now, for this moment in time, Della does. Stefano is becoming addicted to her, or rather, to their lovemaking, which is both intense and deeply satisfying. With each time the scars of the past lighten and fade. With each time Stefano grows stronger. He is grateful to her for this.

Every day that week they make love. Once in the villa when Hunter goes into the city for an evening meeting, twice at midday in Stefano's apartment when he knows Marco is off meeting Bettina in some restaurant for lunch.

On Friday, at lunchtime, all the staff members stay at the villa for their monthly get-together. This is a school ritual that Hunter insists on for the students and staff, so that the different groups can mingle. Della has brought wine and mineral water, packets of crisps and crackers, some cheese and prosciutto. These are spread out on several tables which Hunter has placed on the back terrace, under the shade of the old olive trees on either side. The day is lightly warm, sweet with birdsong and flower scents.

Della manages a few words with Stefano alone, wandering with him, as if discussing work, away from the terrace and garden, along the path through the lime trees leading to the tennis court. 'Hunter insists we go out for dinner tonight, to this place we know out in

Greve. Just the two of us, so I can't even invite you,' Della says.

'I wouldn't go. I've no desire to socialize with my father.'

'I was hoping we could spend the evening together. I don't know if I can bear not seeing you until tomorrow.' And indeed she cannot stop herself from moving into his space, holding him, touching him.

Stefano glances around to make sure they are well hidden by the trees and shrubbery. They have rounded a bend and are at the edge of the tennis court, out of sight of the terrace. In the distance they can hear shrieks of laughter from the students and staff, but they are hidden and alone.

He pulls her down onto the grass verge, under a hedge of jasmine. Above them the lime trees hover, blanketing them with their shadows. 'Tomorrow is out,' he says softly. 'I'm tied up all day. We have only now.'

In minutes they are making love, Della's pale hair crushed against the red poppies, and the scent of jasmine thickening their senses like honey.

That night Della sits with Hunter on a wide expanse of terracotta terrace in the small Chianti town of Greve, outside Florence. The terrace is part of a large, pleasant restaurant and pizzeria, filled with the usual mixture of Italian families with children and grand-parents, stylish thirty-something couples and groups of younger single people. At a table opposite them a dozen or so of the latter are celebrating a birthday with massive pizzas and much wine, beer and high spirits.

Though the excessive hot weather of the previous weeks has cooled, the evening is still warm enough to be comfortable outside. Hunter has taken off his jumper and sits in shirt sleeves, while Della has a yellow cardigan slung over her shoulders. Opposite them, in the light still lingering in the night sky, is the Tuscan countryside: an olive grove and terraces of

197

vineyards. Above this panorama is an accommodating moon.

Della wishes she were anywhere but here. Or that she were here with Stefano. Or that, if she had to be here without Stefano, she were with anyone but Hunter.

She needs to examine this last thought and does so as the waiter brings them *spaghetti alle vongole*, smelling of the sea and garlic. The clams look up at her with open mouths, ready to be plucked out of their shells.

As Hunter discusses the merits of the wine he has ordered with the waiter, Della stares at the vineyards opposite and wonders why she no longer likes Hunter.

She understands, of course, why she no longer loves him. Having met Stefano it has become impossible to love anyone else; having made love to Stefano, making love to Hunter is out of the question.

This last dilemma is a bit of a bother. Della no longer wants to be with Hunter, but knows it's necessary, at least for a time. She wants to be with Stefano, and not just secretly and hurriedly as it is now. For the moment, though, this is impossible; it's too soon. When Hunter learns of it there will be a scene, a catalyst; everything, for all of them, will change. It will have to come. Della knows this, but it's too early now. She doesn't want to lose Stefano, to have him storm back to London perhaps, driven away by a confrontation with Hunter. She will have to wait until she has become so necessary to Stefano that whatever Hunter says or does Stefano will stay with her.

With a shock Della remembers that this is what Hunter did: made sure of her before he left Chiara. The irony of it nearly makes her laugh out loud. But she is unrepentant. Chiara hadn't deserved to be lied to, but Hunter does. In the end the first lie was his. But Della, suddenly saddened, wonders when the last lie will finally be spoken and finished with. She hopes it will be soon.

Hunter has dismissed the wine waiter. 'A bit of a

know-it-all, but he hadn't a clue; it was obvious when I started questioning him. I soon put him right,' he says, pouring Della a glass. He drinks more of his own. 'Mmm, a Pinot Nero, one of the best. The waiter was trying to tell me—'

Della doesn't want to hear. 'You should eat your clams; they're getting cold,' she interrupts.

While Hunter eats his clams he keeps talking, commenting on their quality, looking at her lovingly and asking if she's enjoying them – though she has hardly touched them – once reaching under the table to caress her calf which rests beside his. Della realizes why she doesn't like Hunter any more. It's because you never know where you stand with him, she decides. He deals out love and kindness, charm and graciousness, only when it suits him. This is much more dangerous than down-and-out nastiness and unpleasantness. At least there, you know where you stand.

'Hm, not bad.' Hunter chews thoughtfully on a clam. 'What do you think, darling? Are they as good as the ones we get at the other place? You know, our special restaurant, in Fiesole.' He looks at her with those smiling grey eyes with the coloured flecks in them, twinkling love at her like stardust. But it's as cold as stardust, as distant.

She stands up suddenly. 'Excuse me, Hunter, I'm not feeling well.'

She rushes off inside the restaurant towards the bathrooms, but doesn't go into them. Instead, she sees another door leading outside and goes through that into the road, zigzagging down the hill into Greve itself, where, sick in her head and heart, she walks up and down the cobbled, funnel-shaped Piazza Matteotti until finally, twenty minutes later, Hunter finds her.

Hours later, back in the villa, Hunter wants to make love to her, but once again she tells him the lie she has used all week, that she has a bad case of cystitis and it's too painful.

Hunter is grumpy. She ruined their dinner with her funny turn, running off like that to get some air rather than simply being sick in the Ladies and getting it out of her system, whatever it was. Now he's willing to forgive and forget with a good long session in bed, but Della's already asleep, slightly snoring even.

It's too early for Hunter to sleep; it's barely ten o'clock. He is feeling restless, bad-tempered, his dinner ruined and no prospect of sex for another night because of Della's various ills. Even though they had a run this morning he decides he will go on another one. He needs to do something to still the vague unease that has been annoying him for several days now. He can't put his finger on what it is, and it's bothering him. Perhaps another run will clear his head, focus him. Changing into his shorts and running shoes he leaves a note in case Della wakes and goes out into the street.

This time he runs up the Via San Leonardo instead of going down into the city centre. He goes up and crosses the road and carries on down the more rural streets, past dark vegetable gardens and the lights of set-back houses, past stone walls shimmering in the moonlight and the silvery branches of olive trees. He realizes that he has cut up towards Sadie and Marino's house and he sees a light still burning in the kitchen. He is about to run past when he feels, in his chest, the beginnings of a suffocating pain, very like the pain that struck him so forcibly in the Piazza della Signoria a week or two ago.

It's only indigestion, of course, come back again after their interrupted meal in Greve. But perhaps he should stop for a bit. He can call in on Sadie and Marino, get a drink of water from them and sit down for a few minutes to get his breath back, while waiting for the strange, aching pain to go.

He veers off up their driveway, through the iron gate, which is open, and on past the low stone wall marking off Sadie's herb garden. He can see Marino through the lit window, and Sadie too, standing with a cup in her hand. Hunter is about to call out to them when suddenly he's on the ground, slumped against the stone wall, the silver of his long, thin hair slicing like knives through a cluster of red poppies.

19

As Hunter's blood, from the cut on his head as he fell
against the stone wall, seeps into the poppies, staining
them a darker crimson, Stefano dances savagely in a
kaleidoscope of bright lights and sound and colour.
He's a good dancer, precise yet abandoned, graceful yet
slightly brutal, as if he would pound the earth and
punish it for putting him on it.

He, Bettina and Marco, and other mutual friends, are
in a club at the entrance of the Cascine park. The room
they are in is vast, mirrored and crowded. A DJ plays a
mixture of reggae and hard rock, which keeps most
people on their feet rather than at the few tables scattered around the edges.

When Stefano dances his mind empties, letting
waterfalls of sound and movement cascade freely into
it. But tonight stray thoughts gather in the hollows of
his brain and refuse to seep out. Images whirl through
his head: Della, her pale hair threaded like silk
amongst the poppies, her hands speckled with the sun
peppering through the lime trees.

Bettina whirls by, tosses Stefano a smile and rocks
away. Her long hair dances with a life of its own.

Della's shorter hair seemed to dance too, among the
flowers, as they made love quickly and silently.

They will be found out, Stefano thinks, if they keep
on like this. For a week they've been taking chances,
too many chances. Hunter will begin to notice, will
find them out one day.

Perhaps it would be better if he did.

This thought so surprises Stefano that he stops

dancing and makes his way through the hot, moving bodies to the bar. He orders a beer and drinks half of it quickly.

If Hunter were to find out it would all be over. He, Stefano, would have to disappear, and Della and his father would have to sort out for themselves whether they intended to go on or not. Stefano can get on with his life, get out of this fruitless, secret relationship.

Then another thought strikes him, so dreadful that he drinks the rest of his beer quickly. Jesus, Mary and Joseph, what if Chiara found out? His *mother*, for the love of God, his mother learning of his affair with his father's . . . what? What *was* Della? In another day and age Hunter would have married her as soon as his divorce had come through, and she would now be Stefano's stepmother.

No, Hunter must never find out, for then Chiara would too. This, to Stefano, is unthinkable. Apart from everything else she would feel it was a second betrayal. First her husband, then her son – no, she cannot find out. Stefano orders another beer and tries to think.

Sipping his second drink more slowly, Stefano asks himself why, if he craves the relief of getting out of his affair with Della, if the lull, the peace, of their initial stage is ending, why does he not end it himself?

There is no reason why not. Yes, he has become as eager as she is to pursue their lovemaking, but he doesn't love her. He hopes she feels the same way about him, despite her words of love that one time in Sadie and Marino's garden. He doesn't want to hurt her, though the thought comes unbidden that her hurt will only be a fraction of what Chiara suffered after Hunter left her.

A designer redhead in a micro-miniskirt comes to the bar and stares boldly at Stefano to see if he will do. He does and she urges him out onto the dance floor, where she moves about as elegantly as her gold chains and her translucent pearl silk blouse. Yet her dancing promises something much more earthy than elegance, and her body language is telling Stefano he would be a fool not to take her up on it.

But when the music changes and they finally stop dancing, Stefano makes his excuses and walks away from her. His life is so complicated right now that to take anything else on would do his head in.

He thinks again about finishing it with Della once and for all, yet strangely, the thought of doing so gives him no relief. In truth, he doesn't want it to be over; not yet, not like this. He may not love Della, but he still wants her. And it's more than just sex; he finds that he looks forward to seeing her during school hours, to the occasional lunches they share together in the villa kitchen, to her no-nonsense bluntness, and her refusal, now that they are lovers, to play games with him. She wants him, and wants him to want her, and he likes her honest assertiveness. His growing affection for her has certainly made him forget Bettina; all that seems years in the past now, rather than just over a week ago.

The music grinds and clashes in the crowded room; the dancers around him are lost in their own world, their own space. Stefano doesn't see them; instead, in a bolt of self-awareness, he sees in his head the illuminated figures of Della and Hunter, with him in the centre between them. *Tra due fuochi*, between two fires, as they say in Italy. He is torn between the two of them, or rather the emotions they kindle in him. Perhaps it's not quite over with his father. Perhaps there's still something that Stefano is waiting for.

And then, with a shock, he knows what it is. He's waiting for Hunter to discover them. Despite Chiara, he's waiting for Hunter to find out.

Hunter, at that moment, knows that he's alive from the throbbing in his head and the scratchy feel of wild grass on his face.

Inside the house Sadie says, 'Marino, *ascolta*. Do you hear that? Right outside the kitchen window. It sounded like an animal of some kind.'

Marino goes to the open window and leans out to look. '*Santo Spirito*, it's a man, sprawled in the herb garden.'

They rush outside to find Hunter, groaning as he slowly pulls himself up to a sitting position.

'*Gesù, Madonna, che cosa?*' Marino exclaims. 'Are you hurt? Should we go to the hospital?'

'*No, grazie.* I'm all right.'

'You have blood on your face,' Sadie cries. 'Were you hit by a car?'

'No, no, nothing like that. I was running, and I happened to be passing by, so I . . . I decided to stop for a drink.' Hunter feels his head and the soreness there. The pain in his chest has gone.

'But you're bleeding, Hunter. What happened?'

'Nothing, a scratch. I'm not quite sure what happened. I must have tripped. Yes, look, one of my laces is untied. I must have tripped over it and hit my head against the wall here.'

'Come inside,' Marino says. 'Have a drink, then I'll take you home.'

'Are you sure you don't want a doctor to look at that cut?'

'No, no, I'll be fine. I will have that drink though.'

They go into the kitchen, where Marino pours them each a glass of brandy. Sadie says, 'Where's Della? And why were you running at this hour of the night?'

'She's asleep. Not feeling too well. In fact, she's not been herself all week.' Hunter stares broodily into his brandy glass, then drinks. The alcohol warms and comforts him.

Marino and Sadie exchange glances. They'd been talking about Hunter only moments before they heard his moaning in the herb garden. They had been discussing whether there was anything they could do to prevent the crisis that Della and Stefano seemed to be bringing on themselves and Hunter, not to mention Chiara. There is no doubt in Sadie's mind that Stefano is having an affair with Della.

Hunter accepts another glass of brandy. This one makes him expansive. 'I'm a bit worried about Della, to be honest,' he says as Sadie finishes washing the blood from his head and disinfecting the cut, which is not very deep. 'She hasn't been right since the beginning of the spring session. Not herself, if you know what I mean.'

Marino grunts, looking helplessly at Sadie.

'Do you, er, do you have any idea what could be wrong?' Sadie asks.

'Yes, actually, I do. I know exactly what's wrong. It's Stef, of course. I realized it tonight.'

Marino whistles softly, pouring himself another brandy. Sadie exhales slowly. This is for the best, she thinks. Hunter knows, so we can get it all out in the open at last.

'So you know,' she says.

'Hm? Oh yes.' Hunter drinks more of the brandy. 'Good stuff, this. One of the best. A good choice, Marino. I don't think much of the French, but you've got to give it to them, their brandy can't be beaten.'

Admiration for the English fills Marino's head for a few seconds. This Englishman has just discovered that his lover is secretly making love to his son and he's discussing the virtues of French brandy. Such cool, such poise.

Sadie says evenly, 'Hunter, how did you come to all this? To Stefano and Della. And what are you going to do?'

'Oh, nothing. God, this even smells like nectar. Vive la France!' He finishes his glass in one gulp.

Marino gapes. This is not cool, this is a travesty. The man is a robot, devoid of all emotion, all passion.

Hunter goes on, 'I've got it all figured out, don't you worry. You see, if I leave them alone they'll just have to learn to live with it.'

'Ah, I see. Or rather, no, I don't quite see.'

'Their envy.'

'Envy?'

206

'Della's and Stefano's. As I was lying, stunned against your garden wall, it came to me that the reason we're all so edgy at the school, and why Della is so changeable, is that she and Stefano are jealous of each other.'

Sadie controls an impulse to laugh. 'Jealous?'

'Of my affection. My love. Each is vying for my attention, envious when the other one gets more.'

'Ah.' Sadie cannot meet Marino's eye. She wonders if he has managed to catch all of Hunter's English, then decides he has. He looks as if he's stifling a giggle too. Sadie says, 'So that's all that's wrong, is it?'

'It's enough, by Jove. It's ruining the morale of the whole team. But I've decided to ignore it. And I want you to do so too. It will pass, Sadie. Don't let it worry you.' He leans over and pats her hand.

Later, when Hunter's gone and Marino has returned from driving him home, and he and Sadie are in bed, Sadie says, 'There's no point, is there, in trying to do something, warn somebody. It wouldn't do a bit of good to anyone. It seems to be the curse of the Villa Tiglio: no-one can face the truth there.'

'Or even recognize it when it cracks someone's head open in the herb garden.'

They begin to giggle, and laugh and laugh, until finally they calm down and go to sleep.

They are all asleep now: Della and Hunter at the Villa Tiglio, Chiara at her home in Siena. Even Bettina and Marco have left the club early and, tired after several late nights, are sound asleep in Marco's apartment.

Only Stefano is awake. Restless and not wanting to be alone with his thoughts, he stays at the club until it closes, then walks the long distance back into the city centre, roaming the empty streets for an hour before finally heading back to the Piazza Santo Spirito.

20

Hunter stays in bed all morning on Saturday. He feels fine but extremely tired. He blames it on the stress of the past week, the atmosphere that has hung around the school after 'the incident', which is how he thinks of Chiara's outburst.

But the week is over. Everyone seems to have forgotten last Sunday, and today is a new weekend. He gets out of bed and pulls on his clothes. It's midday and glorious, sunny but not too hot. He should have been up early, running in the fresh new morning with Della, instead of sleeping in like this, but he had been tired out by his fall last night and the brandy Marino kept plying him with. What he needs is exercise, movement.

Della has left the house. When she brought him a cup of tea at nine o'clock this morning, she'd said she was going shopping and didn't know when she'd be home. Hunter had gone straight back to sleep, but he still feels somewhat lethargic. What he needs is some fresh air and brisk activity to wake him up again.

On impulse he picks up the phone and dials the number of Marco's apartment. It rings for a long time. Hunter is about to hang up when at last Stefano answers.

Stefano had nearly not answered the phone. Della, in bed beside him, had urged him to ignore it, but it rang so long and persistently that Stefano began to worry it was Chiara, that she was ill perhaps and calling off the lunch at her place later that day.

'Stef, hello. I nearly hung up. What took you so long to answer?'

Stefano closes his eyes, then opens them. He is standing naked in the living room where the phone is. He wonders if he double-locked the door of the apartment after Della came in, but then realizes there's no point: both Marco and Bettina have keys that unlock both doors.

'I was in bed.'

'Good grief, on such a beautiful day?'

Stefano is silent. He's waiting for Hunter to ask if Della's there. He wonders how he will answer.

Hunter says, 'In fact, it's such a perfect day that I thought you and I could play some tennis. Care to come up to the villa? Whenever you like; we're free today. Della's out shopping somewhere, but I'm expecting her back any minute. Come for a light lunch.'

Stefano wonders briefly how Hunter can think he'd want to see his father again, other than when strictly necessary at work, after last Sunday. He wonders if Hunter is even on the same planet any more.

'No,' he says. Then, 'I'm going to Siena.'

'But that's where Sadie and Marino are going.'

'Yes.'

'Oh, I see. Family party, ha ha. At Chiara's. Except that Sadie and Marino are not family, of course. Though I suppose old friends count as family.'

'Yes, I suppose they do.'

'Well. How about tomorrow then? Come on, Stef, show some spunk. Don't you want another go at your old dad? Aren't you itching to pay me back for the thrashing I gave you last time?'

'Dad.' Stefano's voice is almost kind. 'Stow it. I don't want to play tennis with you. Not any more. Not ever.'

'That was Hunter,' Della says when he goes back into the bedroom. 'I heard.'

'I thought he was looking for you.'

209

'How could he know I was here? I didn't even know I was coming here myself until I rang your doorbell this morning.'

'Jesus, Della, you're taking risks. You couldn't have known Bettina and Marco would be out early today, that I'd be in on my own. On Saturdays they're usually in bed till noon. I was the one who planned to get out early. If my mother hadn't phoned to change the plans around I wouldn't even be here.'

Della smiles. It was pure impulse that had made her ring Stefano's doorbell that morning; she'd done it without thinking, without even wondering what excuse she would make if Marco or Bettina answered. 'It worked, though, taking a risk. And you didn't mind my waking you up, that was obvious.'

Stefano is getting dressed, looking out of the window as he does so at the piazza, vibrant with shoppers and pigeons, dog-walkers and families. Tourists too, of course, but not nearly as many here as in the centre of the city. 'Come on,' he says to Della, who's lying there as if she would stay all day. 'Marco and Bettina could be back anytime now. We're lucky they didn't walk in and catch us at it.'

'You didn't seem worried at the time.'

'No. Well.' He looks over at her and grins affectionately as he pulls on a black T-shirt and black jeans, then stares out of the window again to make sure Marco and Bettina aren't on their way back up. Della looks at the way the cotton of his shirt smooths over the muscles in his back and says, 'I love you, you know.'

He keeps staring out of the window, as if he hasn't heard her. Finally, after a few moments, he says, 'Don't, Della.'

'Say it? Or feel it?'

'Both.' To soften the word he goes to the bed and runs his fingers through her hair, tenderly, affectionately.

'I can't not—'

'Shh,' he says, putting his hand lightly over her

210

mouth. 'We're in deep shit already, you and me. What we're doing just isn't on.'

'Who cares? I don't.'

'I suppose I don't either. But there are prices to pay, Della. You know that. And one of them is keeping things under control, keeping a lid on it.' He pulls her up gently. 'Now come on, get a move on. Sadie and Marino are picking me up here in half an hour to take me to Siena with them. You need to be well out of here before they arrive.'

'Stefano.' She doesn't move from the bed.

'Yes?' He's becoming impatient now.

'Do you love me? Even a little?'

God, how he wishes women wouldn't ask this. He'd thought that Della, being so much older, would know not to ask a question like that.

But isn't that what he finds refreshing about her? Her honesty? Her candidness? The mature way she stopped flirting and playing games and simply got on with it, once their affair had started? Despite himself, despite Hunter, he's finding that he's becoming more involved in this relationship than he had anticipated. Not that he'd anticipated anything; not that he'd even wanted this to begin. But now that it has, he's beginning to like it more and more.

She's still looking at him, waiting for an answer. The woman in front of him seems entirely without guile, unlike the woman she seems to be when she's with Hunter. She seems so much more natural, so much more *real*. Perhaps it's because there is, or was, all that stuff that Della and Hunter felt they had to prove, to both themselves and to others, to justify the fact that they were together.

But it's early days for Stefano and Della, far too early to start talking about things like love. He says gently, 'You want it all, don't you. I remember when you told me you just wanted *now*.'

'It never works that way, does it. Yes, I suppose I do. Want it all.'

211

Stefano shakes his head. 'Don't ask, OK?' he says softly. 'In a situation like this, it's best not to say anything. Who knows what will happen.' This time he succeeds in pulling her up, adding, 'C'mon, Sadie will be here soon. Out you get, before we end up with a hell of a lot of explaining to do.'

Della, to his surprise, seems content with this. She too is thinking that it's early days yet. If Stefano doesn't love her now he's getting close; he will one day. In the meantime, she has enough for them both.

Chiara begins preparing lunch in Siena: an antipasto of mozzarella, tomatoes and avocado; a first course of creamy mushroom risotto; a second of Florentine beefsteaks. There will be a salad to follow the beefsteaks and then fresh cherries and strawberries – bowlfuls of them.

As Chiara works in her spruced, tidy kitchen, which she repainted this week in a sudden surge of energy and inspiration, she realizes this is the first party of any kind she has given since leaving Hunter.

By the time all the preparations are made – the place brimming with fresh flowers, Verdi on the stereo and the smell of thyme in the kitchen – Chiara has decided that if today's a success she will do it again next weekend, this time for two or three of the new acquaintances she has already made in Siena. There's nothing like an informal meal round a kitchen table to turn acquaintances into friends, she thinks. She is ready for that now, for new friends to blend in with the old ones she's rediscovering.

When Sadie, Marino and Stefano arrive she's relaxed and bubbling. 'Welcome to Siena,' she says as she kisses them each in turn. 'Welcome to my home.'

Stefano stays at his mother's place that night after Sadie and Marino have gone. That evening mother and son go out to walk around the narrow streets, and they stop for a Campari and soda at a bar off the Campo. The night is warm and still, and even the few tourists left on the sloping piazza don't seem to be moving, but stand motionless, indolent. Small groups of younger people sit on the stones themselves, quiet and still, as if they were absorbing history from the cobbles of the square and the medieval buildings surrounding it.

'Should we sit too?' Chiara asks.

Stefano spreads the sweater he's carrying on the stone of the piazza for his mother and sits next to her. 'I love this square,' Chiara says. 'Do you know that my earliest, my very earliest, childhood memory is of the Palio, the horse race? Imagine that for a first memory: the horses thundering round the Campo, the riders bareback, the piazza so crowded that my father had to carry me on his shoulders, not only so I could see, but also so I wouldn't be crushed.'

Chiara talks and Stefano listens as the sky deepens in colour above the Campo, turning from blue to lavender to a deep indigo. From her childhood, Chiara's reminiscences move on to Stefano's boyhood, and he's glad that she speaks of Hunter without anger or vengeance.

'Is everything all right between you two now?' she asks suddenly, turning from the Campo to look at Stefano.

'We haven't exchanged blows, if that's what you mean. Or even many words. Mostly we carry on as if nothing happened.'

'*Grazie a Dio!*' Chiara's exclamation of relief is one of pure joy, and Stefano realizes how worried she has been. She confirms this by saying, 'After last Sunday I was terrified there would be a permanent rift between you and Hunter. It would be dreadful for a father and son to fall out. I'd hate that. Especially if it was because of me.'

Stefano is silent. He thinks again of his mother finding out about him and Della and is appalled.

Chiara goes on, 'I've had enough, Stefano. We all have. Of past hurts, bitterness, recriminations. But

213

thank God it's all over at last. Hardly once, since I left Sadie and Marino in Florence last week, have I thought of the unpleasant events of the past two years. It's the future I think of now. Don't spoil it for me, for all of us, please, by holding grudges against your father.'

Still Stefano is quiet. Chiara says, 'I know, despite what you say, that everything isn't all going smoothly between you and him. How can it, after all that's happened? But promise me, Stefano, that you'll do nothing to make it worse. It's time, now, for us both to begin all over again.'

Chiara turns to search her son's face. He looks so troubled that she's frightened for him. '*Per favore*, Stefano,' she pleads. 'Promise me just this. No more trouble, *d'accordo*?'

Stefano takes a deep breath. 'I promise, all right? Now stop worrying.'

Later that night, alone in his bedroom in his mother's home, Stefano lies on his bed, awake and desperate. He's not so much thinking about what he must do as letting random images explode in his head without any apparent order or logic: Hunter, his father, so far away from him now that all the bridges of Florence wouldn't be enough to close the torrent between them; his mother, Chiara, and her new-found peace; his parents together, a unit, a single entity to Stefano, and then, suddenly, two disparate souls with nothing in common but him; and Della. Brazen and loving, bold and endearingly vulnerable in her love for him, her unashamed desire. Della, with her pale hair flowing like water over a bed of red poppies, or standing at his side watching a crimson sunset splatter the Arno like raindrops of blood.

Stefano knows, of course, what he must do. He allows himself a night of regrets, recriminations and confusion, but as the morning light wafts gently through the thin curtains of his bedroom he feels suddenly relaxed and tranquil. As he falls asleep, at last, he realizes that the decision he has made is not only the right one, it is, in the end, the one he's happy with.

By the time Stefano gets the bus back from Siena the next day and walks from the station to the Piazza Santo Spirito it's four o'clock. He goes into the apartment, changes into some shorts, puts on his old, well-worn trainers and leaves the apartment. He gets his scooter, parked in a side street, and goes up to the Villa Tiglio.

Both cars are there, as he expected. It was too much to hope that Della would be there alone, that he would have plenty of time to tell her quietly and firmly that it was over.

He finds them outside, in the front garden. Della is fiddling with the plants in the terracotta pots, plucking away dead leaves and flowers, and Hunter is tidying up the border of roses.

Hunter sees Stefano first. 'Stef! What are you doing here?' he asks suspiciously.

'Just got back.'

'Well, well, well.' Hunter glares at his son, but is secretly pleased. Stefano had upset him yesterday, making that uncalled-for remark about never playing tennis with him again.

Della's face is radiant with the happiness she feels at this unexpected visit. It's all she can do not to tell Hunter there and then that she's in love with his son.

Hunter, though, is already taking Stefano off. 'I see you've come dressed for tennis. You've decided to stop being so sulky and give me my match, then? Right, I'm keen. I'll go and wash my hands, then find the racquets.'

When he has gone into the house Della says softly, 'I hoped you'd come. I was wondering how I was going to get through the whole day without you.'

Stefano shakes his head warningly. The windows in the house are all open; Hunter could be anywhere inside, the words drifting into his consciousness.

'I don't care,' Della says. 'I don't care if he *does* hear. Maybe we should tell him. Maybe it's time.'

'We'll talk later, not now.'

215

From above them comes a shout from a window, 'Della, have you seen that new pack of tennis balls? I only bought them a couple of days ago. Can you find them for us?'

Della says softly to Stefano, 'We'll do more than talk.' She touches him intimately, brazenly, not even looking up to see if Hunter has left the window. Stefano moves away from her with another shake of the head, but she only smiles defiantly, then goes into the house.

Today, Stefano says to himself. Whatever happens, I must tell her it's over today.

21

Hunter's in good form and wins the first set easily. Yesterday, Saturday, he'd rested most of the day, deciding that some kind of a bug – flu, a touch of gastroenteritis, something like that – was the reason he has felt slightly off-colour over the past week. The rest has done him good. This morning, early, before the day became too hot, he had his usual run and felt fit and exhilarated afterwards. Della, for some reason, didn't join him, preferring a lie-in, she'd said. However, when he returned she was up and about and had even cooked him one of her usual fine lunches, the kind of light lasagne that he's so partial to. He hopes this means she's feeling better. He hopes this means that at last they can resume their sex life.

Della has pulled a deckchair from the back terrace and is sitting in the shade of the lime trees, watching the match. After the first two sets – Hunter won one and Stefano the other – Hunter goes inside to get a towel and Stefano squats on the grass next to her. 'We need to talk,' he says again. 'Can you get away this evening? Can we manage some time alone?'

'Leave it to me. I've got some ideas.' She looks at him oddly. 'I thought you said we *weren't* to talk. You said last time that talking only complicated things.'

Stefano, spotting Hunter bounding towards them, gets up and walks back to the court. Hunter throws a towel at him. 'Here, give yourself a rub-down. You're dripping wet. I noticed you were puffing a bit during that last set, Stef. You're letting yourself get unfit.'

'Stow it, Dad. No lectures.' Stefano picks up his racquet and swings it around.

He has said it off-handedly, unimportantly, but Hunter takes umbrage. 'I'm only telling you for your own good. There's no need to be rude.'

'Oh shit. Here we go.'

Hunter has picked up his racquet and is ready to play, but Stefano's words stop him. 'What do you mean?' he says stiffly.

'Forget it. Whose serve?'

But Hunter's rattled. He's not going to begin the next set feeling rattled. Refusing to answer, he walks to the side and wipes imaginary perspiration from the handle of his racquet with one of the towels he has brought out.

'I think it's yours,' Stefano calls. His voice is easy, friendly even. Hunter is about to be pacified, but catches Della looking at Stefano with open admiration. The bitch, he thinks, as rage fills his veins with the suddenness of a forest fire; she's enjoying this, enjoying hearing Stefano insolently talk back to his father, enjoying the boy's rudeness. It confirms what he said to Sadie and Marino the other night, that Della is jealous of his relationship with the boy and would like to cause a rift between them.

Hunter knows he cannot let Stefano get the upper hand now. Walking slowly towards the centre of the court, towards Stefano, he says, 'I think we should get to the bottom of this, Stef, before we start to play again.'

Stefano looks genuinely confused. 'What are you on about? Get to the bottom of what?'

'Your last remark, that exasperated swear word followed by "Here we go again". What exactly did you mean by that?'

'Jesus. Nothing. Can we just play?'

'When you've explained.'

'Oh, for fuck's sake.' The words are said wearily, with no rancour. Stefano suddenly feels exhausted. All

218

he wants to do is finish the game and find some way to talk privately with Della, to end everything once and for all. He doesn't need or want a scene with Hunter; he knows only too well that there'll be one with Della. 'Get a grip, Dad, OK? Just calm down.'

Out of the corner of his eye Hunter can see a sly smile on Della's face. She's still looking at Stefano, a look that stirs something muddy and dark inside him, something he doesn't yet recognize. 'Shut up, Stefano.' The words bounce around the green grass of the court, the lime trees and the poppies in the corner like a brand-new tennis ball. 'Just shut up and stop being so cheeky, so rude. Remember who you're talking to.'

Stefano stares at him. 'You sad old tosser,' he says, so softly that Hunter cannot quite make the words out.

His next words are lost as Della springs up and stands between them. 'Will you two stop this fucking silliness and finish your game? It's getting on and I'm dying for a drink. Stefano, it *is* your serve, will you get out there and start? Go on, Hunter.' She takes his arm and steers him away from Stefano. 'Relax,' she says in a coaxing whisper. 'Finish the game, don't let him upset you.' She presses his arm encouragingly. 'You've practically beaten him already; you're only playing three sets. One more and the game's over.'

Gently manoeuvring him out of Stefano's hearing she tries to calm him. A row between the two of them, with Stefano leaving abruptly, would spoil all chances of her spending some time alone with him. 'Come on, darling, be a good sport, even though Stefano isn't. He's just lost his cool because he's losing, he only barely won that last set. You know how volatile he is. Let's see you thrash him and then we can all relax with drinks and dinner.'

Hunter succumbs, letting himself be mollified. 'Right, Stef. Your serve. Let's see how long it'll take me to beat you. Della, are you timing this?'

*　　*　　*

It takes a long time for Stefano to win the match, but only because Hunter argues over every call, finally asking Della to umpire, and then disputing whenever she calls against him. Often he is so insistent, so enraged, that they give him the benefit of the doubt.

Stefano, who played the first set carelessly, wanting only for the game to be over so that he and Della can be alone, now begins to concentrate. It has become necessary to beat Hunter. It has become necessary to win.

When the match is nearly over, when Stefano is ahead by two games, Hunter stops play. 'Sorry, I've broken a string. I'll have to run inside to get my other racquet; I didn't bring it out with me.' He rushes off towards the house even as he says this.

Stefano says to Della. 'I didn't notice a broken string.'

Della shrugs. 'I don't know. I wasn't watching him, I was watching you. I hope you thrash him.'

'Oh I will. I will.' His voice is grim.

In the house Hunter changes racquets, hiding the one he has just been using in the cupboard, so Della won't find it and notice there's nothing wrong with it. He needs this respite to regain his concentration. A few moments away from the court will break Stefano's sudden lucky winning streak. There's no way his son can possibly win; Hunter is not only a far better player, he's also fitter.

Before Hunter goes back outside he makes himself take several deep breaths to centre himself again. 'Sorry about that,' he says breezily as he returns to the court.

It's Hunter's serve. 'Ace,' he shouts, at the same time as Della's and Stefano's: 'Out.'

'It was not bloody out.'

'Dad, it was.'

'I saw it; I watched it.'

'So did I,' Della says. 'It was out, Hunter. I'm sure of it.'

'I can't believe you're saying that.'

'Hunter—'

'All right, all right! But you keep out of it from now on, Della. Stef and I can call the shots, like we'd do if you weren't here.'

'Listen, Hunter, it was your idea for me to umpire and be linesman. Don't start getting stroppy with me.'

Stefano says, 'Can we get on with the game, please?'

Hunter serves again; this time it's good, fast and in the corner, but Stefano returns it with an easy back-hand. There's a short rally before Stefano wins the point with a low stroke into the back of the court, which Hunter cannot reach, though he nearly falls over trying.

'Love, fifteen,' Della says. Hunter glares at her. Then he serves a double fault.

'See what you did?' he explodes at her. 'I told you to keep quiet. How can I concentrate when you keep babbling?'

Della presses her lips together. She's not going to say anything and blow her chances of meeting Stefano later.

Stefano says quietly, 'Love, thirty.'

'I know, I know, for fuck's sake.' Hunter turns his back on Stefano and tries to compose himself.

The next rally's short. Hunter serves well, but Stefano returns it easily and hard, so that Hunter puts it in the net.

Hunter takes his time before the next serve. He dries his racquet, takes a drink of water and does a few squats to loosen his legs. He's waiting for Stefano or Della to rush him, then he'll lay into them. Between the two of them they've completely put him off his game.

But the other two are silent, waiting. No-one speaks. A bird sings in the lime trees.

Finally Hunter, after what seems like hours, serves.

The rally is a long one, long and fierce. Della hears the men's grunts, the clump of the ball on the court, and remembers the first time she saw Stefano. There's still a lingering scent of lime blossom in the air.

And then it's over. Stefano wins the point and breaks Hunter's serve with a spectacular return just inside the corner lines. Della cannot help it; she bursts into applause.

Hunter's head explodes in a fireworks of rage. 'Damn you, Della, try to control yourself! I know you wanted Stefano to win; I know you wanted to see my own son humiliate me, but I wish you wouldn't be so bloody obvious about it. Don't think I'm unaware of what you're up to.'

'Hunter, what are you on about?'

'"Hunter, what are you on about?"' Hunter mimics Della's words with nasty precision. 'I'll tell what I'm on about, as if you don't know already.'

'Stop talking in circles, Hunter. Just spit it out and get it over with.'

'You're jealous, Della, that's what. You're fucking jealous of me and Stefano, of our relationship. The fact that I have a son and you don't.'

'Dad, just leave it.' Stefano's the only one not shouting, but his voice is tight and controlled with the effort of preventing himself either telling Hunter exactly what he thinks of him or walking away from the Villa Tiglio and never seeing him again. The only thing that stops him is the promise he made to Chiara. He doesn't want to be the one to spoil the new tranquillity she has found.

But Della's angry now. Hunter's remark about her being jealous of the fact that he has a son and she doesn't is so off the mark she cannot let it go. 'Hunter, you are totally clueless. If I wanted children, I'd have had them years ago. God, you're pathetic, the things you come up with.'

'Don't you dare talk to me like that! What do you know about children? What do you know about me and Stefano? I've been watching you, Della. Watching you closely. I've seen you trying to pry me away from my son. I know how you'd like nothing better than to get him out of the Villa Tiglio so you can have me to yourself again, like it used to be.'

Della stares at him and begins to laugh. She laughs loudly, raucously. 'That is so outrageous,' she gasps. 'If you only knew how outrageous—' She stops with a cry as Hunter slaps her hard across the face.

The moment elongates, becomes two moments, three. It's hard to know who of the three is the most shocked. Then Stefano moves, lunges for Hunter. But Della sees him and stops him with a shove, pushing Hunter too, who steps on a tennis ball and falls, sprawling, onto the grass.

'Get up,' Stefano says. 'Get up.'

Hunter holds his chest, waiting for the searing pain that has come twice before, but just when he could use it as an excuse to stay where he is, to howl in agony and despair, it doesn't come. 'Get up, Hunter,' Stefano says again. Hunter notes that it's the first time his son has called him anything but Dad.

But now Della's pulling and tugging at Stefano. 'Leave him. I don't want to have anything to do with him, ever again. Let's go. I want to get away, right now.'

Hunter is kneeling now, but he doesn't get up; Stefano still has both hands clenched into tight fists. The enormity of what he has done roars in Hunter's eardrums and his eyes seem to fill with blood. But the blood is not on him. What fills his sight is Della's blood, trickling slowly down the side of her mouth, which is twisted in pain and disbelief. 'No, please, Della, don't go,' Hunter gasps. 'I'm sorry, I . . . I shouldn't have done that. Don't go.'

Della backs away from him, as if from a serial killer. Her eyes have darkened with shock. 'Do you think I could stay with a man, any man, who hit me? I hope I never set eyes on you again.' She turns and runs towards the house.

Hunter slumps down with a groan. Stefano says, 'I think I won, don't you, Hunter? I think the game is over.' Then he turns and follows Della into the house.

She's throwing things in a suitcase when he finds her, upstairs in the bedroom. Angry tears are coursing down her face, burning her left cheek, which is a bright red, as bright as the poppies. 'The bastard. The bastard *hit* me, Stefano.'

'I know, I should've hit *him*.'

The sound of a car starting stops their conversation. Della goes to the window. 'It's Hunter, he's driving away somewhere. Thank God.' She sits on the bed, spent.

Stefano goes to her and touches the bruise forming on her cheekbone. 'Christ, he's a shit. That's a nasty cut.' He takes a tissue from the bedside table, dampens it in a glass of water by the bed and begins wiping the drying blood from her face.

'And for no reason at all, either, except that he was losing at tennis.'

'There is a reason, Della. We both know that.'

'*He* doesn't know. You heard him, he thinks I'm jealous of you and him.' Della gets up again and continues her packing.

Stefano says, 'What are you doing? Where are you planning to go?'

She looks at him, bewildered. 'Why, I'm going with you. Where else?'

'Della, you can't. I'm sharing with Marco, you know that. It's not as if I've got a place of my own. If I did you'd be welcome to stay there, at least for a while, at least until you could find your own place. That is if you're determined to leave him.'

'What do you mean, for a while?'

'I don't blame you,' Stefano says gently, 'for wanting to go. He shouldn't have hit you like that, even if he knew. What about Sadie and Marino? Can you stay with them?'

Della begins to shake. She can feel her body vibrating, like the earth before a quake. 'Stefano, what are

224

you saying? I want to stay with you, be with you. We can stay at a hotel tonight, for longer, a few days, a week, more even, until we can find somewhere to live together. I've got money saved – quite a bit now, enough to rent a nice apartment. I could even buy a flat. Not just for me, for both of us—' She stops as she looks at his face.

'I'm sorry, Della. It's just not on. *We're* not on. I can't hack it any more, it's no good. That's what I came up here to talk to you about.'

'But it's OK now; it's out in the open. Or rather it can be, now that I'm leaving Hunter. You're free, and now I'm free.'

The eager hope in her face saddens Stefano and he has to look away. 'No, Della,' he says quietly. 'It won't work.'

'It *will* work. I'll make it work, you'll see.'

'I don't want it, Della. Don't make this harder. I was up all night thinking about it, about us. It shouldn't have happened, but it did, and it's time to get out now before anyone finds out. We're both fucking lucky not to have hurt anyone else by it.'

Both Della's cheeks are like poppies now. Stefano knows this second blow, the one from him, has wounded her far more deeply than anything Hunter has done. 'I'm sorry,' he says again. 'While it lasted I wanted it as much as you did. But it couldn't last, Della. I tried to warn you, tried not to make promises and give you false hopes. You must have known.'

Like Hunter falling onto the grass by the tennis court, Della collapses onto the bed, face down, and begins to sob. Stefano goes to her. 'Don't, please. Come on, I'll help you pack. I'll drive you wherever you want – Sadie's, or anywhere. To a hotel if you like. I can't take you to my place: Bettina's there tonight and it would be awkward for you.'

Della isn't responding; she's making muffled kitten-like sounds into the pillow. They are beginning to wrench Stefano apart. He doesn't love her, he knows that now, but for a moment he wishes he could.

'Please get up,' he says, lying down beside her and stroking her streaky hair. 'Look, if you can't face Sadie or a hotel, you can have my room tonight. I'll sleep on the sofa. It just means explaining to Bettina and Marco that you've left Hunter. I don't know if you're ready to do that yet.'

He turns Della over to look at her face and try to calm her. She reaches for him and pulls him down to her. 'I don't care what I do, where you take me tonight. Just hold me, OK? Stay with me one more time, like this, Stefano. Please, please?' She's pressing up against him, running her warm hands over his back and buttocks, opening herself up to him for the last time. There's a tiny smudge of fresh blood in the corner of her mouth, where the cut has reopened. Moved, Stefano kisses it, then kisses her mouth, again and again, and then he's making love to her, quickly, as she seems to want, as she's urging him to.

But not quickly enough. They haven't quite finished when the bedroom door opens and Hunter walks in.

22

Hunter stands immobile in the bedroom doorway. He tries to shout, to rage, but the words, instead of bursting forth, drip like icicles from the roof of his mouth and stay there. He tries to move so he can tear into Stefano, rip him away from Della, but his legs are incapable of action.

And so he stares. In a few seconds, which to Hunter is timelessness itself, it's over. He hears Della's cries and sees Stefano slump weakly over her, spent. In a moment of illumination he sees defeat looming in a game he didn't know was being played, and hatred unlocks his legs as he takes a step towards them.

But Della hears something: a click, a gasp. Lifting her head she sees Hunter and pushes Stefano up, crying out loudly. Hunter is on the bed, his hands around Stefano's throat, but Stefano hurls him away with such strength that the older man falls off the bed and lands, sprawled, on the soft, cream carpet on the marble floor. Della goes to him and tries to turn his limp, prostrate body to see if he's all right, and as she does Hunter grabs her arm with one hand and starts hitting her with the other. Stefano cries out and pulls him away and hits him soundly in the face. Hunter falls again and rolls towards the door, his body curled away from the other two in a foetal position.

For a few seconds there's complete silence. A soft wind which began earlier is the only noise, but it sounds like a typhoon in the heavy silence of the villa. Then the phut-phut of a motorbike coming up the Via San Leonardo filters through the open window and echoes away into the distance.

Still no-one speaks. No-one has spoken since Hunter came in; the room had been filled with cries and groans and inarticulate shouts, but no words have been spoken. Hunter lies panting and impotent by the door. When the sound of the motorbike dies away into the darkening evening his gasping breath seems loud, overdone in the quiet bedroom.

Della, shaking, sits back on the bed and begins to cry silent tears of terror and relief. Stefano goes to her to see if she's all right, but keeps looking at Hunter tensely, waiting to see what he'll do next.

Hunter pulls himself up by the brass doorknob. His jaw is bruised and cut and his eye is beginning to swell, but otherwise he's intact. He looks at Stefano with hatred. 'Well, you win, Stef,' he says, his voice bruised too.

'This wasn't a game, Hunter. Life isn't about winning all the time.'

'Nevertheless you did.'

'You forced me to. You were so big on winning, even with me, with your own son. Whatever I did you made sure I knew that you did it better. When I was a kid it was basketball, or tennis, or whatever game I tried to have a go at. When I grew up it was women. You didn't care whose life you fucked up – mine, your wife's – so long as you could prove that you were more of a man than I was.'

Hunter makes a noise that sounds like a snarl. He had been leaning against the bedroom door, but now he stands up straight. 'So we're back to Chiara again, are we? Still angry over that, eh, Stef? Everything goes back to her, to your mother. Why didn't you screw her instead of Della? Then you'd have wrecked only yours and her lives, instead of mine and Della's.'

'I'll kill you, Hunter,' Stefano shouts as he lunges across the room. But Hunter is out of the door before Stefano can get to him, running down the stairs and out of the house. Stefano, following, can't quite catch him. This is Hunter's home; he knows every step, every obstacle, every short cut. The house is quite dark now, no lights have been switched on, and Stefano stumbles over a chair Hunter has hurled from the corridor into the path of the stairs. By the time Stefano has righted himself and followed Hunter outside he can hear the car start and see the headlights as Hunter bolts down the drive and through the open gate.

Hunter drives recklessly for half an hour before he becomes sane again. Not wholly sane, though. When he realizes that he's on the road to Siena he drives on, instead of turning back.

Chiara is reading *La Repubblica* by the light of a soft lamp, a Victorian one she'd found in a junk shop and tenderly restored. The cherrywood base warms the whole room with its polished gleam. A vase of lilies sits on an applewood table. As she reads the Sunday newspaper she is also listening to music: Puccini.

The ring of the doorbell surprises her; it's eleven o'clock. Panic circles her throat and tightens in on it. Stefano? An accident?

When she sees Hunter standing in the door, still in his tennis shorts, one eye swelling and beginning to close, all she can think of is that there has been some dreadful accident, and Hunter has come to tell her that Stefano is dead, dying. She cries, '*Dio, oh Dio! Stefano? Che è successo?*' Her babble of Italian punctures the quiet night like the rattle of a machine-gun.

Hunter thinks fleetingly of hitting her too, but his voltage of rage has weakened. 'Can I come in?'

'Stefano? Where is he? What has happened to him?'

'Let's go inside. I'll tell you when we're inside.'

He follows her through the narrow hallway into the living room. 'Tell me,' she says, her mouth wobbling and trembling as she bites her lips, pressing them together, then she gives up and lets them quiver. He wants to slap her, to stop that uncontrollable mouth.

He would like to tell her Stefano is dead, so that he can take her in his arms, console her and be strong as she collapses in grief and helplessness. He says harshly, 'Always Stefano, isn't it. Always the Italian mother, worried about *him*, instead of being concerned about me. It was always like that, from the day he was born. He always came first with you.'

Chiara cries, 'Hunter, *per favore*, don't torment me, tell me—'

'He's fine, for heaven's sake! Stop looking like that!'

'Then . . . what's happened? Why are you here? What *is* it? What has happened to your face?'

Hunter begins walking around the room, looking at the paintings on the wall, picking up a ceramic vase and putting it down again. 'Nice place, this. You've done a lot to it since your sister left; it looks different from the way it did when she lived here. How is she, by the way? Still in California?' He sits in the armchair where Chiara had been reading the paper.

'*Gesù, Maria*, what is this, Hunter? A social call? What are you up to, coming here like this? Either tell me or get out.'

'Temper, temper. I see your Italian tendency towards hysteria hasn't mellowed with age. And speaking of age, you're looking well, Chiara. I would have told you last Sunday if I'd had the chance.'

Chiara looks at him carefully. The realization that Hunter's not quite right in the head filters through her anger at him, her relief that this has nothing to do with Stefano. 'You've been hurt,' she says. 'Your face is a mess; it's swollen terribly. I'll get some water, a cloth.'

'No, Chiara. You won't. You'll stay here and look at my face. See the blood on it.'

'Hunter . . . I don't understand.' Chiara is beginning to feel afraid again, but not for Stefano this time. She doesn't want to be alone in the house with Hunter. 'Let me get some things, I'll wash it off for you.' She wants to get to the kitchen, to use the phone there to call one of her nearby friends.

'Stay, Chiara.' His voice is low, ominous. 'Look at me. See the blood?'

She nods.

'Do you know who put it there? Your precious son, that's who. Stefano. He did this to me.'

Chiara sucks in a breath of air, gasping, as she struggles with the shock of what Hunter has said. So that's what happened, she thinks. Stefano, still brooding about last Sunday, still angry at his father for so many things, finally took a swipe at him, despite his promise to let it be.

'He shouldn't have done it,' she says when her breathing is even again. 'It was wrong of him.'

'Oh, you think so? You think your precious son has done something wrong?' Hunter leans forward in his chair. His opal eyes glint in the lamplight. 'Well, listen to this, Chiara. Do you know why he hit me? Why he tried to kill *me*? His father? Because I found him in bed with Della.'

Chiara stares at him. Hunter shouts, 'Oh, for fuck's sake, don't you understand? Do you want me to spell it out for you? He was screwing her, Chiara. He was screwing his own mother.'

Chiara's lips move slowly. She seems to have no control over them. 'Della is not his mother.'

'She's the woman I live with, and I'm his father. Bloody hell, Chiara, I'm his *father*.' Hunter stands up and smashes the wall with his fist. A small painting near his hand falls off, the glass breaking on the parquet floor. 'I saw them. They were in the bedroom at the villa. *My* bedroom; mine and Della's. The big one, remember? It was yours too once, Chiara, yours and mine. Remember the balcony, how we used to stand in the summer evenings watching the sun rolling down the hills, blood-red behind the poplar trees? The sky looked like fire, we used to say, threatening to burn up the city, but we felt so safe in our cool haven, remember?' He's murmuring softly now, his rage seemingly forgotten, standing in front of her, too near. Chiara feels

231

the stickiness of his fingers on the soft spot between her neck and shoulders.

She moves away quickly and tries to leave the room, but his arm stops her. His voice toughens. 'Listen, Chiara, or I'll make you listen. He was screwing her on my bed, on *our* bed. Your son, *our* son. He's a monster, Chiara. You've raised a monster.'

She pulls away from him and falls onto the sofa behind her. She cannot talk, cannot think. Whatever Stefano has done it's not as monstrous as Hunter himself, raging over her, abusing her with words, terrifying her with his madness.

'Go away,' she whispers. 'Please.'

He's at her side, wrapping his rope-like arms around her, tightly, tighter. 'I don't want to go. I can't go. I want you, Chiara. I should never have left you. You're my wife, you belong to me. Stefano can have Della; she's a slut, worthless. You're the only one I've ever truly loved.'

He doesn't even notice Chiara's struggles and cries as he kisses and caresses her. His arms tighten around her like cords, their angles and sinews pressing against her, hurting her. '*Lasciami!* Hunter, stop, let me go!' But her voice is muffled against the sharp, hard pressure of his body as he pushes himself down on her.

He takes no notice of her, but carries on talking, crooning to her, his words becoming soft again, at odds with what his body is doing. 'I'll take you back to the villa tonight. You can tell them both to go, that you've come back. We'll ban them from the house and the school and never see them again. It will be just like it was before, you and me. Just like the old days, Chiara.'

He has pinned her down on the sofa with one hand, covering her mouth with the other. She can feel him trying to thrust through her clothes, trying to push away her skirt with his knees. She feels his frustration as he tries to free himself and her from their few summer garments.

'No,' she cries as his hand slips from her mouth and she tries to push free of him.

'Oh yes, Chiara. Remember how it was? Like this, remember? No, don't fight me, Chiara, you know you want—'

But he doesn't finish. His words break with a shrill cry, which flies around the room like shards of glass, and his tensed body slackens, falling on her.

For a moment she doesn't move. She is frightened that this inanimate form on top of her will come to life again, that this is some kind of sick game Hunter is playing with her. She closes her eyes, playing dead herself, until his light weight, made heavy by his limpness, begins to make breathing difficult. She eases herself out from under him and he moans, moving his hand to his chest. 'Help me,' he whispers. 'Help me.' His eyes close and he is still.

23

Bettina knows something is wrong the minute she turns into the gates of the Villa Tiglio the next morning.

She's early; it's only eight o'clock, but she's worried about Stefano. He didn't come home to the apartment last night, though she and Marco knew he was back in Florence after his weekend in Siena with Chiara. There had been a scrawled note for them saying that he had to go out for a while but would meet them later that night as planned, to go for an hour or two to the new jazz club Marco wanted to try. Stefano had not shown up, so they went on without him, thinking he'd join them there. When they'd returned there was still no Stefano, nor was there any sign of him this morning.

It's not like Stefano to cancel plans without an explanation. It's also not like him to stay out all night, unless he's at his mother's place in Siena. Marco had said that Bettina worried too much, that Stefano had probably found a girl of his own at last, and just as well too, maybe he would stop mooning over Bettina. He had said this with a smile, though. He was fond of Stefano too, and more worried than he'd let on. He couldn't believe that Stefano would stay at some girl's place all evening and all night without at least a brief phone call of explanation.

When Bettina sees Stefano's scooter she's relieved, but is perplexed to see both Hunter's and Della's cars gone. Sometimes they are out running when she arrives early, but they're never out in their cars.

Her relief turns to unease when she walks through the unlocked front door and sees a chair turned over at the foot of the stairs. '*Stefano? Dove sei?*' She calls out to him loudly, telling herself he must be around somewhere, but her words bring no response.

The villa seems hollow, though the perfume of lime and jasmine tries to fill the vacuum. Before Bettina even begins to look methodically in each office and classroom, the kitchens and bathrooms downstairs, she knows the place is empty.

The phone in the office rings but by the time Bettina, who by now is in one of the far classrooms trying to find Hunter or Della, gets to it, it has stopped. She goes into the corridor, picks up the fallen chair and sets it in its proper place against the wall. She doesn't know what to do next; she suddenly doesn't want to be here.

The front door opens and Bettina cries out involuntarily. '*Madonna*, Sadie, I didn't hear your car come in. You frightened me.'

'I just phoned the apartment and talked to Marco. He said you'd already left. Is Stefano here?'

'No, though his Vespa is. I've looked everywhere. Not upstairs, of course. But he wouldn't be there.'

Sadie says, 'So you haven't heard? Chiara hasn't phoned?'

'The phone was ringing earlier, but it stopped before I got there. Heard what?'

'Is Della here?'

'Not unless she's still upstairs asleep; I've looked everywhere else. But her car's gone and so is Hunter's. Sadie, what's happened?'

'First let me make sure they're not upstairs. Make us some coffee, there's a dear, *per favore*. I've been up most of the night and I'm whacked. Then I'll tell you everything.'

Bettina makes coffee while Sadie searches upstairs. She sees the rumpled bed, Della's clothes strewn on chairs and the unmade bed, the wardrobe door open and the contents half gone. An overhead light still glows, though it has been light for hours. Sadie shuts it off and goes back downstairs.

Bettina meets her in the corridor with the coffee, which they take into Hunter's empty office so they can see if anyone comes in the front door. Sadie says, 'Hunter's in the hospital. He had a heart attack last night, but he's all right. The doctors say he'll recover.'

'Poor Hunter! So that's where Della must be. I couldn't think where her car was gone at this time of the morning.'

'No, Della's not at the hospital. Chiara is. He's at the hospital in Siena.'

'I don't understand. Why in Siena? And where's Della?'

'No-one can find her. Or Stefano. Chiara has been trying to find them all night. She couldn't get an answer either here at the villa or at Marco's apartment.'

'We were out quite late, and Marco turns the ringer on the phone off when we go to bed. He hates to be woken by any calls.'

'Well, I talked to him just now. He said Stefano didn't come home.'

'I know. We've been worried about him.'

Sadie drinks her coffee in one swallow. 'Wonderful, Bettina. I needed that.'

Bettina hasn't touched her own coffee. 'There's something more, Sadie. Something you're not telling me. Why is Hunter in Siena? Why is Chiara with him, instead of Della? And where's Stefano?'

Sadie runs a hand through her hair. She was too flustered this morning to run a comb through the frizz of orange and it's running riot, straining straight upwards from her scalp. 'God knows where Stefano and Della are. Probably ran off somewhere together. Hunter found them last night in bed together.'

Bettina stares. Her purple lips open and shut like an exotic tropical fish as she gropes for words. '*Santa Madonna. Non ci credo.*'

'It's true. Chiara told me. Hunter came to her in quite a state, half mad, raging. From what I gather, he wasn't very pleasant to her.' Sadie doesn't add the details.

236

Chiara, in her dazed, shocked state, has told Sadie everything, but there are some things Sadie will repeat only to Marino.

'Della and Stefano? I can't believe it,' Bettina says again.

'Well, they're both gone. Stefano never came home, and there are clothes strewn all over the bedroom upstairs, as if Della packed in a hurry. They've obviously gone away together. Goodness knows what we're going to tell the students. I managed to find a supply teacher for Hunter's classes; she should be here soon. I'm waiting to hear from someone else to see if he can take Della's classes. I'll have to cover the rest by putting them in with my class.'

Bettina's shaking her head in disbelief. 'Stefano wouldn't go off with that woman. It's just not possible.'

They are both startled by the sound of someone coming in the wide front door. Sadie and Bettina stand up and go into the hallway. 'Stefano!' Bettina cries.

He looks rough. His hair is matted and, though his face is washed, small bruises are growing like mushrooms under his skin. He hasn't shaved and his clothes are still the tennis shorts and T-shirt of yesterday. 'Where's Hunter?' he asks brusquely. 'I need to see him, right away.'

Stefano has been up all night with Della, in a family-run *pensione* in Impruneta. She chose to go there because she vaguely knows the owners and knows they have apartments to let. Luckily one will be free at the weekend, so Della has said she will have it. In the meantime, she has a small single room in the hotel itself.

Stefano stayed with her all night because he was afraid to leave her, afraid that she would either harm herself or make a scene in front of the *padrone* and his wife. There were enough explanations to make anyway, with Della and Stefano looking the way they did, as if they'd both come out of a brawl. But finally they'd got past that and were left alone at last in Della's room.

She had cried, then raged, then cried again. She'd tried to persuade Stefano to at least give it a try and move in with her for a time; she'd tried to convince him that, now that Hunter knew, there was no reason to stop the affair. It took all night for Stefano to make her realize, as kindly as he could, that it was over.

When the sky began to lighten at five this morning, Stefano disentangled himself from Della's arms and began to walk quietly towards the door. He had thought she was asleep, that she'd finally fallen into an exhausted slumber as he held her while her last tears fell and dried. But as he turned to look at her one more time, her eyes opened. 'You're going?' she'd said, almost as if she were asking him whether he was going out for a pint of milk or the morning's newspapers.

But he knew what she meant. 'Yes. I'm going now.'

'It was good, though, Stefano. Wasn't it? For a time, wasn't it good?' Her voice was hoarse, pitiful, resigned.

He'd looked at her dishevelled hair and blotchy, swollen face, bruised from Hunter's blows; the crumpled hotel bed, the tawdriness of it all. Then he'd shut his eyes for a moment, blotting it out. He'd let himself think of the Villa Tiglio, of the scent of the lime trees, of making love to Della in their shade, eagerly and intensely, his passion matching hers, at least momentarily, at least for a time.

'Yes,' he'd answered her. 'It was good, Della.'

He didn't know whether she'd heard him or not, for by then she had closed her eyes again so as not to see him go.

He'd had to wait for the first bus from Impruneta to Florence. When it came he sat in the back, staring out at the grapevines as the bus began the climb up through the vineyards. Everything outside the bus seemed clean, fresh and flagrant with colour: the red of the poppies in the meadows and on the verges; the deep green of the cyprus trees; the silver of the olive leaves. It made him feel old and sick and dirty.

He wanted a shower, a shave, a change of clothes.

When the bus stopped at Due Strade he had got off and walked quickly down the Via del Gelsomino to the school. Now, here in the villa for the last time, he's in a hurry to see Hunter, face him as he knows he must, before he can wash the night away. He doesn't know what they'll say to each other, but it has to be done. Then he will take his bike and go home to the Piazza Santo Spirito and sleep. He has no illusions that Hunter will want him to teach today, or ever again. That at least is a relief. He would like nothing better than to never see the Villa Tiglio again. Later there will be Chiara, but he can't think about that now.

He says again, 'Where's Hunter?' Bettina says nothing, just stares. She cannot believe this is Stefano – sweet Stefano. She looks at him as if he has turned into a werewolf.

Sadie says, 'Where's Della? I thought she was with you.'

'Hunter told you? He didn't waste any time. No, she's not with me; she's staying at a hotel. On her own. I've come to collect my scooter and see Hunter. Then I'm going back to the apartment.'

He sounds so weary, so full of regret and sadness, that Sadie would like to put her arms round him, comfort him as she would comfort Marco. Instead she says gently, 'Hunter's in hospital, but it's OK, he's fine. He had a coronary, but not a huge one. The doctors say he'll be out and about in no time.'

'*Gesù.*' Stefano slumps into an empty office chair and puts his face in his hands. Bettina goes to him and cradles him in her arms, as Sadie wanted to do.

'Should I go and see him?' he asks Sadie when at last he lifts his head. There are streaks on his face where tears have washed through the dirt on his face.

'Maybe not. Not yet, anyway. He's still . . . upset about last night. But don't worry, he's really not in any danger. He doesn't want to see Della either, but she

239

should know about it. Chiara has been trying to find you both.'

'My mother?' Stefano's head drops in his hands again. 'Oh Christ.' His voice is muffled and broken. 'Who told her? About . . . about me and Della.'

Bettina and Sadie exchange a look of compassion. It's Sadie who says, 'Hunter did, Stefano. He went to Siena to tell her. It was in her house that he had the attack.'

Stefano struggles for a moment with more tears, which are threatening to completely undo him. Then he regains control and gets up slowly. His face is pale under the night's black stubble. 'I'd better go back to Della and tell her about Hunter.' He doesn't want to go back there. He doesn't know how he can face anything more.

Sadie says, 'No, tell me where she is and I'll go. She might need me, as a female friend. I've got my car, I can drive out there right now. Bettina can brief the supply teacher.'

Sadie gives Stefano a motherly, affectionate shove. 'Don't just stand there looking dozy, lad, we need you here. No time now to mope about all this. You go home, shower and quickly change, then come back before the students arrive. Go on, you can just about make it.'

Stefano stares at her as if she were off her head. 'Sadie, I can't. Not today.'

'I need you, Stefano. I can't run this school single-handedly. We've got to finish this one week; the students have paid for a four-week course. We'll worry about next week – the next session – later.'

'But Della? You don't think . . .?'

'I don't think you should be the one to tell her about Hunter. I'll handle it. I'll be back as soon as I can. Bettina, tell the students that Hunter is in hospital, but classes will go on as usual. And make some excuses for Della's absence – anything, I don't care what you say.' As she talks there's the sound of a car coming up the drive. 'That will be the supply teacher.' She gives Stefano another small shove. 'Go on. You can't sleep now, my boy. But you're young, you'll survive.'

It doesn't take Sadie long to drive to Impruneta. Stefano has told her Della's room number, so she strides right upstairs and bangs on the door. It seems to take a long time for Della to answer the door.

At last she does. She doesn't seem surprised to see Sadie, but Sadie is taken back by the bruises on Della's face, her swollen eyes and cheeks. 'Good grief, you look a complete disaster area,' she says, then puts her arms round Della as the other woman crumples into them gratefully.

First Sadie lets Della cry a bit and tell her about Stefano. Sadie listens, murmurs inadequacies, does all the things women do for each other at times like these. Then, after Della has calmed down, Sadie tells her about Hunter.

For a moment, there's no reaction from Della, she merely looks down at the floor, not moving or speaking. Then she lifts her head and says dully, 'I suppose I should be grateful that he isn't dead. I've got enough guilt to carry around regarding Chiara, any more would have just about finished me off.'

'That's a bit hard, isn't it?'

But Della's face does not look hard. It looks soft, bruised, swollen and vulnerable. She says, 'You weren't there, Sadie. You didn't see him last night. He tried to kill us, both of us. And don't say we deserved it. Nobody deserves that.'

'No.'

'Anyway, in the end it wasn't about me and his son. It was really all about Hunter. He first hit me before he found out about me and Stefano, you know. He hit me because he was losing, because he lost the tennis match.' She begins to laugh, and her laughter is, to Sadie, even sadder than her tears. 'All this happened because Hunter is such a fucking awful loser.'

Sadie stands up, 'I'd better go,' she says. 'I've got a class waiting.'

Della stands up too. 'I can't come back, Sadie. To the villa, to the job. I can't face it. Not just today, not ever.'

'I didn't for a minute expect you to, nor does anyone else. We'll cope; it's nearly the end of term.'

Della nods. 'About Hunter . . .'

'Yes?'

'Do I need to go and see him in hospital?'

'On the contrary,' Sadie says, 'he has asked Chiara to keep you away. You and Stefano.'

'Thank God for that.'

'I'll come back tonight, see how you're getting on. That's if you want me to.'

Della looks at her with vacant eyes. 'Thanks. I would, yes.'

When Sadie turns at the door to say goodbye Della is huddled once again on the bed, her face to the wall.

24

Chiara visits Hunter in hospital because he won't see anyone else. Sometimes she horrifies herself by wishing the attack had killed him. She hasn't forgotten the events before he was taken to hospital, though he seems to have. Or rather, he has reinvented that night to suit himself, believing that he and Chiara had been on the point of a reunion when he'd been knocked down by his attack.

Sadie and Stefano between them, with the help of two supply teachers, finish the week at the school, but have postponed the new courses starting the following Monday. They blame Hunter's health as Bettina returns deposits and writes letters of explanations. Bettina has already had an interview for another job and Sadie has decided that she'll take the summer off and start thinking about the wedding in the autumn. She'll wait until that is over before looking for another teaching job.

Chiara has one last ghost to exorcize. When everyone, both students and staff, have gone, but before Hunter has returned from hospital, she comes to the Villa Tiglio. Stefano is expecting her. He seems to be in charge of the place somehow, unlocking it for the students and staff first thing in the morning, locking it at night. He doesn't stay overnight, though. He would rather go back and stay in the apartment with Marco, even though the villa is empty.

Stefano meets Chiara outside, under the lime trees. 'They still smell as sweet,' she says as she kisses his cheeks. 'The lime trees. Some things don't change.'

The evening's bright and clear, looking as if the day will last for ever and not succumb to night. Swifts fly about the garden, catching insects. It all looks perfectly innocent.

'Is it strange?' Stefano asks. 'To be back here, after all that's happened?'

'*Sì, molto*. But it's comforting somehow. It is so *ordinary*. Beautiful, yes, but not more beautiful than so many other places in Italy. After I left here, the villa and the grounds became some magic place in my head, some kind of paradise from which I was excluded for ever. I needed to come back one more time to see it for myself.'

'You belong here, don't you. You always did, more than *he* did.' Stefano puts his arm lightly around her shoulders. 'When I'm rich, *Mamma*, I'll buy it from Hunter and give it to you.'

Chiara smiles mischievously as they walk round the back and look out over the hills. 'If I wanted the Villa Tiglio I could have it, Stefano. I don't need you to buy it for me, though I appreciate the offer.'

'What do you mean?'

'Hunter wants me to come back. For good. He wants to marry me again.'

Stefano turns away so she doesn't see his face. But she says, 'Oh, don't worry, I wouldn't think of it.' She doesn't say the rest: that she hopes she'll never set eyes on Hunter again after he leaves the hospital.

'But . . . why does he want you back now? Because Della left him? Because of me and Della?'

Stefano's aware that his questions sound insensitive. 'Sorry, it's none of my business.'

'He's afraid of being alone, I suppose, with Della gone.' They are quiet for a moment, watching the light of day slowly begin to bleach out the colour of the hills, the trees and the vineyards. Chiara says, 'It's none of my business, either, but do you want to tell me about it? You and Della? Do you still see her?'

244

Stefano doesn't want to talk about it, but feels he owes his mother at least this. 'No, not since that night. She's OK, Sadie's keeping an eye on her. She seems to be coping.'

'What about you? Are you coping?'

'I didn't love her, if that's what you're getting at. Or even mean to . . . to get involved. But I did, and I'm not too proud of myself for it.'

'It's done, Stefano. Don't punish yourself any more.'

He's grateful to his mother for the way she has taken all this. He says, 'It wasn't about Della; it was about my father.'

But Chiara knows. She knows too not to push it, and to Stefano's great relief she changes the subject.

Hunter comes home to the Villa Tiglio, now empty of students and teachers. For a week or so he has a paid nurse and then a live-in housekeeper to do the heavy chores he's not yet capable of. Bettina stays on for another week to wind up the paperwork.

Hunter says that he'll start the school up again, but when, he can't envisage. He has lost all his staff, except possibly Sadie, who might be persuaded to come back in the autumn. The students have found other language schools, of course. But he can build it all up again, in good time. For the moment, to keep himself in funds, he has ordered beds for the classrooms down-stairs and will be renting them out as rooms to tourists and students. Accommodation in Florence is always sought after. It will only be a temporary measure, of course, until he can find the energy to start all over again. Which he will, naturally; but right now he seems to want nothing more than to sleep on the ter-race in the new full-length garden recliner he bought when he came home from the hospital.

Della comes to the Villa Tiglio late one sultry after-noon, weeks later. It's summer now, and is hot, even hotter than the recent unseasonable springtime. She's wearing a short summer dress the colour of cappuccino, and sandals with a little heel and spaghetti straps. Her hair is darker, many of the blond streaks have been cut away into a shorter hairstyle, and her pale English skin is darker too, bronzed and somehow startling. She looks sturdy, healthy. Hunter feels weary just looking at her.

'What do you want?' he says curtly as she stands on the back terrace looking at him. He doesn't get up from his seat at the garden table, where he's eating the early dinner the housekeeper prepared for him.

'Aren't you surprised to see me?'

'No.' He had been ready. He'd heard a car drive up and her voice calling him from the front of the house before she finally found him in the back.

'You don't look too bad. Bloody good, actually, for a man who's been ill.'

'I've gained weight. Need more exercise.'

'It suits you.'

Conversation curdles and dries. Della's not fazed; she sits without being asked in front of Hunter. 'Carry on eating,' she says.

Hunter, who had been, puts down his knife and fork. 'What do you want?' he says again.

'Oh, to see if you're all right. I thought of visiting you in hospital, but I was told I'd be thrown out on my ear. Me and Stefano.' She takes a cherry tomato from his plate and pops it in her mouth.

Hunter's face tightens. 'You dare to mention Stefano to me. You dare.'

'Oh God, Hunter, mellow out a bit. And I thought you might have changed, stopped being so stressed out about everything, after all that's happened. Why shouldn't I mention Stefano? We had an affair, as you well know; it's over; that's that. I'm not going to pretend it didn't happen.'

'It's over?'

'Of course it's over. Not that it really took off in the first place. Didn't you know?'

246

Hunter did not. But how could he, when he refused to hear either of their names spoken. He says, cautiously, 'You never see him? At all?'

'No.'

Della turns her back on him and walks across the terrace onto the lawn. She still cannot control her face or emotions when she thinks of Stefano. She has heard from Sadie that he's still in Florence, still living in the apartment in the Piazza Santo Spirito, but she hasn't seen him. She thinks it would break her heart if she did.

Hunter is standing, following Della across the lawn. The heat of the day is like a sticky ocean he must swim through before he gets to her. But he does.

Together they look at the overblown, blowsy summer hills, covered in the white haze of summer heat. Hunter puts his arm around her shoulder, tentatively at first, and then confidently, joyously. He's not to be alone after all. He has not lost everything.

Della feels his other hand turning her round, feels his face on hers, his body against hers. She lets herself be kissed and touched. Why not, she thinks. She doesn't want to be alone either.

But after a time, when Hunter urges her upstairs, still holding her, caressing her as he pushes her towards the house, Della knows it's no good. On the terrace she pulls away from him, walks to the edge of the stone paving and looks out towards the heavy, dusty lime trees. Hidden behind them is the tennis court. She imagines Stefano there, newly arrived from London. She imagines that it's all beginning, not ending.

Hunter says, 'I was going to ask you to stay. But it's no good, is it.'

'No. I'm sorry. I thought it might be.'

'Just as well, I suppose.' He suppresses a sudden urge to yawn. How tiring it is, all this heat and emotion. He looks longingly at his recliner, sitting so temptingly under the shade of one of the old olive trees at the edge of the terrace. 'Sit down, if you like,' he says generously, sitting on the recliner and motioning Della to a garden chair. He supposes he should be angry at her, coming like this to disturb his convalescence, but anger is so draining, and it's far, far too hot.

Della sits on a chair at the table and picks another cherry tomato off his plate. Hunter, eyes closed, says, 'You could come back and work for me, you know. When I get started up again. I can always use good teachers. But I suppose you've already found a job with another school?'

'I'm doing supply work at the moment.'

'Well. If you need a job . . .'

Della takes a last look around her at the Villa Tiglio. The haze on the hills has blurred the contours, made them dreamy, far away. 'Actually,' she says, 'I'm moving back to Rome. I've still got quite a few friends there, and I like the city. I lived there for a long time, remember.'

Hunter opens his eyes sharply. 'You've changed your tune. I thought you hated Rome, all those memories, that man who jilted you—'

'That's enough, Hunter. Let's not say goodbye on a sour note.'

'Well, it's true,' Hunter says petulantly.

Della looks over the fields and valleys and vineyards, over towards the hills, and feels that she could float right through the haze of the day into the cool branches of the cyprus trees on the horizon. 'It's not true any more. Maybe I'm growing up, Hunter. Maybe I'm beginning to see that there's more to life than pining for the men you can't have, and making do with the ones you don't want. Maybe I'm beginning to see that there's more to life than fucking men, full stop.'

But Hunter hasn't heard her. Overcome by the heat of the day and the drowsiness he always feels these days after a big meal, he has fallen fast asleep in the garden recliner.

* * *

248

Stefano finds him there half an hour later, still asleep. By some freak coincidence he'd thought he passed Della in Due Strade on the way, getting into her car in front of the greengrocer's, arms laden with peaches and nectarines. He was on his scooter, coming from Galluzzo, and it gave him a start, like suddenly seeing a ghost in strong bright sunlight.

But he must have been mistaken; Sadie said Della never went into Florence these days. And as Stefano raised his hand in a stunned greeting, the woman had turned her face quickly away from him, so that he'd seen only a fleeting glimpse of brownish hair, too dark for Della's, and too short as well. It couldn't have been her.

Hunter wakes when a shadow passes over him. He looks up to see Stefano standing in front of him. For a split second he thinks Stefano is there to kill him, but he cannot summon enough energy to care.

'*You*,' Hunter says, finally stirring himself. 'I wondered when you'd show up. Wondered when you'd be man enough to show your face.'

Stefano looks at his father. Strangely, Hunter looks better than he did when Stefano first saw him last May, when he'd first arrived from London. His hair is cut short, and it makes his face look younger, fresher. The lines are still there, but his colour's more rosy, less grey and pasty. His eyes are the same. Nothing will change Hunter's eyes, Stefano thinks.

'I would have come sooner,' he says, 'but I was told you didn't want to see me.'

'Well, is that so strange?'

'No.'

'So why are you here now?'

'To tell you I'm sorry.'

'Oh, really?' Hunter's voice is resonant with sarcasm. 'And that makes it all just dandy?'

'No, of course not. But I wanted you to know. I'm sorry about me and Della.'

Hunter doesn't reply. There isn't, after all, anything

to say. He should give Stefano an earful, a good blistering, but it seems such an effort.

'Well,' Stefano says after a moment. 'I'll be off now.' He starts to walk away.

'Wait,' Hunter cries, sitting up in his recliner. 'You don't have to go, you know. Do you want a drink? A beer or something?'

Stefano stops. 'No, I don't think so.' His voice is polite, even kind. 'I think I'll go, if that's all right with you.'

It's not all right with Hunter, but he nods and Stefano goes, trying to keep the relief from showing on his face as he leaves the villa.

Hunter tries to go to sleep again, but can't this time. There's nothing to do but stare at the hazy hills as they darken and disappear, until one by one the stars come out and the hills are gone.

25

In the Piazza Santo Spirito a crowd of young people sit on the church steps, listening to the music of an itinerate Dutch traveller playing his guitar. He sings Sixties Bob Dylan songs in a strange, harsh accent, though he wasn't even conceived when the songs were written. Despite his poor English, he's a good imitator. Hot, tired, elderly tourists who remember the songs, put money in his hat and sit on the steps with the youngsters who don't notice them. The Sixties are gone – long gone. The Nineties are almost over too. A new young century's beginning.

Stefano sits on the steps with Bettina and Marco, planning a beach trip for the next day. Marco's on holiday and Bettina's new job doesn't start for another week, so they're planning a camping trip by the sea for a few days. Stefano, as yet, hasn't found a permanent job, but is keeping solvent by giving private English lessons. He has already put in several applications to various language schools in Florence for a full-time post in the autumn.

'And you, Stefano, you still haven't got a tent,' Bettina says sternly.

'The one I was supposed to borrow, the one promised me, is useless, full of holes.'

'*Madonna*, imagine discovering this today. I told you ages ago to check.'

'No problem.' Stefano leans back on the stone steps to grin at her. 'I'll share yours and Marco's.'

Marco takes a mock swipe at him. 'Fat chance. No

way. You find your own woman, stop trying to keep stealing mine.'

Next to Bettina a young woman with the flaxen hair, light-blue eyes and olive skin of the northern Italians says, 'I have a tent. Brand new. Small. Fits two. You can use it if you like.'

Stefano recognizes Anna, one of Bettina and Marco's crowd. She's sitting on the step above them with her own small group, but now edges towards Stefano. Her face is round, lovely, open, and her eyes are smiling.

'You don't mind?' Stefano says. 'If I borrow it?' He slides closer to her.

'On one condition.' She's smiling all over now, and her smile seems to come from everywhere: skin, eyes, mouth and body. Stefano thinks that even Bettina's smile is not as spectacular as this one, and he wonders why he hasn't noticed before.

'Yes?' he says. 'The condition?'

'That I go with it. The tent, that is. You can have the tent as long as I'm in it.'

'You're on,' Stefano says. 'We're leaving tomorrow, though. Early. Can you and the tent be ready?'

'Oh yes.'

Bettina and Marco, listening to this, look at each other and wink. Anna moves away from her group to join theirs. The wide steps of the Gothic church fill with more reclining young people as the evening begins to cool and darken. On the piazza in front of the church small children reach up to splash in the fountain, their mothers and fathers standing in lively, chattering groups of two or three or four.

Only the old are sitting tonight. The stone benches of the piazza are heavy with the aged and ageing, watching the antics of the young, remembering.

On the steps of the church the Dutch guitarist abandons Bob Dylan and begins a composition of his own: original, contemporary. It's not as imaginative or memorable as the Sixties songs he has been singing, but he's young. He has plenty of time.

THE END

A Patch Of Green Water

Karen Hayes

'WEAVES RUEFUL HOPE, VENETIAN CANALS AND CARNAL SENSUALITY INTO A BITTERSWEET *BRIEF ENCOUNTER* ROMANCE'
She

As a tour guide for Comet Trail Travel Company, Callie Miller is used to spending most of her time with complete strangers who gather round her like knots on a string necklace. And she has come to know destinations like Venice and its Hotel Isabella better than her own base of Whitstable – where a dust-filled empty home awaits her.

City of myth and melancholy, part reality and part reflection, Venice is a natural port of call for all wanderers. It is here that Callie breaks her golden rule about married men *(don't),* when she meets Tomaso Venturi and becomes the 'other woman'. With its labyrinth of dark narrow alleyways that lead nowhere and its shops full of carnival masks, Venice itself lulls the lovers into dreaming of a life together as they develop their own *Brief Encounter* against the deceptive backcloth.

While the members of Callie's Venetian tour painfully confront, in the city of fantasy, their own past illusions, she and Tomaso, wary of causing a tragic outcome are forced to make choices which will alter their lives irrevocably.

'A POWERFUL STORY ABOUT LOVE AND THE ILLUSIONS PEOPLE WEAVE ABOUT IT'
Home & Country

0 552 99778 1

BLACK SWAN

Cloud Music

Karen Hayes

Down the pitted road from the Irish harbour village of Ballycaveen nestles a ramshackle house. Behind it, like a ribbon wrapping a special parcel, runs a narrow river where swans swim.

To musician Troy O'Donnell, who has inherited Heron's Cove from a spinster aunt, it is a setting which is 'no less than paradise'. To brilliant harpsichordist Alina Montgomery, it is a retreat from the outside world as she convalesces from a serious accident like a damaged Celtic princess. To Troy's elder sister Steffie, who longs for a daughter at forty-two, it is the place where she experiences the exhaustion of motherhood before she even has a child. And to their photographer brother Ivo, last of the three 'Ginger Nuts', it is a magical landscape where the energy of each summer's spectacular electrical storms offers the only release he knows.

Into this arena of sea, mountains and music, from far away in a soft, mystical forest in Brittany, come the connections that spell the passion of unrequited love, of soul-healing, witch-doctoring, and of altered destinies.

0 552 99754 4

BLACK SWAN

Still Life On Sand

Karen Hayes

To an artist's eye, the receding sea leaves the boats
in the harbour looking like abandoned water toys
after the bath has been drained. Living in the
harbour community of St Ives, sculptor Esme
Cochran has watched both her sons fall in love
with that sea – Hugo with the surfing and Crispin
with the fishing. But here, in the company of the
tides, the mists and the extraordinary local light,
other love affairs are also begun.

Affairs that divide husband from wife and artist
from canvas take place alongside budding youthful
romances, whilst one old sailor, Percy Prynne, is
haunted by the tragic echoes of the past and
watches over Esme's own growing turmoil with
uncanny foreknowledge.

In this beautiful and perceptive story, in which the
sounds of the sea mingle with the smell of oil
paint, Karen Hayes has drawn an evocative and
lasting picture of the lives and loves of members of
a small community.

0 552 99724 2

BLACK SWAN

A SELECTED LIST OF FINE WRITING
AVAILABLE FROM BLACK SWAN

99830 3	SINGLE WHITE E-MAIL	Jessica Adams	£6.99
99821 4	HOMING INSTINCT	Diana Appleyard	£6.99
99768 4	THE RIGHT THING	Judy Astley	£6.99
99687 4	THE PURVEYOR OF ENCHANTMENT	Marika Cobbold	£6.99
99755 2	WINGS OF THE MORNING	Elizabeth Falconer	£6.99
99770 6	TELLING LIDDY	Anne Fine	£6.99
99795 1	LIAR BIRDS	Lucy Fitzgerald	£6.99
99760 9	THE DRESS CIRCLE	Laurie Graham	£6.99
99774 9	THE CUCKOO'S PARTING CRY	Anthea Halliwell	£6.99
99724 2	STILL LIFE ON SAND	Karen Hayes	£6.99
99754 4	CLOUD MUSIC	Karen Hayes	£6.99
99778 1	A PATCH OF GREEN WATER	Karen Hayes	£6.99
99736 6	KISS AND KIN	Angela Lambert	£6.99
99771 4	MALLINGFORD	Alison Love	£6.99
99812 5	THE PHILOSOPHER'S HOUSE	Joan Marysmith	£6.99
99701 3	EVERMORE	Penny Perrick	£6.99
99696 3	THE VISITATION	Sue Reidy	£5.99
99814 1	AN INNOCENT DIVERSION	Kathleen Rowntree	£6.99
99764 1	ALL THAT GLISTERS	Mary Selby	£6.99
99781 1	WRITING ON THE WATER	Jane Slavin	£6.99
99753 6	AN ACCIDENTAL LIFE	Titia Sutherland	£6.99
99788 9	OTHER PEOPLE'S CHILDREN	Joanna Trollope	£6.99
99720 X	THE SERPENTINE CAVE	Jill Paton Walsh	£6.99
99723 4	PART OF THE FURNITURE	Mary Wesley	£6.99
99761 7	THE GATEGRASHER	Madeleine Wickham	£6.99
99797 8	ARRIVING IN SNOWY WEATHER	Joyce Windsor	£6.99